MW00773283

Gaseous Clay and Other Ambivalent Tales

by

John Travis

Gaseous Clay and Other Ambivalent Tales
by John Travis

ISBN: 978-1-913766-12-2

Publication Date: September 2021

Publishing Credits

We, the Remedials originally published in *At Ease with the Dead*, 2007

The Monkey, Not the Organ Grinder original to this collection

Everything originally published in *Supernatural Tales 12*, 2007

The Flit originally published in *All Hallows 34*, 2003

Tequila Mockingbird originally published in *The Monster Book for Girls*, 2012

The Cure originally published in *Horror without Victims*, 2013

Rated X originally published in *Wordland 4*, 2014

Networking originally published in *All Hallows 29*, 2002

Cuticles originally published in *Dark Horizons 40*, 2001

King of the Maggots originally published in *British Invasion*, 2008

Reflections from a Broken Lamp originally published in *Darker Minds*, 2012

Less Ahead Than Behind original to this collection

Links Ain't What They Used to Be originally published in *The Urbanite 11*, 1999

The Tobacconist's Concession originally published in *The Second Humdrumming Book of Horror Stories*, 2008

In Bleed original to this collection

Gaseous Clay original to this collection

www.eibonvalepress.co.uk

Acknowledgments

A HUGE thank you to the following: Barbara & Christopher Roden, David Longhorn, Des Lewis, Debbie Bennett, Ross Warren & Anthony Watson, Christopher Golden & James A Moore, Tim Lebbon, Mark McLaughlin, Guy Adams & Ian Alexander Martin, Steve Bacon, Simon Clark, Steve Harris, Gary McMahon, Marni Scofidio, Allyson Bird, Donna Thornhill, Peter Straub, Gary Fry, Jim Jarmusch, the late Joel Lane, Ramsey Campbell, TED Klein, the Pixies, HP Lovecraft, David Renwick, Kate Bush, Phil Cool, Jan Svankmajer, Luis Bunuel & Salvador Dali, Maya Deren & Alexander Hammid, The Crusty Exterior, The Baggage Handlers, Mum, Dad, Sharon, Andrew, Sam, Catherine and Peter McAuley. An extra special thank you (again) to Tim Lebbon for his wonderful introduction and for being so encouraging about my writing over the years, Terry Grimwood for more reasons than I can shake a stick at, and David Rix for making such a beautiful book from my attempts at storytelling.

For my writing family, with love, respect and not a little awe.

Contents:

The Guy Who Nailed Himself to the Blank Page

Introduction by Tim Lebbon

I've known John Travis for a long time. Not so long that I still had hair when we met – not *that* long – but he's one of my oldest writing friends. Back in the distant, dazzling days of a thriving home-publishing industry in the UK, when magazines came self-printed and saddle-stapled and submissions were by post and included a stamped addressed envelope for a response, a publisher called Tanjen rose above the ranks. Run by Anthony Barker, for several years they published a selection of novels, collections and anthologies from writers such as Neal Asher, Derek M Fox, Paul Pinn, Rhys Hughes, and Stephen Savile. They also published my first novel, *Mesmer*, and it was soon after this that Gavin Williams, another old writing mate, and I negotiated to edit an anthology for them.

Tales From the Teeth Park was conceived, but it was never born. Even though we collected together a wonderful selection of stories from established names and talented newcomers, the dreaded hand of doom fell on Tanjen – otherwise known as 'a decision from the bank' – and the publisher ceased trading. It was a real shame, and we tried to place the anthology elsewhere, but it was not to be. It resides now only in that great Anthology Graveyard of memory, where many such projects dwell.

One of the stories we'd accepted was *The Guy Who Nailed Himself to the Bench*, by John Travis. It was one of my favourite stories in the anthology, surreal and startlingly original, and it's the one that stuck in my mind for years after. John and I would bump into each other at various writing events over the years that followed, most often the British Fantasy Convention (more affectionately known by regulars as FantasyCon), and at some point we chatted about him publishing a collection of short stories. He asked if I'd ever be willing to write an introduction, and I said of course. That guy and his bench had always been with me, and John continued writing unique fiction that really built on that early promise.

And now, here we are.

I'm sorta disappointed that *The Guy Who Nailed Himself to the Bench* isn't included herein, but that's just me. As for you the reader, you're in for a treat, because everything that was promised in that early story is served up here, and then some.

John's tales work as spells. They lure you in and take possession of you, and all the while they're weaving a particular type of magic in your mind. They're preparing you for twists that don't always come, at least not as you might expect. They're guiding you one way whilst readying to spin you around and shove you in another. That's not to say that, sometimes, you don't have a rough idea of where they might be going – or where you might take them if *you* were writing them – but he has a real knack of pulling the rug out from under you and sending you elsewhere. And that's not tricksy writing or fooling the reader. Part of it is skilful writing, but a lot of it – most of it, I'd say – is down to John's unique vision. The stories in this collection jump and jig with originality, because his way of telling them is filtered through a singular, quirky voice.

John's been around and writing for some time, working away at his craft, finding and developing and refining his style, and he's got to a place now where many writers strive to be but not all manage to attain – because I'd say that there's a good chance you'll know a John Travis story when you read it. That's the mark of someone who has found their true voice. That doesn't mean to say that he's become comfortable. What writer wants to be *comfortable*? But there's a confidence to his writing that shines through, and a feel to the writing that's always just a little off-kilter. His stories create surreal tapestries of strange lives haunted by doubts and insecurities, fears and twisted desires, and the reader is taken along for the ride and offered, for a moment, a glimpse into worlds we should be grateful we don't inhabit.

A good story can change you, and the idea of transformation appears to a lesser or greater degree in many of these tales. It could be argued that speculative fiction often involves transformation to some extent – the physical changes of body horror; mental changes leading to, or from madness; altering outlooks. And transformations occur – and sometimes erupt – throughout this collection, either in a physical form such as the grotesqueries of *We, the Remedials* or *The Cure*, or more philosophical transformations such as the guilt-ridden tale *Rated X*, or the superb novella from which the collection takes its title. In fact, *Gaseous Clay* is so skillfully wrought that it would be worth the price of this book alone. Spooky, intriguing, unexpected, and laced with veins of dry humour, it's placed perfectly at the end of this volume as it will stay with you for a long time.

A good twist does not necessarily make a good story. That's something I learned when I first started writing, and most of my very early stories grew from last lines or twists which were then reverse-engineered. Occasionally that works, but it's also mostly obvious, and it's a clumsy and dishonest way to construct a tale. No fear of that herein. John's stories do often reveal a twist, but it's always, always honestly earned. Some are surprising, some perhaps less so (if you're paying attention), but that doesn't detract from their effectiveness. More than once I closed the Kindle with a smile and spent a few minutes thinking about the last few lines of a story I'd just read. That's not merely a reflection of a twist, but how such an ending can sometimes rewrite much of what you've just read. Try reading *Networking* or *The Monkey, Not the Organ Grinder*, without spending a while thinking about them afterwards.

One aspect that unites these stories, and is a marker of John's style and voice and his outlook, is humour. It's not always overt, and it's rarely in your face – these are dark tales through and through – but whether it's a wry line here and there, or a deeper, playful humour built in as part of the foundation of a story, there are plenty of places throughout this volume where you'll find yourself smiling. That's not to say it's light, and for me the best, most rounded humour is rarely light and fluffy. Sometimes it's dark. *Dark*. **Dark!**

So welcome to the world of *Gaseous Clay*. And no, I'll not explain that title. It's up to you to find out, and doing so is something you won't regret. These stories flow, slipping from the page into your consciousness, and it occurred to me whilst reading that a smooth *flow* to the writing doesn't mean *easy* writing. On the contrary, it's a fine wordsmith indeed who creates stories where the effects are wholly positive. There's nothing jarring here, no stylistic bumps, no clumsy turns that pull you from the page. John's writing is artful. Surprising. Thoughtful. Surreal. Original. After my first taste of his fiction almost a quarter of a century ago, I'm so glad he became the guy who nailed himself to the blank page, and filled it again and again.

Tim Lebbon
Goytre
October 2020

We, the Remedials

I used to have no confidence.

I was the shyest, meekest, most introverted, undemonstrative person you could ever meet in your life; debilitating so: I couldn't put myself forward, I couldn't offer up opinions, I couldn't even *contemplate* complaining if something wasn't to my liking, such as a hotel room for instance.

I am, or rather was – a salesman. I used to traipse around, going from town to town, trying very badly to sell substandard goods to people that did not want or even need them in the first place. I barely scraped a living together, and the money that I did take I felt guilty about taking. In short, it was no way to live: an inadequate man living a life he did not enjoy, his soul shrivelling away to nothing, until it came to the Final Day, when his body would shrivel up too and both would vanish, blow away, remembered by nobody, with nothing to show for a life that promised so much when it began.

Am I depressing you? Good.

It's said that life is a journey; mine certainly was – a journey that found me hoping that the inhabitants of the next town would be more gullible than the last, a journey from hotel to hotel, each one a little shabbier than the last as my money dwindled.

On arriving in the capital, I had imagined I'd end up in a hostel or something like that, the prices down there so ludicrously expensive I doubted that I could even afford a half-decent hotel. So leaving behind the cavernous train/subway station, I held out little hope of better luck here than anywhere else; I was already thinking of where to go next.

Outside, everything was grey and wet, people with bent heads staring at the pavements to avoid eye contact, their feet kicking at the rubbish, careful to avoid the wild eyes that stared above moth-eaten sleeping bags, empty polystyrene cups at their sides. In a strange way, I fitted in.

I must've wandered for the best part of half an hour, through dingy back streets, past grimy-looking café's and dimly-lit newsagents, skirting the odd entrance to a tube station along the way. By now I was absolutely soaked, and wanted nothing more than a place to put my suitcase down and have a rest.

It seemed an unlikely place for an art gallery, but when I looked up from my watch, there it was. I knew nothing about art, but as there didn't seem to be an admission fee I went inside, into a large airy room with perfect white walls and a high ceiling.

I immediately saw my mistake: despite being in such a run-down area, the patrons of the gallery were all well-to-do, successful, *confident* people; and when they saw little old bedraggled me standing there with my suitcase tucked under my arm, well, they did what came naturally.

You know that expression, 'so-and-so made me feel *this* big?' Well, this bunch of unadulterated so-and-so's did exactly that; they had a field day. It must've been like shooting fish in a barrel.

In the centre of the room were a series of brown wooden benches. With all eyes on me I headed towards them, my every step resounding through the room like flatulence in a church, my shoes squelching. The high ceiling seemed to get higher, the benches further away – the gallery became almost as big as the train station. When I eventually arrived at the nearest seat, I laid my case on the end of it, and picked my sopping shirt from my chest so its creases hung against my jacket instead.

They were still watching me.

Sitting down beside my case, I removed a soaking handkerchief from my pocket and wiped my face with it. When I looked up they were still watching me.

A more confident person would've said something at that point, along the lines of 'what are you staring at?' Maybe that was why they looked away *en masse*, back to the paintings. For a minute or so I tried to compose myself, determined that I *would* look at the pictures, instead of running away with my tail between my legs.

Taking a deep breath, I got up off the bench.

Unfortunately for me, my case decided to do the same thing a fraction earlier, which meant I tripped over it, my outstretched hands hitting the floor a split second after my nose did, resulting in a horrible sickly pain spreading across my face, my head full of unwelcome noise.

As the noise began to clear, I stood up, leaving a set of comical handprints on the floor. Another noise intruded – the sound of perhaps a dozen people laughing. Dusting myself down, I stepped over the case and headed for the nearest wall, still determined to take a look around.

The first canvas was evidently the result of a five year old going mad with a paint-box. Completely bewildered by *Psychedelic rampage by two chimps (No. 4 Jungle)*, I walked along to the next painting.

To my eye, I was looking at the same canvas I'd just passed, when one of the patrons walked towards me. I could sense others watching. I knew what was coming.

"Do you come here often?" a short man with a red face said. Behind him the room seemed to crawl with sniggers.

"N-not really," I said.

"Do you approve of *Vomiting without tonsils,* if I may be so bold?"

"Pardon me?" I followed his gaze to the title. "Oh, r-right. The name of this er –"

"You *don't* approve?" the man said.

"No, it's just it's … it's a bit highbrow for me, I'm afraid."

"A bit *eyebrow,* did you say?" Stifled laughter around the gallery.

"No, I said highbrow. You're trying to twist my words –"

"Well, if it's *eyebrow* you like, follow me my good man."

Without touching me, he was dragging me over to the other side of the gallery, pointing at a painting ahead of us. "There," he said winking back at his audience "what do you think of *that?*"

It was a painting of a man in suit, perfect only except for the fact that both eyes weren't where they were supposed to be; one was on his knee, while the other was on the end of his big toe, the space below the brows empty.

The laughter at my back bubbled up like noxious fluids in a steaming hot cauldron, scalding my flesh. With my face bright red, my clothes sopping, my nose throbbing and the feeling that I wanted the world to swallow me up, I went back for my case, tucked it under my arm and left the gallery with the laughter still echoing around the room.

It was raining heavier than ever now, and the streets were empty. I didn't relish the prospect of trying to find lodgings. But turning a corner away from the gallery, my luck seemed to change.

Next to what looked like an abandoned tube station was a square, grey, flat-roofed building with the letters REME stencilled above the top windows. Wiping my face, I crossed the road and headed for the door.

"Good afternoon Remedial can I help you," a man who looked too cheerful for his own good said to me without punctuation. It took me a second or two to realise it wasn't meant as an insult.

"I'm sorry, I thought this was a hotel. I'm sorry to have wasted your –"

"Yes, this is a hotel, sir. How many nights would you like?"

"Y-you're called the –"

"We are the Remedials, yes sir. At your service. How many nights?"

I was a bit flustered, not having thought that far ahead. "Well, I'm not sure. I'm a salesman, you see, and –"

"We'll leave that blank for the time being then, shall we?" the man grinned. Suddenly he began to look me up and down, even going so far as to lean over the desk. Then he began nodding, mumbled a few "uh-huh"s before saying "I have just the room for you, sir. Top floor. S'cuse me a second." When he turned his face, I saw what looked like a long hosepipe coming through the ceiling. Taking one end in his hand, he started speaking into it. "One two seven straight away," he said. Putting the hose to his ear, he listened for a few seconds, then nodded. Putting it down, he turned back to me. "One two seven will be ready the time we get up there," he said, coming from around the reception desk. "We don't have any lifts, so if you'll follow me."

"I hope I'm not putting you to any trouble," I said as we marched upstairs.

"No trouble," he informed me, puffing and panting like an old horse fit for the knackers yard.

Going up seemingly endless flights of stairs (it hadn't looked this big from the outside), I saw that without doubt this was the most dilapidated hotel I had ever set foot in; I passed at least three walls with running water, the paper peeling so low it acted as a second carpet (in one or two places it *was* the carpet). The ceilings discoloured to the point it looked like somebody had painted them with wet earth. The place was so miserable that it even made me confident – confident that even I could afford to stay there.

"Here we are," the man said, standing before a door that failed to reach the floor by a couple of inches. "Room one two seven. I'm sure you'll have a happy stay with us. Here's your key. Goodbye!" With that he was off, trotting back down the stairs as though expecting a sudden influx of trade to walk through the mouldy doors.

Standing outside the peeling door of room one two seven for a second, I wondered why the odd man had handed me a baton; but then, at the end of the long metal pole, I saw the smallest key I'd ever seen in my life, barely a quarter of an inch long. Without much hope I pinched the tiny key between my thumb and forefinger and turned it in the lock, opening the door onto the most depressing hotel room I have ever seen.

The first thing to hit me was the smell, an incredibly oppressive odour of staleness, the dust hovering throughout the room; stepping across the threshold, it felt like I was walking through the screen of a badly-tuned television set.

Inside, the walls were done in *grey* wallpaper. What remained of the carpet had once been burgundy; now it was mostly a series of dubious stains and muddy footprints. The single bed was covered with a faded woollen blanket full of horrid knotted tassels dangling off the ends to the floor like strands of greasy hair. The bed itself was unusually low to the ground, its shortened legs perhaps only three or four inches from the floor to the mattress. Despite the dryness in the room, the far wall looked as damp as some of those I'd passed on the way up. Hadn't the receptionist said they were getting this room *ready?* Closing the door behind me, the latch clicked with a clank like a cell door. As I gazed around at the rest of the room, something small and brown with multiple legs scuttled away under the door's large gap.

Putting my case down on the bed, ignoring the small cloud of dust that flew up around it, I saw that the room also contained a cracked wall-length mirror, a badly-varnished wardrobe, a white wicker chair that looked like it would collapse if I sneezed near it, and a small chest of drawers.

Opening the top drawer, I found a handwritten leaflet inside:

> Hello! We, the Remedials, welcome you to our humble hotel. We trust you will have a pleasant, comfortable and enlightening stay with us, however long it may last. If you find that you need anything, be sure and ask – that is why we are here, after all!
>
> May you have an illuminating stay with us!
>
> - The Remedial Hotel

Something about the message seemed a bit odd, but at that point I was too dispirited to care. Looking through the rest of the drawers, the only other thing I found was a Gideon's bible in the bottom drawer, its leather cover full of what appeared to be tiny teeth marks.

It'd taken me my entire adult life, but I had finally, finally hit rock bottom.

Flopping down on the bed with a *whumph*, I closed my eyes and waited for the dust to settle back on top of me. I didn't expect sleep, just a brief respite from the world and its awfulness.

When I opened my eyes, I was sure only a few minutes had passed; but according to my watch it was morning – I'd slept for something like sixteen hours straight through. Rather shocked, I sat up and saw a man in the mirror opposite the bed who looked like he'd been rolled in stale breadcrumbs. Dusting myself down, I got off the bed and headed for the door.

After finding a bathroom secreted at the end of a dingy corridor and attempting to wash myself with the postage stamp of soap on the edge of the bath, I went downstairs for breakfast.

"In the basement," the same overly cheerful man said from behind his desk. "And today, it's tinned mushrooms! How about that?" Without saying anything, I headed for the basement.

It was a bit of a surprise to find that it was crowded, not having seen or heard a soul since I arrived. But it was full of people sat at single tables hunched over bowls and plates beneath the harsh lights. Looking at the long table full of self-service breakfast I decided to give the speciality of the house, the tinned mushrooms, a miss, instead opting for a couple of slices of dry toast. Finding an empty table, I sat down.

Crunching a piece of toast, I tried to take my mind of it and my problems by doing a bit of people watching. Without exception, I saw every person looking intently at their plates, as if they could sink into them and disappear from view. They all looked as miserable as I felt. My spirits, if possible, nose-dived; the last thing I wanted was to be around people like this. Finishing my toast, I went back to my room.

"Good night, sir!" the man on reception chirped. "Don't let the bedbugs bite!"

I was just about to contradict him on the time when I opened my eyes and found myself in bed. The room was in darkness, except for the light coming under the gap in the door. Even in such poor light everything looked strange somehow, as if my eyes had still to adjust to the sudden change.

If there'd been a sudden change, that was.

Laying there, I tried to think about it. If it'd all been a dream, then it was an extremely vivid one – I'd felt the toast softening in my mouth, seen the second hand on my watch whirring round, the basement full of people with downcast eyes; but if it wasn't a dream, then that meant I'd blacked out; and I had fallen in the gallery. But I couldn't remember –

I also couldn't remember changing into my pyjamas.

But there wasn't any doubt – I was lying there in a set of baggy clothes, so I *must* have got changed. To be doubly sure, I felt the material: the soft shirt, the buttons, my collar and tie –

What on earth was happening? Swinging my legs onto the floor, it felt like they landed a split second later than they should've done. Slipping my feet into my shoes, I stumbled towards the light switch, managing to trip before I got there and sprawling hands first against the wall. The damn cotton wool I had in the back of my shoes must've slipped, which made the shoes too big. Kicking them off, I stretched up towards the light switch and clicked it on.

As the room lit up, I felt a movement beneath my hand. It was as though the wall had turned into a blind, and was spinning up out of my grasp. But then I saw that the reverse was true – I was sliding down from *it*, further and further from the light switch I'd had to grab for. Terrified, I looked down to see the enormous shoes I was standing between, *my* shoes, which were quickly covered with my clothes, *not* my pyjamas, my clothes which were now falling from my body all around me, then my tie plummeted past me, *over* me, like a large grey lasso, landing in a perfect circle on top of the huge mound of discarded clothes, its long tongue fluttering to the floor in slow motion. Following its descent past the mirror, I saw the full horror of the situation.

"So-and-so made me feel *this* big"

Imagine it happening for real.

I didn't have long to look at my rapidly diminishing naked body – as I watched, I sank, and my head was soon beneath the mirror's cracked frame. When I turned round I was looking up at a dirty woollen blanket, its frilled edges apparently leading to the ceiling.

I don't know what happened for a while; I shrieked, I shrank, I ran around naked on the carpet, through the dust, eventually through the curtain of fringes so I was under the bed itself, running through a grey desert of dust-balls the size of boulders, the black hessian of the bed's bottom just above my head like a lowered ceiling.

I don't know how long it took – my watch was out *there* somewhere, no doubt lying on its side like a rusted car – but eventually I became less hysterical, got the panicking down to a manageable level, and started – or tried to – think.

The first conclusion I came to, which was a great relief, was that I seemed to have stopped shrinking. Then I tried to judge what height I now was: six inches? Less than that, I'd never have gotten under the bed otherwise. Four inches then? No. Three? Yes, I decided three was about right.

Somehow, I was now three inches tall.

Then I remembered the dream.

That was it, I was still in the dream – or in *a* dream. An *extremely* vivid dream. Which meant that this wasn't really happening. I calmed down a bit more. All I had to do then was last the dream, nightmare, whatever it was, out – it was only one night, I just had to play along with it. Knowing that I couldn't be hurt, I walked through the piles of dust and assorted rubbish towards the fringed curtain overhanging the bed.

Approaching the frills, I found that the floor must be slightly uneven, as I had to bend to stop my head touching the hessian. Grabbing a gnarled thread in each hand, I parted the fringes and looked out into the room.

At the other end of it, several miles away, a single eye was staring at me under the door.

Startled, I fell backwards, letting go of the fringes, expecting to knock my head on the bed's ceiling; but instead I toppled over, landing among the dust balls. Without giving myself time to think I ran through the dust to the other side of the bed. I was nearly there, the other set of fringes in sight when something grey with a shell scampered between the fringes towards me.

At first I thought it hadn't seen me, as it darted around the dust balls, stray hairs and sweet wrappers, but then it did see me, and it was heading straight for me like an armour-plated car.

A woodlouse, my mind screamed out, *I was going to be eaten alive by a woodlouse.* I began to sprint back the way I came, but the woodlouse was gaining on me, despite the dust and the stray carpet fibres, the solitary hairs and eyelashes –

I pulled up quickly and looked down at it; a long blonde eyelash, laying there in the dust. In what felt like slow motion, I picked it up, hefting it in my tiny hand as if it were a baseball bat.

I looked up to see the woodlouse almost on top of me, its tiny feelers reaching. Lashing out, I struck it, the eyelash bending, springing out of my hand; but the shock of it was enough; the woodlouse stopped, turned and scurried back the way it came, out from under the bed.

Planting my hands on my knees, my face now barely an inch above the carpet, I looked at the tangle of things trapped in the carpet fibres as I tried to get my breath back. I wasn't safe down there – I remembered the gap under the door, and what I'd seen scurrying under it, not to mention what was under it now. The room was filthy too – and I doubted that the woodlouse was on its own. What else would be waiting for me?

I needed weapons.

The situation, bizarre and terrifying as it was, was bringing something out of me – for the first time in my life, I had the will to survive; my reactions were quickening, my thoughts clarifying; I was down on my hands and knees looking for suitable objects to defend myself with. The dust balls were no good if even I could punch a hole through them. The blonde eyelash had been okay but it was too willowy. But there were other types of eyelash down there, eyebrows too – the bed must've been in a different position at some point – that'd probably been there for years. Using the little weight and strength I had, I began to yank them free from the carpet, testing them for strength. I found that ginger eyelashes and grey eyebrows were the best, because they were the thickest. Soon I had a small arsenal of solid-looking red and grey hairs piled up beside me, male and female; the ones coated in mascara were the thickest of them all but also the heaviest. Putting them under my arm, I marched toward the fringes on the further side of the bed, ready for any attack.

An attack wasn't long in coming. I'd hardly taken my first step through the frills when the woodlouse came at me again. Dropping all of the lashes except the thickest grey one, I waited until it was perhaps a half-inch from me, then levered the hair beneath its body before wrenching it upwards. In fascination I watched as the insect was upended, stranded on its back with its legs scissor-kicking the air in front of me. Dragging myself away from this obscene spectacle, I began picking up my collection of weapons once more when the air above me suddenly began to hum.

I looked up to see a fly the size of my face coming straight at me.

Again, I dropped my weapons, this time in panic. The fly was so fast I had no time to get back under the bed. As I scrabbled around among the lashes, I could feel the warm air from the fly's wings ruffling my hair; I didn't even have time to raise a lash and aim.

Again, my newly awakened senses rescued me. The thickest red eyelash I had was almost completely smeared in mascara. Standing it up on end, I went behind it and bent it back quickly as far as I could before letting go of the end and closing my eyes. Almost immediately a cloud of dried mascara flew from the hair, and my face was pelted with thick flakes. Around me the sound of angry buzzing was deafening. I crouched, waiting for the fly to pick me up or start chewing my head, but nothing happened. Slowly, I opened my eyes.

The fly was nowhere to be seen.

I decided then that I'd hung around long enough; the sooner I got up onto the bed, the better – at least up there I could hide under the blankets. Picking out the thickest of my remaining weapons, I clamped them between my teeth and started to climb the frills.

The climb wasn't as bad as I'd imagined – I was grateful that the bed was so much lower than most, and I made quick progress. At one point, I had to slow down a bit to circumnavigate a large dried-up bogey stuck to one of the tassels, but that was all. Reaching the summit, I pulled myself up the last frill with renewed energy.

Only to find the fly at the top, waiting for me.

With one hand still clenched around the frill, I removed my weapons from my mouth with the other as the fly hurtled towards me in a rush of legs. Like the woodlouse, I waited until it was almost on me before swinging both lashes together at it as hard as I could. I was still yelling with the effort when I saw the body slice in two, the top half spinning into the air and falling barely a centimetre in front of me. Finishing my ascent, I ran around both halves of the fly's corpse to the centre of the bed. Again, the journey was much quicker than I thought it would be. Looking back at the fly, something occurred to me.

Even though it was in two pieces, the fly seemed much smaller than before; in fact, looking at the whole room, everything seemed much smaller.

I'd got bigger again – that was why the climb up the bed hadn't taken so long; it also explained why I hadn't knocked my head when I fell back earlier. *My size was being governed by my reactions to my surroundings* – when I was scared, I shrank; when I felt more confident, I grew. The whole thing had the logic of a –

I was still dreaming – of course. Because everything was so real, I'd forgotten that. I just had to hang on in there. It couldn't last forever.

But when I dreamt a long thin spider web descending from the ceiling, with a big fat, hungry spider dangling from the end of it, such rationality went out of the window. Once more I could feel myself shrinking.

Finding my weapons over by the two halves of the fly, I grabbed one in each hand and turned just as the spider landed on the bed, still attached to its thread.

I looked at the spider. The spider looked at me.

The spider began to move towards me. I thought of running away, but I didn't.

Instead, I charged.

With the red eyelash curved in my left hand like a scimitar and the grey eyebrow in my right like a bayonet, I hurtled across the blanket towards it, faster than I'd ever run in my life, both blades aimed straight at its nasty little eyes. And as I ran, I could feel myself getting bigger, heavier; my tread was now indenting the blanket. All of a sudden I felt a foot tall.

But before I had a chance to attack the spider it began to clamber back up the thread, scrabbling up towards the ceiling like a badly worked marionette. By the time it was a few inches from the ceiling, I found I was tall enough to look over the side of the bed without having to move.

The eye was still there, watching from under the door.

I was about the size of a toddler, but I couldn't see how I could get any bigger now. Following the 'logic' of the 'dream', I knew that I couldn't stay there forever: I had to open the door and face what was on the other side.

Despite everything I'd just been through, I hesitated; the eye was grotesque enough, but it was what it represented, both here and at the gallery. Lying back on the bed to think, I looked up at the ceiling at the spider, now an insignificant little speck of no real danger.

It took me a while but I got there in the end. I let out a small yelp of delight, evidently frightening the spider, which began to swing from side to side.

The implications of my logic made it no easier to go to the door however; and as my doubts began to rise I could feel myself beginning to shrink again. I knew I had to get myself off that bed before I vanished entirely. I had to get out of the hotel, back to that gallery –

The gallery triggered off an idea which in turn triggered off a memory.

Once, in another hotel, I bumped into a much better salesman than me. He told me how he used to go from house to house with a large vacuum in his car and a packet of photographs. The spiel he used was always the same – he'd inform the householder that even the cleanest bed in the world was home to hundreds of thousands of tiny bedbugs, revolting little things they were, and that the only way to get rid of them properly was with his special vacuum cleaner. When the householder, usually sceptical, began to umm and ahh he'd show them the pictures.

The pictures were of bedbugs, magnified to such a size that they filled the whole of an 8 X 10 size picture in glorious colour. Hundreds of thousands of those in your bed, he would remind them. More often than not, the householder would ask him to wheel his special vacuum cleaner into the bedroom.

And I knew that if I didn't get off this bed soon, I was going to shrink. Maybe shrink to such a degree that I would be able to see these bugs face to face. Then be eaten by them. Hundreds of thousands of them.

Don't let the bedbugs bite! the receptionist had said.

As things now stood the bed was like a jungle, full of unseen menaces ready to devour me.

That did the trick.

Still big enough to jump off the bed I leapt, landing by the oversized pile of clothes. Not wanting to meet what was on the other side of the door naked, I roughly pulled the clothes around me, careful not to trip over them as I moved towards the door. Taking a very deep breath and closing my eyes, I slowly opened it. Then, a few seconds later, I slowly opened my eyes.

The receptionist was standing there grinning at me, his fist raised to knock.

"Ah! You're awake! Well, it's a wonderful morning, sir. I trust you had a good night. I hope you're ready for breakfast? It's tinned mushrooms today."

I've never tasted boiled slugs before, but after chewing for the best part of a minute then giving up, I rather imagined that they taste like tinned mushrooms.

"These mushrooms," I said, pointing at the chewed up mess with my fork "they're not *funny* mushrooms, are they? If you get my meaning. I didn't have any that last time and forgot about it?"

The receptionist, or rather the only member of staff I'd seen in the Remedial, smiled. "Oh no, definitely not. Everything you experienced happened. You did very well – you managed to do what a lot of the others don't."

I stopped crunching dry toast. "The ones I saw at breakfast before, you mean?"

He nodded. "Limbo people. They live that existence, or something similar, day in day out … as you have done, in a way. But you used the items around you to change things. They haven't figured that out yet, so they stay as they are. But they will figure it out, hopefully, one day." Over the years, I've often wondered how many managed it.

As I finished breakfast, I asked questions, lots of questions: about the gallery, the seemingly strange dimensions of the hotel, the tube coming through the ceiling, the eyes in the picture, the eye under my door, the people in the gallery, the people in the hotel, the lack of staff in the hotel, the tinned mushrooms, I even considered asking about the tiny bite-marks on the Gideon's bible but decided I didn't want to know.

And I asked the most important question of all: Why me?

The receptionist / whatever he really was just smiled. "Strange things happen sometimes," he replied, as if that was an answer to all my queries. "It's not always best to question them. You found us – most don't. You discovered that you wanted to live. *Really* live. You've been given another chance to look life in the eyes."

After shaking his hand, I went back up to room one two seven, passing door after closed door, wondering what was going on behind each one. Inside my room, I saw that it wasn't as big or scary or as dismal as I remembered it. It was just a room.

Outside, the hotel didn't exist of course; I turned around to find a patch of waste ground next to an abandoned subway station. I knew the gallery would exist though, so picking up my suitcase, I headed for it.

Instead of stumbling into it, this time I strode. The picture was there, but it had changed – the eyes were where they should be, above and either side of the nose, staring straight ahead, out into the room. I stared straight back at them, holding their gaze.

Leaving the gallery, I forgot to look at the very thing I'd gone to check – the picture's title – but I could guess what it was. The reason I forgot was that the picture had changed in other ways too; as well as the eyes having moved to their rightful positions, the man in the picture now had a swollen nose, as if he'd fallen face-first onto a hard surface.

Perhaps even more surprisingly, he had a huge grin on his face.

I raised an eyebrow at that.

The Monkey, Not the
Organ Grinder

They won't let us leave. I've written my statement and handed it in. People are milling around, confused, scared. Me too, but maybe I'm still in the hospital, I don't know. I'll write it out again; they're too busy clearing away the rides and the mess to notice me. Near my foot is a smooth cylindrical hole in the grass where I've pulled out a tent-peg. I'll slip the note down the hole and come back tomorrow to see if it is still there – here.

I discharged myself against orders. They were too busy to see me go, gorging someone else with bright coloured capsules no doubt. Every so often, the world revolved around me and I had to stop. But I kept going through the spitting drizzle.

I don't remember anything of interest; only here. I must have left the hospital by a back entrance as I don't recognise this place at all. Some kind of park I suppose. Maybe I was attracted by the light and the noise at the top of the hill, like a moth to a lightbulb. I knew they wouldn't come after me up here.

All at once I seemed to be upon it. I shuffled forward slowly, raindrops touching my face. The fair looked old; the colours were brighter than the greenery surrounding it, but it still looked tainted somehow.

I was moving towards the sound of a pipe organ, one of my favourite sounds, attracted by its up-and-down notations, hypnotic yet strangely comic. In my mind I could see its pipes rising and falling, the music swirling and coiling around me. Suddenly there was the smell of roasting chestnuts, the heat pushing me back, causing me to stop. Ahead something big and yellow spun before my eyes like a giant plate, then the delighted screams of children. I could feel mud sticking to the soles of my shoes.

To one side of me, I could only see the back of people's heads, raised a foot higher than mine. Every few seconds, someone would yank their right arm downwards and release the dull silver boxes with their single round red stoppers for hands; I heard the sharp tinkle of money landing in front of peoples' groins.

As I jostled forward through the crowds, I saw a mother and a young girl trying to hook a plastic duck bobbing in six inches of water as it rippled past; behind the attendant, goldfish in opaque plastic bags looked on.

Seeing the face of the attendant took me back to childhood; being scared of the fairground workers as a child, losing money in a machine and telling a grizzled-looking man who just swore under his breath and turned his back to me. This man was like that. The girl wasn't having much luck with the hook-game so he was smiling, pretending to encourage her.

I thought I was feeling a bit better at that moment, but just as the girl was about to hook one of the plastic birds, the pipe-music shut down; it was as though the whole fairground stopped, but just for a second. The face of the stallholder was caught in a toothy grin, his eyes locked into place. The girl and her mother successfully leaned over and hooked a plastic duck; then the music whirled once more. The attendant snapped to again, the grin slipping from his face as he saw the girl jumping up and down demanding her prize. His expression changed to a snarl.

36

He reached backwards and grabbed a plastic watch off the shelf, ignoring the goldfish, dolls and vanity mirrors, slamming it down on the counter. As the girl moved away I saw the man shake his head vigorously as if dislodging water. He caught me staring at him; I moved away before he could say anything.

Again I could smell chestnuts. But nothing stays still for long at fairgrounds; as I walked, the smell quickly changed to the sweet aroma of frying onions. To my right I could hear video games, a series of insubstantial beeps and blips. Through it all I heard a corrugated computer voice demanding money. The consoles were closed in by large black lacquered boards of wood painted over with black panthers and lions and dragons. Another wooden board above prevented electrocution.

I regretted leaving the hospital now. Of all the places I could've ended up, I think this was the worst. I watched people squashed into miniature blue and red cars attached to a mesh ceiling with long poles, their sparks everywhere. I was dazzled by jagged shards of strobe lighting off to my left. It seemed to stab into my mind, reacting with the cocktail of chemicals coursing through my brain. I reeled backwards, treading on someone's feet. I apologised, still with my back to them, walked away. As I walked, I noticed the other workers in the fairground. They seemed to move around as awkwardly as I did, as though stiffened with inactivity. I never noticed people in hospital moving like this. But then again, I hadn't been watching.

I carried on through huddling bodies, the sky around us even murkier now as the drizzle continued. The music pulsed on. Red and blue candy-striped awnings were on either side of me now, their supporting ropes twanging with tension as children bumped against them on their way out of the tents. I avoided going in, not wanting the confinement. Ahead were the woman and child from earlier, peering down into some kind of mechanical slide-show. A ragged queue was forming behind them, a boy with a mustard-smeared face and a man with a jet-black beard smiling.

They looked up as the big wheel spun down past them again, faces jarring out of focus in the pale, thin mist.

I was getting nearer the music. I could hear the reedy air passing through the tubes of the calliope, like wind through a milk bottle.

I saw it then. It was quite large, with pipes of varying sizes. On the floor to its left, a small box was draped with red velvet. Inside was a toy monkey, its arm turning the organ's handle round and round, button eyes staring ahead. It was a nice trick, but it worried me; the rest of the fair was old and weather-worn; this toy looked new, and clean. It reminded me of the other toys on the stalls – bears and clothed dolls covered with dust, cheap prizes in a faded fairground. I looked past the organ and saw that the fair went no further. Below were thick bushy trees, presumably cutting through to a main road. I had no idea where I was.

Turning back the way I'd come, I saw the rides I'd missed last time; people spinning around in giant cracked teacups painted pink and yellow, the paint flaking; nestled between this and the Ferris wheel was a small white hot dog stall; then an inflatable castle, full of oversized children. There seemed to be more mud on this side of the fair; I felt it almost lapping against my shoes.

As I approached the target range I saw the mother and child again. Everything seems to repeat in fairgrounds; the smells, sounds and faces, spinning like a roulette wheel. The girl's mother had just paid the stallholder and the girl picked up three darts, leaving two in her left hand. HIT A PICTURE CARD AND WIN A PRIZE said a sign above the red plasterboard, which was full of holes. There was a wider array of prizes at this stall; stuffed bears and blond-haired dolls, others in combat fatigues. Some soft toys were laid flat, their empty stitched faces staring upwards. Suddenly a drop of rain landed in my eye; as I blinked it away, I got the impression that one of the dolls blinked a plastic eyelid at me in return. The girl was just lining up her aim, when a red-faced boy pushed in front of her, snatching a dart from her other hand.

She let out a wail, slapping the boy on the arm; he shouted into her face and held back his dart arm, aiming, his tongue lolling to the side of his mouth in concentration. The girl pushed him, knocking him slightly off balance. His face reddened further and he lined up his aim again, waving his other arm absently in her direction. The mother was appealing to the stallholder, who shrugged his shoulders, moustache bristling. As the boy released the dart, the girl shoved him off balance. The dart whistled through the air.

I watched as it sailed through the drizzle, piercing the left temple of the attendant's head, seeming to go in further than it should, nearly up to the dart's stem. His expression froze, just like the other attendant when the music stopped. I sensed an extra noise added to the cacophony of the fair.

Suddenly the organ music ground down again, like a record played at the wrong speed. It was then I knew where the noise was coming from.

The man's face had frozen in a rigid grimace, the shrill hissing noise clearly audible now. It sounded like someone slowly letting the air out of a balloon.

I couldn't move as I watched the man's face gradually crumple in on itself, the head of the dart trembling. The sound was a high-pitched whistling now, like a boiling kettle. There was movement under his clothes and he pitched forward, his legs folding under him like wet cardboard. His face landed with a soggy thud against the counter. Somehow he toppled backwards and there was a sterile plastic smell coming up from the darthole.

His body was on the floor now, legs shrivelling away slowly. His torso had flattened, his face had turned in on itself; there was still plenty of him left but he was slowly wrinkling inwards. I couldn't see any blood.

A man from behind pushed past me and climbed over the benchtop, pulling out the dart. He shrank away immediately, banging against the counter. The attendant's face and torso continued to sink. His face now resembled an inky screwed-up ball of paper. Then the legs started to thin out.

I came out of myself with a start; behind me, there were a series of screams. I moved backwards away from the target range in a daze. All over the fairground, I saw people looking down towards the mud with horrified faces. At the target range I was just about to turn back, but I saw a ragged brown mess moving forward, jerkily sludging through the mud, its knitted yellow belly getting splashed as it stumbled on. I was starting to move back when suddenly it fell forward into a muddy puddle, face first. As I watched, small brown bubbles appeared either side of its face.

I turned away just as something jumped from the prize-rack on the target range; an impossibly thin plastic doll clacked around on the counter now, its yellow hair spraying off in all directions. Soon the entire counter was teeming with movement, all jerking about with short angry motions. One of them slipped from the red counter and slapped down into the mud below.

I found myself moving into the centre of the fair. Every stall was alive with them now, spinning and jumping, marching awkwardly. I had to kick them away as I moved, and they crashed against chipboard panels and fairground rides with a series of brittle cracks, not woolly thuds. The further I went I saw some of them perched on people's shoulders and heads. One clung to my left leg; I kicked it off with the right, not wanting to touch it with my hand.

Some of the rides were still going; there were lights everywhere, some of them crawling up the hill itself, making me feel trapped. As the seconds passed the toys became more agile, moving without stiffness now; they weren't falling over anymore, and dodged kicking feet with ease. Through it all, somehow, I heard the screech of a van behind me. I turned and there were two of them, three, lights blazing. The vans were metallic grey with blackened windscreens. Men poured out of them in a flood of grey uniforms, black rifles in their arms.

My panic had gone as far as it possibly could. I realised where I was going. Trampling over dolls and stuffed bears, tangling with legs and splashing in puddles, I ran towards the organ. I looked around for the monkey but it wasn't there, its box empty. In desperation, I reached for the organ. If I got the music going again ...

I was just starting to turn the handle when a series of shots rang out in the sky. All the people froze; the others carried on. One of the uniformed men grabbed a bear roughly by its stomach, its legs and arms struggled. He walked purposefully over to the target range and put it on the counter. I don't remember moving over there, but I was stood right behind him. He took a small knife from his pocket, and cut it into the brown fleece of the toy. Its legs stopped kicking.

As he opened it up, there was a terrible smell. Inside it were perfectly formed human lungs, kidneys, a heart, a ribcage – all in miniature. The man jumped over the counter, knelt down over the stallholder. He used the knife again, slitting him down the middle from head to stomach. Then he ripped open the gash with his hands, gagging at the overwhelming stench of plastic. There was nothing inside; nothing but a salmon-pink surface, as smooth as the skin of a baby.

I don't know what happened for a while. I blanked out or something; my clothes were clean, so I hadn't fallen over. The next thing I knew, all the toys were gone. A piece of paper was being held in front of my face; a man, his eyes covered with black sunglasses, said nothing as I took the paper and joined several others, writing on the counter of the target range.

After I'd finished, someone came and took my paper.

We're surrounded by grey vans now. Their sides rolled up, like garage doors. Inside they are empty. People are starting to huddle around each other now, shivering, whispering. There is nothing left to clean up.

Except the customers.

Everything

Kneeling over the porcelain as if in prayer, Eberol didn't know which was worse – the cold, the headache or the hangover. But when the remaining bile in his stomach shuddered up through him and out into the already crowded toilet bowl, he became pretty certain.

The hangover, he thought, wiping his chin. The hangover was worse.

The week had started so well, too – nine months after losing the only job he'd ever had and his increasingly desperate and futile attempts to find another, it finally dawned on him that everybody was right and that severe apathy had set in alongside the depression, which was never far from the surface at the best of times. His visits to the Job Centre had dropped off and feelings of worthlessness ran riot, as seemingly did his appetite, if the rings of blubber around his midriff and under his chin were anything to go by. He realised that he'd let himself go: something, perhaps everything, had to change.

So, he began that Monday morning by walking into town rather than taking the bus, which he couldn't really afford anyway, and headed straight for the cramped (and somehow very unhealthy-looking) health food shop. He told the assistant, a small elderly woman who looked like she could do with a good dusting, that he needed to change his diet. Five minutes later, he was leaving the shop with two bags full of enough seeds to start his own allotment. And when he got home, again after walking the half-mile, he did some gentle exercises, had a quick shower and then settled down to his lunch of seeds, along with a half pot of tea, now minus sugar.

Eberol was going to do this properly.

The seeds, pumpkin and sunflower, were surprisingly tasty and according to the dusty assistant, were good for supplying energy. It was strange; as a child, he'd fed them to his hamster – and now here he was, eating them himself.

He wondered if this new-found purpose, this sudden desire to leave his mark on the world, had been brought on by the graffiti he'd seen the week before. Out of sheer boredom one afternoon he'd gone for a drive along the motorway, enjoying the speed and the brief rush of power the car afforded him. On a wall beneath a motorway bridge, the usual dull grey concrete was covered instead with an enormous psychedelic mural, going right up to the bridge itself. In his glum mood it occurred to him that even vandals left their mark on the world – they didn't see it as graffiti; to them it was art, a sign of public expression.

Buoyed up by the morning's efforts, Eberol continued by clearing his lunch things up straight away instead of leaving them for later, and as a reward he settled down to read the biography he'd started the previous week. Its subject, an unusual man wealthy beyond most people's conception, had certainly led a rich and varied life, full of experiences – 'a veritable rollercoaster of a book', as the cover said. But instead of making Eberol feel inadequate, the man's story had inspired him; it showed just what was possible if you put in the effort. Yes, there was a point to everything. He could see that now.

That was on the Monday.

And so it continued, all through Tuesday and part of Wednesday; gradually, bit by bit, Eberol was beginning to feel better.

That was until the sniffles began.

By Wednesday evening, he had an absolute stinker of a cold, and all thoughts of health food and an orderly life went out of the window, to be replaced by sneezes and self-pity. So when a friend called to ask if he was going to the party tomorrow night, Eberol said yes. He could start back on the health food and exercise *after* the party and *after* the cold had cleared.

And here he was now, propped over the toilet bowl with various disagreeable bodily fluids pouring from him and a lump on his head the size of a Chinese worry-ball.

A long time ago, when things had been different, Eberol had once spoken to a musician in a band who told him that a good gig should be like a good party – a complete blur. If the way he felt now was anything to go by, then he'd just been to the best party of his life; a shame then that he could hardly remember anything about it. The only detail he was sure of was that he'd spent part of the evening talking to a complete stranger, which, under normal circumstances, he would never have done – that's how drunk he was. So drunk in fact that on leaving the party he'd slipped on the front step and cracked his head against the garden wall, and now wasn't sure how much of his headache was a result of the bump on his head and the hangover.

Suddenly a noise like a parrot squawking after it had just swallowed an alarm clock went off in the living room. With a disgusted grimace, Eberol averted his gaze from the toilet bowl and went through to stop the racket, picking a tissue from his dressing gown pocket on the way and blowing into it with such violence that it managed to blot out the sound of the telephone.

"Hello," he whispered, holding the mouthpiece at a distance as if it had the cold and not him. Whilst listening to the voice on the other end telling him he'd won a prize, he looked absently down into the used tissue before crumpling it up and tossing it in the nearly overflowing bin. Then he hung up on the pre-recorded message.

After a few hours in bed and a long hot bath, he felt ready to face the day. His stomach was grumbling at him but he doubted whether anything would stay down. Getting dressed, he went through to the living room and flopped onto the sofa, trying to ignore the bin brimming with used tissues next to him.

But, like some grotesque road accident, it was impossible; his eyes were constantly drawn back to the evidence of his cold, the tissues scrunched up like off-white clouds within. And as he looked, he spotted something out of place, sunshine among the clouds. Taking the sunshine out of the bin and holding it up to the light, a small smile spread first across his face, then to his eyes, quickly to be followed by a puzzled frown. Where on earth had it come from? And then he had it.

As he dialled his sister's number, he carefully spread the tissue out on the coffee table, smoothing it out.

"Hello?"

Following the usual preliminaries, Eberol asked her when she'd last brought Ian and Kay, his nephew and niece, round to visit. Sunday, she'd said, which was before he got the cold. You don't remember them doing any drawing while they were here, do you? No. Why, they've not been scribbling on your walls again, have they? Oh no, he told her, nothing like that. What's that? No, no luck with a job, I'm afraid. Haven't been feeling well lately. Actually, I banged my head last night, and – well, I don't know if it's worth booking another appointment now – it never seemed to do any good, did it? After they've finished school? I'll look forward to it. Bye, then.

46

Replacing the receiver, he knew that she must've forgotten about it. Heaven knows he was forgetful enough. But it was extraordinary to think that they'd both forgotten such an incredibly detailed and beautiful drawing, bearing in mind the two children – or should he say, artists – involved only had a combined age of eleven. It was just so – well, what could you say? He couldn't take his eyes off it. What a wonderful –

Suddenly, an idea came to him, perfectly in keeping with his newly acquired positivity.

Eventually finding a box of tacks in a drawer, he picked up the tissue by its topmost corners, and carefully pinned the drawing to the wall behind the sofa. After making sure it was straight, he continued to look at it for several minutes more, marvelling at how much it brightened the room.

Certain now that he could chance a bite to eat, he had a handful of seeds for lunch, which, temporarily at least, seemed to quell his stomach's rowdy remonstrations. Then, hoping the exertion would get rid of the last of his hangover, he went out for a run.

Leaving the house, he was determined to see the world in a different light as he jogged along. It was difficult at first, but it got easier, so that when he saw two red-faced men gesturing at a crashed car a few minutes later, he could tell himself their obvious anger was just a way of showing how relieved they both were that the other was unhurt; the dozens of CCTV and speed cameras he passed, along with the police cars and stickers in windows warning of *Neighbourhood Watch* were simply a means of showing that people out there cared; the voice that he thought he kept hearing was probably something and nothing, just an old friend calling out to another. And he was sure the litter everywhere would be picked up *eventually*.

Back home and out of breath, he removed his sweat-drenched clothes, dropped them into the clothes basket and had a long hot shower, which always felt like a luxury. Spreading himself out in an armchair, he let out a series of contented sighs.

He'd been sat for a few minutes when he thought he could hear the voice he'd noticed while out running. Either someone had followed him home (the old Eberol, the one who needed to make 'appointments', would have believed that in a flash, he told himself), or it was some kind of aural trickery, like ringing in the ears. Turning his head from side to side, the noise remained. But when he lowered his head slightly, the noise was louder. He knew what it was now – his stomach!

The way it was gurgling away, it sounded uncannily like a voice, as if there was someone trapped behind the bars of his ribcage demanding to be heard. Another memory of the party came back to him – the stranger saying something about listening to what your insides were telling you. What, literally? he'd replied and they'd said, Yes, if necessary.

Amused by the idea, Eberol sat for a while, listening to this internal monologue, chuckling every now and then as individual noises bubbled to the surface like words. It was only to be expected, he supposed – he wasn't used to eating so little. But his stomach would shrink in time and then the noises would go away.

It wasn't long before his sister came to visit with his nephew and niece, now that school had finished. He'd been about to make them all a drink and tell them about his day when his sister, looking at the picture he'd put up on the wall, told them not to take their coats off as they couldn't stay long. Before he had a chance to say anything, Ian and Kay were pointing at the tissue on the wall. "It's not!" one of them appeared to say and they both started giggling. They were still giggling as their mother frog-marched them from the house, an unreadable look on her face.

He hadn't even had time to let them listen to his stomach.

The next morning, she phoned to see if he was okay. Yes, of course he was, he told her, and he'd be even better once he got rid of this damn cold and sore head. Did he tell her he'd banged it the other day? Are you *sure* you're okay, she asked him before ringing off. Yes, he told her. He was fine. He was sure the headache would fade in time.

But it didn't and an hour later his head still throbbed. Standing in front of the bathroom mirror, he gingerly moved his fringe from his face to see if the swelling was going down and the bruise coming out.

Staring into the glass, it was evident that the swelling hadn't gone down at all. But that didn't bother him. It was the bruise itself that bothered him.

Only its outer edges were black; or more precisely, black, blue and yellow. That was normal enough. But the centre of the bruise, the part that was swollen, was patterned like a kaleidoscope, a dizzying combination of red dots, orange splashes and purple-green flourishes, all swirled together across the bump.

It hurt like hell – he should be worried. He'd heard about head injuries. People had gone on killing sprees after head injuries, started seeing things. Thankfully, he'd been lucky there. And instead he'd ended up with this exquisite bruise! He couldn't stop himself from touching it, brushing it lightly with his fingertips. The pain was the opposite of exquisite. Taking the bottle of paracetamols from the medicine cabinet, he crunched a couple back, the water surprisingly sweet against the bitterness of the tablets.

After five minutes of lump admiration, he found that the pain had eased slightly. He had to keep busy now, take his mind off it. Perhaps if he read his book.

An hour later he closed the covers as quietly and reverentially as if it had been a prayer book. *That poor man,* he thought, wiping his face, aware once more of the noises in his stomach. *All that money but he still wasn't happy. And the way he ended up ...* But it must've meant something to him, the way they'd found him. Everything meant something, after all.

Where had he heard that recently?

The party, that was right. If only he could remember who he'd been speaking to. Who would know?

He supposed that running to Adam's would be the best thing, what with his headache and everything, but it was too far so he drove instead. When he got there, Adam expressed concern for how he looked. A bit of a cold, that was all, Eberol told him. That and the headache. He showed Adam his bump, but Adam wasn't impressed.

The conversation seemed a bit strained to Eberol from here on in – Adam kept narrowing his eyes at some of the things he said and his gaze kept going up to the lump on his head. When Eberol asked who he'd been talking to on the night of the party, Adam said he'd no idea – when he left, Eberol was slumped in a corner either drunk or asleep.

At Adam's insistence, Eberol took a few more paracetamols before he left and promised that he'd see a doctor on Monday if his head wasn't any better. Adam also tried to persuade him to get a taxi home but he refused.

Ten minutes later he wished he had taken a cab; his headache was so powerful now it felt like his head would burst, as if something inside was trying to break free. Every time a car whistled past the bruise seemed to pulse, making him screw up his eyes, blurring his vision. More than once he found himself perilously close to the hard shoulder, and he nearly struck a motorway bridge just before his turning.

But somehow he got home and staggered inside to his bed, taking a couple more tablets before he went.

He awoke in darkness.

He realised it wasn't the pain in his head that had woken him but a series of shouts, so loud they appeared to be coming from the bed. His stomach again: he was starving. He'd eaten nothing but seeds since Monday.

But it was too late – or too early – to have anything substantial now, so he fumbled his way into the kitchen and grabbed two fistfuls of seeds and knocked them back with a glass of water, followed by two paracetamols. Grabbing his waistline he was dismayed to find that it wasn't receding. It would come. He had to be positive.

He'd hoped that the seeds would've lessened his stomach's constant chatter but instead its noise increased, becoming so loud it made his headache even worse. His eyes were wet, his head throbbed, and he felt dizzy. But the noises in his stomach grew louder still, words were becoming recognisable among the gurgles and groans.

Listen to what your insides are telling you.

What, literally?

Yes, if necessary.

Making his way to the bedroom, his senses bombarded him like litter in a storm. Sweating, he lay on the bed. His stomach cramped and instinctively he curled himself into a foetal position, the noises in his stomach so close now he could hear them as clearly as if listening to them through a stethoscope.

Leave your mark on the world his stomach seemed to be saying, *Be positive. BELIEVE. Everything is something. Leave your mark ...*

The words were forming a pattern around him, lulling him at last into a deep and comforting sleep.

He awoke, and the sun was shining. Today, he knew, was the rest of his life.

He washed, got dressed, had something to eat, then set to work. Some parts of the house he tidied, other parts he added to, giving them their finishing touches. Eventually, it was perfect. It had to be.

He was about to leave his mark on the world.

He picked up his car keys.

Out on the open road the world was a different place, an enormous canvas on which everyone filled in a small section for themselves, like a piece of graffiti. All he had to do was find his own section of canvas.

As he sped along, he reflected on how easy it was to miss what was under your nose – he'd only had to look around his house this morning to see what was really happening: he was changing, body and soul, as was everything around him; the noises in his stomach might've *sounded* like voices, but he knew now exactly what they were – they were the sounds of *growth,* of *progress.*

Then, in the distance, he saw his canvas.

Flooring the accelerator he glanced at the speedometer: a hundred, a hundred and ten, a hundred and twenty, the blank grey canvas of the bridge growing larger in his windscreen, the engine roaring. Turning the wheel sharply to the left the tyres shrieked, and he bumped onto the hard shoulder.

They say your life flashes before your eyes at such times. For Eberol, it was his belief that flashed before his eyes.

He was back at the party, sitting on the floor – and he'd known all along; deep down inside he'd known. He'd convinced himself he'd been talking out loud but of course he hadn't.

Life is essentially meaningless, a part of him had said.

No, that isn't true at all. Everything means something. Listen to what your insides are telling you.

That my life is pointless?

That you have to believe. What do you want to change about yourself?

Anything, everything. From the inside out.

The only stranger he'd been talking to that night was –

He struggled to regain control of himself. He mustn't think these things, not now. He *was* doing the right thing – at least it would be if he believed it. Everything was about belief in the end –

And at that moment, as the car crumpled and he crashed through the windscreen to leave his mark on the world, Eberol believed.

He was watching the remains of the car being towed away when he saw it. It was just a visual trick of course, like seeing a face in a cloud. Still, he'd feel better once they'd hosed it off. Poor devil never stood a chance.

Thankfully the cars' registration plate was intact, if nothing else was. The vehicle belonged to a Mr Eberol; whether that was him splatted across the side of the motorway bridge like a fly on a windscreen there was no way of knowing; nothing remained that even looked vaguely person-like. It was as if whoever it had been was so frail to begin with that every trace of humanity had been obliterated by the crash. In all his years, he'd never seen anything so ... *complete*. As always in these situations, he set out for the address with a heavy heart.

The front door was open – not a good sign. He called out, but nobody answered. This whole situation felt *wrong*. Reluctantly, he went inside. A few seconds later that feeling of wrongness had intensified.

He was looking at the living room wall, which had dozens of soiled tissues and pieces of toilet paper tacked to the walls with drawing pins. A more normal sight was a book open on a coffee table; at least it was until his gaze fell on a paragraph about someone keeping urine in jars. Howard Hughes, the cover said. A veritable rollercoaster.

After the living room, the bathroom wasn't half as bad as he'd expected – there were a few dirty towels and some sweaty clothes laid out as if they'd been freshly laundered, but that was all. That and an empty bottle of paracetamols in the sink, surrounded by an assortment of nail clippings, body hairs and luminous globules of phlegm.

In the kitchen the cupboards were well stocked. On the table were two large seed packets, and he recognised one immediately – his daughter's hamster nearly overdosed on them. That packet was almost empty. The packet of pumpkin seeds next to it was almost full.

Picking up the empty packet, an image of the crash scene came back to him. Strange how your mind made pictures: the way the poor sod's guts were spread across the wall, a thin line at the bottom like a stalk, blossoming out into a garish explosion of colour at the top like the head of a giant discoloured –

But he realised he was being ridiculous. He was overworked, that was all. Wondering if Eberol had a hamster, he went back into the living room to check.

The Flit

"Would *Madame* like to see inside the box?"

Sandra sighed with mock despair. "What on earth have you got now?" She indicated the rest of the cluttered living room. "It's not as if we don't have enough already."

Placing the box down on the table, David Lyle lifted the cardboard flaps. "Aha! Wait and see ..." Removing wads of brown tissue paper and cardboard, he grabbed the object inside with both hands and placed it on the table. "There. You said we didn't have a decent clock."

Sandra bent forward and looked at it: an old unvarnished thing shaped like a cottage, the pointed roof alive with splinters. Inside the large face of numbers were two closed shutters. She looked at her husband. "I'd say we still don't. A *cuckoo* clock? How m-"

"Going cheap, in a manner of speaking," David interrupted her. "An old antique shop in the town. The owner assured me it worked perfectly, but it wasn't worth a bean, despite its appearance. A bit of work and it'll look great. Shall I get it going?"

"If you like," Sandra replied. "And while your about it, I notice Boris is still there."

David looked over at the far wall. They'd moved in a week ago, but the spider hadn't moved from its dusty web in the corner of the room. "Sandra, I'm pretty sure it's dead. It hasn't moved for days."

"I don't care. You know how much I hate them."

"Okay, okay; I'll get round to it. I thought I'd put the clock over here though, on this wall."

Finally getting a nail into the wall, the clock was positioned. It was a minute to the hour. "Hope it works," David said, rubbing his hands.

"Big kid," Sandra mumbled to herself.

From inside the clock came a sharp click and the chimes rang out, in four sets of four. The shutters opened slowly. On the end of a coiled spring came a small shabby wooden bird, before going back into the clock and re-emerging twice more. David couldn't help smiling.

"You're a very sad man, David Lyle," Sandra said, standing on tip-toe. "But I love you anyway." She pecked him on the cheek. "Want a cuppa?"

"Yes," he called to her as she headed for the kitchen. "But remember, you're every bit as sad as I am."

Turning away from the clock, he looked up in the corner where the web hung. *Tomorrow,* he told himself looking at the spider. He wasn't that keen on them himself.

"Uh!" David blinked and looked around stupidly.

Sandra turned to him. "What's the matter?"

He scanned the bedroom in confusion. At the foot of the bed, two cardboard boxes yawned open at him, revealing kitchen utensils. "Eh? Oh, I just had this really odd dream. The police were arresting me. And you were one of them."

She smiled at him slyly. "Oh yes? What for?"

"I don't know. Your colleague was just about to tell me when you *nudged* me." He dug her in the ribs.

Sandra laughed. "Hey –"

"Shh!" David held a finger to her lips. "Listen."

Through the open bedroom door, the sound of the clock was just audible. Getting out of bed, David went to the living room and watched its performance. "I'll never tire of it, you know," he called back. Sandra faked a noisy yawn.

Over breakfast they decided where unopened boxes of books and ornaments were going – onto shelves. Which meant that David had to go out to get some.

He was new to Acrebridge. It looked a fairly ordinary place, but he enjoyed the walk through the leafy streets full of three-storey Victorian houses alongside the college, past the town hall and various red-bricked legal offices, the old courthouse slipping behind him. Soon he was in the town centre, facing row upon row of shops. Standing at the traffic lights, he looked across the busy road and saw exactly what he was looking for; a shop window full of cabinets and chests of drawers and shelving units.

In front of the shop was a knot of pensioners, oblivious to the fact that they were taking up almost all of the narrow pavement. One head was turned in David's direction, an old-fashioned hat obscuring part of the face.

Hearing the bleep of the lights, David crossed the road and saw that the face was still looking – no, glaring – at him. Perhaps he has a funny eye, he thought, and wasn't staring at him at all. Although he was standing among the other pensioners, he didn't look a part of them; he was badly dressed, his face sooty, like a miner's. And there was no doubt about it: he was staring at him. David hated that. He had every intention of staring him out, but approaching the group he felt his resolve slipping. The man was nowhere near as old as the others he saw now, and he didn't look like the kind you'd want to get into an argument with; his face was creased and leathery, thick black hair tufting out from under his hat. *Where did you get that hat, where did you get that tile?* David hummed to himself as he jostled through the assembled group, all the while feeling the man's gaze on him as he went into the shop.

Sandra had got through three boxes when the knock at the door came. "Just a minute!" She called.

Downstairs, she opened it to an elderly woman in a burgundy cardigan. "Hello!" she said, the light from above reflecting off her spectacles. "Sorry I haven't been before now, we've been on holiday. I'm Margery, from downstairs."

"Oh, hello!" said Sandra, offering a hand. "Please, come in. Would you like a coffee?"

In the kitchen Sandra raised her voice above the noise of the boiling kettle. "It's David's work, really. We've moved several times over the past few years. Never this far north though."

"You don't mind? I think the stress of it all would be too much for me." Margery wrestled with the biscuit tin.

"No," Sandra replied. "For some reason that kind of thing bypasses us. It's like a big adventure, particularly to David." She smiled to herself. In the living room, she saw Margery eyeing the cuckoo clock. "Do you like it? David got it yesterday. Brightens the place up a bit, doesn't it?"

"You didn't get it in town, I trust," Margery asked.

"Excuse me?"

"Oh, it's just a silly local law. It was in the papers a few years ago, along with some other funny by-laws: 'It is illegal to sell or purchase cuckoo clocks in Acrebridge.'"

Sandra laughed. "Whyever is that?"

"Who knows? You know what people were like way back then. Passed all manner of petty, silly laws, and no one's ever bothered getting rid of them. Not as if its doing any harm these days. And cuckoo clocks are hardly a sought-after item. I suppose it's like taking sheep across Westminster Bridge. Nobody ever will."

"I got some," David said, coming up the stairs. "I'll tell you what though, you don't half see some funny things when you look for them." He put the box down in an already-crowded corner of the room.

"Such as? Oh, we've had a visit from our neighbours downstairs. Well, one of them. The husband was at the shops. They weren't round earlier because they were away, and *not* because they were miserable old devils as I remember somebody saying the other day."

"Oh good. Yeah, in town … some bloke with a blacked-up face and a weird hat, eyeing me up like I was the devil. God knows why. What did she have to say then, this neighbour?"

"Oh, welcoming us to the area, and they'll be in the Fox and Hounds around seven tonight and they hope to see us there. What on earth is that?"

As David was taking off his coat Sandra grabbed at the arm. "Ugh! Where did you say you'd been?"

David looked at the oily smear on his sleeve. "I've no idea where *that* came from."

Sandra sighed. "Well, it'll have to go in the wash. You can wear your light jacket to the pub tonight."

By the time Margery – with some help from her husband George – waxed lyrical on the history of the town, David was wondering at the elderly couple's stamina after six rounds. They must have hollow legs, he mused.

"Oh yes, it goes back a long way Acrebridge, you know," Margery was saying. "Settlements going back donkey's years –"

"They've just dug up some more remains a few weeks past," George put in. "Reckon they might be important."

"– and some rum doings in the cathedral, but we don't talk about that."

"Why ever not?" Sandra asked.

"*'Cos we don't know what they are!*" Margery slapped her husband on the arm, nearly dislodging him from his stool. David and Sandra exchanged glances, but Margery was still cackling.

"Ooo! *Anyway,*" she said at last, "time we were getting off back. That thing's on at quarter to that George likes and the box is playing up again."

David was raising his arm to order another pint, unaware last orders had been called half an hour ago. "And I think we'd better go back with you." Sandra, who'd been on tomato juice all evening, tried to winch David up by the forearm, getting George to help her.

The air outside the pub was scented with cigarettes and fish and chips. "So then, Marge," said David, "what dark and terrible secrets does this here town hold, eh?"

"Well –"

"You mean you haven't heard of Stanley Winship?" George finished.

"Who?"

"Oh, he was a – evening," George nodded to a couple across the street. "Right devil he was. Bit of a joker by all accounts.

There's this one tale about –"

"– a woman who left her washing out in the middle of the night," Margery said. "And, looking out of her window, saw it waving about at her. Only it *wasn't windy.* So she went outside to have a look at what was flapping it about. At that moment, it's said that the pegs *pinged* off the washing line and *flung* the sheets at the poor woman –"

"– only that wasn't all –" George put in.

"– only that wasn't all, as George says. As she stumbled back with the shock of it, she saw faces in the linen. Didn't know any of them, except one: that of Stanley Winship. And that," she smiled, pleased with her rendering of the tale, "is why it's illegal to hang your washing out after dark in Acrebridge, apparently."

"No!" David said.

"Oh yes. Me and Sandra were talking about this earlier, weren't we love? There's all these silly laws around here, the rumour being that they were all brought in to curtail Winship's mischief."

"Is he responsible for the cuckoo clock law then?" Sandra asked.

"What cuckoo clock law?" David said.

"Must be, I suppose." Margery shrugged.

"What cuckoo clock law?"

"I'll tell you later; we're home now. *David,*" she shook her head at him, pointed. "You forgot to close the curtains before we left."

"Well, it wasn't dark then, was it? Hey, I'm not the –"

"Aye, aye – what's that in your window?" asked George, narrowing his eyes.

As they all looked, a thin, silver line seemed to pass before the glass from right to left. Suddenly it appeared to shoot back across, and then was gone.

"I've no idea," David said. He turned and looked at the sky. "Shooting star. It can't have been in the house; it was a shooting star or a comet or something reflected in the glass."

Sandra wasn't convinced. "Anyway, we'd better go." She was reaching for the door key. "Thanks for a lovely evening; goodnight."

"Goodnight."

"Aye, goodnight love."

In the kitchen, Sandra watched David drunkenly pour himself a glass of orange juice. "They're odd, those laws, aren't they?" he said. "I think they're making them up. Did you see how many G&T's she put away?"

"Well, I'll see tomorrow," said Sandra. "I think I'll pay a visit to the library. It'll give me a break from the house."

David woke to the sound of the washing machine thundering away, as though it was trying to leave the floor like it did in the old house. Putting his head back on the pillow, he realised it wasn't just the machine.

"Oh, *David!*" he heard Sandra snap.

"What?"

"Didn't you think to empty your pockets? This whole load'll have to go back in now!"

"Why, what have I done?"

Sandra came in and stood at the foot of the bed, waggling a greyish piece of card in one hand. "*This* was in your coat pocket. The ink's run everywhere. I'll have a devil of a job getting it out."

"I didn't know I had anything in that coat." He peered up at the card Sandra was holding in front of his face. It looked soggy, and ready to fall to pieces. "That isn't mine. I don't use red ink. Anyway, what does it say? I can't read it without my glasses."

Sandra squinted at the watery script. "Er, it says something like 'Do you', blank, lots of inked together words for two lines and then 'but out of'. I can't make out the rest."

"Eh?"

"Well, whatever it said, it messed up an hour's washing."

"Thought you were going to the Library?"

"I am. You know where the soap powder is, don't you? Margery said last night we could borrow her line downstairs. It's a nice day. Bye now."

Before David had a chance to answer, Sandra went to the living room and grabbed her sunglasses from the table. She glanced up at the corner, noticing that the spider and its web had gone. *David must've done it after I fell asleep.* She tucked the glasses into her pocket. *Lucky he didn't fall off the chair, the state he was in.* She slammed the door shut behind her.

David looked at his watch. A slight smile played across his face. If he was quick –

Jumping out of bed, he went to the living room and stood before the clock. The second hand came round, and a small click sounded from inside.

The bells chimed, but the cuckoo came from its housing slightly late; when it did, it lurched forward instead of springing. Underneath the chimes he heard a faint scratching. The cuckoo lurched forward seven times, each time more sluggish than the last; the eighth time, the shutters opened but only the head of the bird emerged, dangling and wobbling like the tongue of an overheated dog; the chime struck for nine, but the cuckoo went back inside when it should've been coming out. As the chimes stopped he heard the scratching sound clearly; it was if the mechanism had suddenly become rusty.

God, they'd only had it a day. He'd have to have a look at it later. He went back to the bedroom and got dressed.

"Of course you can *look* at the books in the meantime," the rather officious man behind the counter told her. Sandra couldn't have a ticket *just* now, but she was free to browse.

"Do you have any books on local law?" she asked.

"I believe there is one, yes. In the local section. Through that alcove and next to the filing cabinet."

It didn't take her long to find the book in question: *Nowt So Queer: Strange Laws and Occurrences in the West Riding* by Bill Charlesworth. Taking a seat, Sandra opened the book and started looking through it; but before she could do much more than glance over a few pages she found it impossible to concentrate. A school party was either coming in or just leaving; students jostled one another and chattered. She was about to turn back to the book when she saw, above one of the nearby shelves, a rather sour-looking, dark face staring in her direction. It winked at her, the eyes gleaming.

Creepy old boy, thought Sandra, looking away. She felt as if someone had just walked across her grave.

There it was again.

David walked into the living room with an armful of sheets and looked at the clock. It had stopped chiming altogether now, but on the hour – and at irregular intervals in-between – there was that scratching sound from inside.

Putting the clothes into the basket, he went slowly down the stairs and, knocking on Margery's door, listened to the sound of footsteps approaching.

"Washing line, is it? How's your head?" she asked, leading him through to the back garden. He didn't answer her; it throbbed like hell.

After pegging out the clothes – checking first to see that the stain had gone from his coat (it had) – he was invited back into Margery's front room for a mug of tea. "Do you take sugar, dear?" she called from the kitchen. "We tend to use that sweetener stuff but – oh my goodness …" David heard the back door open.

"Is anything wrong?" he called out. Getting no answer, he went through the kitchen and stopped at the door, staring out into the garden.

"Don't know what happened there," said Margery, picking up another piece of washing and pinning it to the line. "I looked through the window and all your washing was on the ground. Good job it's not windy; they'd have been in the next street by now! Where did you get this jumper from?" she asked, turning the garment in question over in her hands. "It's very realistic, and – oh!" Frowning, she turned it over again. "Must've been a trick of the light."

David smiled. Perhaps she wasn't so immune to the sauce after all.

Ah, here we are.

Sandra smiled at the heading of the page, done in Olde-worlde script:

Stanley Winship – 'The Devil's Caught Jester'

I daresay the name Stanley Winship is a new one to some of you (the book informed her). But his antics have become part of West Riding folklore. The wayward son of a well-to-do Acrebridge businessman, Stanley Winship liked nothing more than to torment and terrorise his neighbours, to, as he put it, 'relieve them of their stuffiness'.

His trickery usually followed a familiar pattern. First, he would pick someone out who offended his sensibilities (childish as they were), and disappear into his murky abode off what was Jacobswell Lane (now derelict field land) and, according to local superstition, "Cook up something fiendish".

Sandra stopped, aware of someone coughing nearby. One of the school party, no doubt. She continued reading.

Before I get onto Winship's fiendishness, however, I should perhaps describe the man himself.

By all accounts, Winship was a thief and con artist – a general bad lot. Overshadowed by his father's success (and subsequently that of his two brothers), he became bitter and took to drinking heavily. One day a large sum of money vanished from his father's home, as did Winship himself. When he returned years later, his father was dead; and Stanley Winship himself was a changed man.

Sporting a fine tan, he arrived back at his old house with several large crates, and was rarely seen in public again. He did, however, have regular visitors – evidently people whom he'd met on his travels, and certainly not locals. There were reports of strange shouts and screams late at night, bright lights shining through upstairs windows, and odd banging noises. Then the pranks began.

Sandra lifted her head again. She suddenly realised she hadn't seen any dates in the book indicating when all these things had happened. The account was so detailed ... flicking the idea away, she noticed that the coughing had stopped. Looking around, she saw that the school party had also disappeared.

> The first evidence of mischief I uncovered seemed to fit the pattern that became apparent later on. A Mrs. Alice Mexborough, local gossip and busybody, awoke one morning to find the following ditty on her doorstep:
>
> > *I should look out Alice, my dear*
> > *Who knows what strangers you'll meet?*
> > *A man or woman, child or a thief*
> > *Or a face with no head but a sheet*
>
> Mrs. Mexborough had a habit of leaving her washing outside overnight to dry in the summer. One night she was disturbed by noises coming from her yard. Looking out of her window, she saw the washing dancing and darting about; but, looking at the trees in the lane, she saw they were motionless. Mrs. Mexborough, a hardy woman, went outside to investigate. As soon as she opened the door she was assailed by her washing, which reputedly "leapt off" the line and tried to smother her. At the same time she saw dozens of ugly faces leering at her from the assorted linen – one of which was the face of Stanley Winship.

Sandra wondered idly where Mr. Mexborough was while all this was going on. The coughing had started again, worse than before; but no-one else seemed to be bothered by it. Thinking that whoever it was could be in trouble, Sandra got up from her seat and left the alcove, walking past several aisles of books. In a shady corner next to a grimy radiator sat a dark figure, its face indiscernible. She was just about to speak when a voice asked, "Did you find what you were looking for?"

Sandra's heart leapt to her mouth. Turning, she saw the man from the counter towering above her. "Yes, thanks. I ... I thought I heard someone coughing." She indicated the dark corner.

"Well, nobody there now," the man answered robustly. "And thank goodness for that. Can't abide splutterers."

Sandra returned to her seat and picked up where she'd left off, reading more about the jokes played on various 'Stiff shirts of the community'.

It was fairly obvious to the townsfolk who was behind these pranks. However Winship was nothing if not clever, and there was nothing specific with which he could be charged; indeed, he rarely ventured out of doors at all. But when the 'Sheet Trick', as it came to be known, had been reported more than half a dozen times, it was clear that something had to be done. A law was quickly passed which forbade the hanging of linen after nightfall. This law still stands today, although it's doubtful whether anyone would be arrested for breaking it. The idea was to reduce Winship's avenues of attack, as it were; and, for a time it seemed to work. Then the jokes got nastier, and there came the incident concerning Sidney Butterfield ...

Butterfield, a blacksmith with a fiery temper, heard unearthly noises in the rafters of his roof; at around the same time, a card was pushed under his door, which he promptly tore up. Although he was advanced in years, Butterfield had the heart of a lion, and he climbed up to his attic expecting to find a bird's nest. According to his son (also called Sidney), what he found was much worse: a selection of gigantic insects crawling over the floor and roof; insects so large, indeed, that they were thought to be tropical in origin. These insects proceeded to attack Butterfield senior, who had a heart attack and died.

Equally malicious 'pranks' soon followed; mirages of falling masonry, coffins mysteriously appearing and then disappearing on people's doorsteps. And at least one gravestone from the local cemetery had its message altered to such an extent that it was libellous, if not to the person below the ground then at least to several still above it ...

Winship eventually met his match, although the cause of the event which saw his downfall is a mystery. A huge fire destroyed his house, presumably with him inside it; for within the wreckage was found the charred remains of a body. However, it would seem that Winship had played one last trick, which resulted in the final law to be passed on his account: the banning of the sale of cuckoo clocks in the Acrebridge ...

Sandra read on, her expression alternating between amusement and vague apprehension. *Well, it would explain why they were banned,* she thought as she reached the end of the chapter. That is, if it were true. She tried to re-arrange the letters of the author's name to see if there was some hidden joke there, but found nothing. Perhaps it *did* have some truth in it, after all.

"Hi, I'm back ..."

"I'll be with you in a minute."

Sandra put her bag down on the table as David walked through, putting an arm around her shoulder. She leant back and kissed him on the cheek.

"What was that for?" he smirked.

"For moving *him*," she replied, indicating the corner. "I thought I was going to have to use the vacuum extension on it."

David scowled. "Oh! Actually –"

"I'll put the kettle on," she continued, not hearing him, and headed towards the kitchen.

David started to say something then changed his mind. What she didn't know wouldn't hurt her.

It'd been a long and productive day, but David couldn't sleep. Sandra rolled over and looked at him.

"What are you listening to?" She asked. He didn't reply, and Sandra was about to repeat the question when she, too, heard. "What is it?"

"I meant to tell you earlier," he said, putting on his slippers. "The clock's broken. It keeps making that funny noise. The bird wants to come out but can't."

They went through to the living room, and David switched on the light. They both looked at the clock; then they looked at what was directly below it.

"Good God!" Sandra pointed at the thin black lines creeping down the wall. "Look at that! It must be from when you hammered in that nail! Mind you, you'd think we'd have noticed …"

"You're right. You saw me put that nail in; the wall was fine."

"Well, tomorrow you'll have to get in touch with the surveyors or someone. Hell, what a mess!"

The scratching sound became increasingly regular as the night drew on. Finally, unable to sleep, Sandra got up, leaving David in bed. She dressed quickly and went into the living room, where she frowned at the marks on the wall. She got a duster and rubbed half-heartedly at them. Perhaps they were just dirt …

A knock sounded at the door, and she tutted impatiently. She moved across the living room, but as she did so turned and looked back at the wall, feeling momentarily uneasy. Somehow it seemed different to the way it had looked in the night. She shook her head and went down to the door; but when she opened it there was no one in sight.

Shrugging, she bent to pick the milk up, and felt her blood boil when she saw that the tops had been pecked open. Damn magpies! She went back upstairs and got her purse, deciding to go and fetch a paper. Back downstairs, she closed the door behind her. As she did so, she became aware of the faint sound of someone singing. She put it down to a radio or TV playing in one of the houses along the street; but the noise seemed to stay level with her, neither increasing nor decreasing in volume as she made her way to the shop.

When she left the shop, paper in hand, the singing seemed to be in front of her, a faint, sing-song rhyme such as children would chant. Turning the corner near the house, she saw a figure across the street, standing in the shade of a tree and staring up at their living room. As she drew closer, she recognised the darkened face.

"Can I help you?" she asked, as much to steady her nerves as be polite. The figure turned to face her.

David awoke, and felt a draft of air on his legs as he got out of bed. Was the main door open? He headed towards the top of the stairs, and heard Sandra outside, calling "Who are you? What do you want?" The door into their rooms hadn't closed properly again; another thing he'd have to sort out.

After putting the kettle on, he went through to the living room. The time was approaching the hour. *One last chance*, he thought, standing in front of the clock. *One last chance.*

Despite the morning sunshine, Sandra felt the hair on her neck prickle. The figure across the road was singing louder and louder, and she didn't dare get any closer. She looked around in vain to see if anyone else was nearby; but nobody was. The figure was booming the song out now, laughing between each line and looking above Sandra's head as he sang. Bit by bit she caught the words, piecing them together in her mind:

> *Now dear lady, do you see*
> *What I have in store for thee?*
> *A bug that flew not from a tree*
> *But out of time, with legs hung free!*

There was a scream from above. The figure standing opposite laughed uproariously as Sandra darted for her front door, which stood open. Thundering up the stairs, she heard a vile swishing sound, and feet scuffling against the floor. Through it all, the clock was doing its best to chime. She turned the corner in the passageway, and heard the song again in her head as she burst into the living room.

David was standing at least two feet from the clock, and the spring was stretched almost to breaking point. His head was covered in a sticky, silky net, through which she could see the rustling of several pairs of long, black spindly legs; the plump body to which they were attached clinging to her husband's face.

Tequila Mockingbird

Why you need *less* sleep as you get older instead of more I've never understood; one of God's little jokes I expect; heaven knows he has plenty of them. As a result, I'm usually up and about by five thirty. In the winter everything's black as pitch; summer and you can see up and down the length of the street. And for the past few days I'd had my eye on one house in particular.

It'd been a sticky, breathless night, and would turn into a baking hot afternoon. I sat there on my porch at quarter past six, watching the world slowly open its eyes as the birds sang, perched on their little tables as they always were, hopping around, taking food from each others' beaks.

But birds tended not to bother with 'Cilla Abcott; they knew which houses had cats and which didn't. And even if Cordelia was knocking on a bit (by my reckoning she's the sixth generation of Cordelias in that house), she could still catch the young 'uns off guard.

There was this one bird though that didn't bother about any cat. It sat patiently on Prescilla Abcott's lawn for most of the day, as though waiting for something. Once in a while, 'Cilla's shroud-like net curtains would re-arrange themselves.

One morning I thought it was a goner. It was hopping about and Cordelia came out. My heart leapt into my throat. It doesn't matter how many times I see a cat catch something, it still pains me. I was frozen to the spot; something like that always seems to hypnotise me. I needn't have worried – I watched in disbelief as the cat walked straight past that bird and they casually glanced at each other like a couple of swells saying 'Hi' to each other in the park. The bird looked away then buried its head back in the soil.

Then around noon 'Cilla would come out and tip some bits off her pinny onto her lawn, go back inside, and peer round the side of her nets watching the bird with a queer look on her face, like someone who's had something good happen to them but they don't know how to react to it. The bird would hang about most of the day, occasionally flapping off for a while. But whenever I looked out it was usually there, peering in at that shabby front window.

'Cilla Abcott was a strange one, no doubt about that. She shunned people and they shunned her and it'd been the same ever since I could remember. Over sixty-five years we'd lived across from each other and not spoken since we were girls. She got a lot of stick for being different in those days, and things never really changed.

That morning though the bird wasn't the first to appear.

'Cilla Abcott was instead.

Out she came, glancing this way and that like some Shakespearean villain, shoulders all hunched up, wearing a long black dress and wrinkled tights (in this weather!), her face all screwed up against the sun. She had something in her hand and was walking down the yard.

When she got out to her garden, she looked around again, like a young child should before crossing a busy road (they soon stop *that* after a while) and stooped and put whatever-it-was down on the gravel. From this distance it looked like a bottle. I'll bet

I screwed my face up too when she put something in the bottle's mouth. The old coot had stuck a straw in the top of the bottle.

With a husband gone and children scattered all over the place, there's nothing much else to do in a small town but wonder. I certainly did that. After a while though, I got angry with myself. I always sat there on a morning in the summer so that was no different; staring into someone's garden though … had I nothing better to do? Is this what my days amounted to, watching silly old women leaving bottles in their gardens? I decided it was not; my yard needed tidying up. I went round back, got the broom and started to clean the place up a bit.

Maybe half an hour later, I heard shouting. It was still early, remember, and at that time of day you sneeze too loud and half the neighbourhood hear it. But there were two voices, shouting. Leaving the broom propped against the side of the house, I made my way to the front. I thought I recognised one of the voices. Rounding the corner, I saw I was right.

Standing beneath the branches of a tree was the heavy bulk and beet-red face of Henry Dwight. If there's ever any noise in the area, look no further. That man could cause a riot in a boneyard. He stood looking up at the branches, shaking his fist comically. He looked about ready to pop.

"Hey!" I shouted as I made my way over to him. "What's all the noise about?"

Dwight opened and closed his mouth a few times. "That, that –" he pointed a shaky finger up into the leafy branches. "*That damned bird called me an asshole!*"

His language didn't shock me. Some men think you swear in front of a woman and you gotta apologise else they faint or something. Well, I can swear with the best of them.

"*Who* did?" I asked.

"That goddamned bird!" he said, spittle flying from the corners of his mouth.

Looking up through the greenery I could see the bird. I know all birds probably look the same to those of us with untrained eyes, but I was sure I recognised this one.

"Don't be ridiculous!" I told Dwight. "It's sat there minding its own business."

He glared down at me, impatient to speak. He hadn't been listening. "Do you know what it did?" he said, his neck muscles bulging. "I was walking along, minding *my* own business, and there's a bottle in the witch's garden," he lowered his voice slightly. When we'd been kids there'd been this story that 'Cilla could take the lids off trashcans by 'thinking' them off. The story, as stories sometimes did, stuck. "And there's only a goddamned straw in the top! A damned blue and white striped straw." I'd been right after all – my eyes weren't deceiving me. "And there's that bird, waddling around the bottle, like it was doing an inspection. I was wondering why when I saw the worm in the bottom and realised – it's a bottle of tequila; it's after the worm. So I stood and watched for a minute. Then, suddenly, it looks up and sees the straw floating about in the top.

"And no word of a lie Ellen, it pecked at the straw, and started to drink the tequila! Honest to God! You go over and look at that bottle, there's a good two fingers gone from it!" Dwight glanced back at the bird, which had its head on one side, listening.

"I started to laugh at it – it was comical. Then it let go of the straw and fell back against the pavement, staggered a bit, then noticed me. It waddled forward a few steps, and I'll swear it on anything you like Ellen," he stopped to catch his breath, "it looked at me all cocked-eyed and said '*What's the matter with you, asshole? You want some?*'"

He stared at me, waiting for sympathy as I shook my head. Dwight's a well-known boozer and, sure enough, his breath smelled of mints as usual.

"Henry Dwight," I said, as though to a kid. "Do you realise how that sounds –"

"*It's true enough, lady!*" said a voice from above.

Well, I thought my time had come. Dwight had to catch me before I fell. He wasn't too steady either. We looked up at that tree as if the Lord himself were perched in it. After a few minutes I got my composure. "Best just to leave it Henry," I whispered. "Come on, it must be the tequila or something."

After a few minutes, I persuaded him to move away. We got about six paces down the road and the bird hopped onto a lower branch to watch. "*Hey, fatso! Hey, I'm talking to you! You listening fat man, huh?*"

There was something in that bird's voice at that moment that took me right back to being about nine years old. The voice was kind of comically childish, naive, mischievous … like someone who hasn't mixed with the wider world and never properly matured … something raced across my mind and then I started to think about trashcans …

I was disturbed from my thoughts by Dwight's yelling.

"Ellen, Ellen! *Look!*"

I looked. Unbeknown to me the bird had fled the tree and was now in 'Cilla's garden. It waddled uncertainly up to the bottle and *pinged* its beak against the glass. I could just make out the shrivelled little thing at the bottom of the bottle. It hadn't moved any nearer the top.

So, just as Henry Dwight said he'd seen, that bird went and grasped the straw in its beak (standing at 'Cilla's wall, I noticed it was candy-striped like a children's party straw), and took three big – and I mean big – slugs from the bottle. You could hear it glugging it down. By the time it had finished, more than a quarter of that bottle had gone. By rights that bird should've been dead.

A sudden movement caught my eye. I was sure I saw those wraith-like nets of 'Cilla's wavering about slightly. They were absolutely filthy, too – the muck was probably holding them together. But the room behind the nets was so dark that you couldn't tell if anyone was standing there or not.

There was a belch from the pavement. The bird was really in its cups now, staggering about like some clown in a silent film. It let forth a torrent of abuse, most of which I can't remember. But it got Dwight even more steamed up, and a couple of others in the street came out to see who was cursing at such an ungodly hour.

"Heavens above!" someone sounding like Alice Dorchester exclaimed behind me. "I haven't heard language like that since – *what the hell is that bird doin'?*"

Me, Dwight and a few others watched as the bird started to fly. It weaved and spun, twisted and corkscrewed like some kamikaze pilot. It dive-bombed us four or five times, and we all ducked in unison as the bird cackled overhead. *"You small-minded sons of bitches! I hope you rot in hell!"*

It soon got bored of this as we knew to duck in time. It flew as quick as a flash over to the other side of the street and rummaged about in one of the gardens there, then hopped onto a wall, watching us. We watched back. It was like something from a western. For a few seconds there was absolute quiet.

Suddenly it seemed to take a sharp intake of breath and flew towards us at high speed; only this time it didn't dive. As it got near you could see something in the back of its throat, its eyes glistened, and it spat – didn't drop, *spat* – a mouthful of gravel chippings right onto us, flew back to the garden, reloaded and did the same again, three times in all. Nobody got hurt any worse than a few scratches, except Alice Dorchester who lost a few locks when it crash-landed her bouffant, yanking out a few hairs at the roots on the last of its attacks.

"You sorry bunch of losers!" the bird screeched at us from a safe distance. *"All so God-damn high and mighty with your nice homes and fancy cars, all clean and spotless –"* It burped again, sounding more like a bullfrog than a bird. *"Well, clean this! Ahahahahaha!"*

And it went past every car that was out in the street and did its business on all of 'em. Of course, that's not a lot of business, not like a horse or nothin', but when you consider there must've been more than ten cars out that day, and this was your average-sized mockingbird … well, it must've been storing it up special is all I can say. It was unnatural.

Dwight snapped then, went crazy. His wife was telling me before about his high blood pressure and how the doctor warned him to take it easy – at that moment it looked as though Henry was going to erupt like a volcano; he was practically purple. After he'd fired off a few curses of his own, Louisa must've heard him and came running out in her nightgown and fluffy pink slippers. Given the circumstances, nobody batted an eyelid.

"Henry, I heard you shouting, what's going on?" she said.

"Fat man! Hey fatso, wanna drink?"

Dwight stared at the bird as though his eyes would roll out of their sockets.

"Bars ain't open yet, but there's a bottle here –"

"Why you little –"

And Dwight charged at the bird. He only got so far because it flew at him and squawked and shrieked and hollered and flapped like a demon. Henry squealed like a stuck pig, shielding his eyes with his hands, backing off all the while. Once he was out of the way, the bird went back to the bottle and took another swig. It was starting to bloat terribly. The bottle was nearly half empty.

Louisa let out a shriek. "My God, Henry! Look what it's done to you!" she said.

It had certainly made a mess. Nothing permanent, but ugly nonetheless. Good job he wasn't entering any beauty pageants. His face and neck were covered in a series of little red crisscrosses, like cuts from a razor. Louisa put her arm around him (as far as she could) and led him away home. The bird shrieked its approval.

"Bye, asshole! Be seein' ya!" it shrilled, its beak snapping open and shut like scissors.

However, the bird decided it hadn't finished. I suppose I was hoping that it was just Dwight that had rattled it and once he was out of the way it would get bored and go. But it didn't. Instead it started to peck at car windows and house doors, marking them with spit and scratches and dirty footprints, all the while calling us all every name under the sun. When it wasn't getting any reaction it would pick up some more gravel and spit at us, or dive at us again.

How long this lasted I don't know. But Dwight emerged after a while covered in little bits of tissue paper. Louisa was still in her nightwear.

"*Hey, nice outfit!*" the bird squawked, "*those pink slippers are really cute!*"

We all looked towards Louisa as if seeing her for the first time. Nobody looked particularly shocked at her dress, but she blushed and dashed back inside, more than once losing a slipper and having to go back for it.

"That damn bird is always in the witch's garden. I reckon she's something to do with all this," Dwight said stupidly, trying to fill the embarrassed silence.

And she'd spent all those years alone in that house brooding, putting up with the taunts and whispers ...

"Well I don't know about anyone else," Dwight announced, rubbing his stomach. "I'm gonna get that bottle. Get rid of the bottle, get rid of the bird." We murmured agreement. It sounded reasonable enough.

So Dwight marched forward, trying to look as macho as can be, and for a big guy with a paunch, not doing too badly – until the bird figured out what was happening and flew at him again.

"*You leave my goddamned bottle alone you fat piece of shit!*" the bird yelled (and I mean *yelled*) amid a frenzied blur of flapping wings and needle-sharp claws. Dwight managed another two steps before he backed out, the bird keeping up the attack until he was almost back alongside us again – just so he'd got the message, I suppose.

We all looked at Dwight then. He stood there re-arranging his shirt and hair, little bits of white paper stuck to his face like dried spitballs. A more ridiculous sight you could not wish to see. He had an indignant look in his eyes which said *If you think I'm gonna be beaten by some stupid bird, then think again.*

Taking a deep breath, he rubbed his hands on his shirt. "Okay," he said with a kind of sigh. "Okay … if that's what has to be done, then so be it." He marched away from us quickly, leaving us all staring at each other. He was halfway down his drive when it struck me what he was going for.

Once inside his house, Louisa started shouting and then Dwight yelled back at her: "*You ain't gonna stop me, Lou. I've been humiliated in my own street!*"

He came out of his front door brandishing his shotgun. We all drew in sharp breaths as we saw the thing, draped over his arm like a mink. I could feel my heart pounding, my breaths shortening. This was getting *way* out of hand. Maybe 'Cilla would see how silly this was all getting and stop.

"What the *hell* is going on here? Henry Dwight, what do you think you're gonna do with that gun?"

We all looked around. When I saw Roberta bustling up the street in her usual busy manner I could've kissed her.

'Cilla hardly got any visitors. Well, she only got the one – Roberta. Over the past fifteen years or so 'Cilla Abcott has had many home helpers and managed to drive away every single one; that was up until about five years ago when Roberta Freeman said she wanted to see this old woman who was causing so much trouble (there was a story that a couple of the helpers had fled from the house in tears) and that she'd be able to sort her out. Nobody believed her of course, but, try as she might (and according to Roberta she really did *try*), 'Cilla couldn't do anything bad enough to get rid of her. Nowadays Roberta said that 'Cilla tolerated her, and I suspect had a grudging admiration for her for staying around so long.

"I asked you a question, Dwight. What are doing with that gun?"

Dwight was speechless. Roberta, when she put her mind to it, could cut anyone down in their prime, Henry Dwight included. I suppose dealing with 'Cilla toughened you up some. But she was never other than friendly with those who treated her right.

Dwight blustered. "That damned bird called me an asshole!" he spat out.

"Well I'd say that bird is a mighty fine judge of character," she answered. "Now, what's going on?" Only Roberta Freeman would have the nerve to say that to a man who was pointing a loaded gun at her.

So we all chipped in and told her bits and pieces until the story was complete. Halfway through, a sly smile started to play across her face. I've never seen such a knowing look. *So that's what the old devil's been up to,* is how I read it.

"Well something's triggered it all off," she said when we'd finished. "I know 'Cilla pretty well and she wouldn't do something like that without reason. So –" she looked at each of us in turn, "– who's upset her lately?"

We all mumbled and looked at each other.

"Dwight …?" Roberta said.

"Okay, okay. I *may* have upset her last week, but she brought it on herself!"

Roberta stood, arms folded. "What did you do, Dwight?" she said quietly.

Apparently one day he'd been walking past her garden and looked in at it. He'd stood there awhile, tutting at the mess. 'Cilla had showed at the window and signalled for him to move away.

"I told her if she was such a good witch she should put a spell on me and make me leave," Dwight told us. "I had a piece of gum in my mouth and spat it into her garden." Roberta shook her head. "But that was nothing compared to what she's doing now!" he added quickly, pointing to his face.

"Oh, it's not just that, you idiot!" Roberta snapped back. "She's had this all her life, all because of some stupid rumour when she was a girl. You've never given her a chance. I know she's an old devil, but she's like that because people round here have made her that way."

That touched a nerve. Heads hung down. Dwight had been the straw that broke the camel's back. There was an awkward silence for a few minutes.

"Okay, okay," Roberta said. "I'll put a stop to it for you. But you've all got to promise – you as well Dwight – that you'll never torment or annoy her again and just leave her be. And you've all to pass the word around too."

We all agreed.

"Okay then. I'll go now."

Dwight wasn't finished yet. "Hang on a minute. How do we know you'll have sorted her out?"

"I'll take one of you with me – not you Dwight, she hates your guts – you Ellen, you're a sensible type."

"Me?" I said, suddenly getting all jittery like a child in a ghost train.

"Yes, you. You'll be perfectly safe with me in there. Now come on."

I started to say something about the bird but she waved that away. "You'll be fine with me," she said again, like a schoolmistress.

With an eye on Roberta and one eye on the bird I made my way into 'Cilla's garden. Roberta bent down and grabbed the bottle by the neck, its contents sloshing against the sides. I tensed, waiting for the bird to attack.

But it didn't; although it looked like it wanted to – it stared down from a tree in the garden, jerking about like a dog on a leash. Roberta's face had a look of sheer concentration on it. "She never locks her door so we can go straight in," she said over her shoulder. *No*, I thought, *she doesn't need to*. We stepped inside quickly. Roberta slammed it shut with a sigh of relief.

Suddenly all hell broke loose. There was a wild banging on the door and flapping of wings which sounded much bigger than they were. Roberta even fastened a few chains in place. Later on people said the bird damned near killed itself bashing that door to get at us.

I was dumbstruck by the noise behind me. In front of me dust motes swirled around, an old faded black and white portrait picture sat crookedly in its frame above the light switch.

"Come on," Roberta said.

We went down the hall and turned right at the end into the living room. It smelled like the inside of a musty wardrobe.

I'd heard that 'Cilla didn't allow Roberta to do any cleaning, but even so … everywhere seemed to have a thin film of dust on it. The wallpaper was stained grey and yellow, the nets looked as though they'd had years of cigar smoke blown on them. As for furnishings in the room, it was all pretty sparse and old fashioned; I saw a table just like we'd had when I was a girl, full of fancy designs and scratches, a moth-eaten light shade with a slender stem underneath it. On a coffee table were three or four days' worth of newspapers curling down towards the filthy carpet.

And stood in front of one of the heavy curtains was Priscilla Abcott.

It was the first proper look I'd had at her in years, and I didn't like what I saw; there was only a few years between us both, but looking at her made me feel young. The skin on her face hung and creased like pieces of well-battered leather; she had no teeth in, and when she breathed in it was like looking at a balloon a few days after Christmas, shrivelling like a prune. She was almost a living skeleton, her eyes sunk right back into her head, hidden in the room's murk. Later on I'd see they were a large baby blue, like a newborn kitten. Her clothes hung off her like they didn't want to be there at all.

"What the hell are you doin' in my house?" she demanded. My heart raced a bit quicker. I could smell tequila in the air.

"You know damned well," Roberta answered her. "You been acting strange for days and I wondered what you were up to."

"You've no idea what I have to put up with round here!" the old lady spat back.

"Yes I do," Roberta answered her, her voice barely above a whisper.

"Hey!" 'Cilla looked down at Roberta's hand. "What are you doing with that? Give it here!"

She shuffled forward at quite a speed, thin arms grasping out for the bottle. Roberta moved away from her, towards a back room. "Come on Ellen," she said. I followed.

We were in the kitchen, a room even more dismal than the living room. The sides of the taps were clogged with dew, a burnt pan sat at an angle on the stove.

"Hey, *you leave that goddamned bottle alone!*"

Roberta had removed the straw and started emptying out the tequila. It glugged away down the filthy stained sink, which in turn gurgled back at her. 'Cilla was just about to grab the bottle when she stopped mid-action and stared straight ahead. "Oh no," she said in a quiet voice, on her face a look of defeat and regret.

"You knew that'd happen," Roberta said to her. I'd no idea what she was talking about. "It's a sin as well. I hope you're happy."

I was just about to ask what was going on when 'Cilla screeched again, making a grab for the bottle. As she did the worm unstuck from the bottom and slid its way out of the bottle, landing with a soft plop in the sink.

"Now, 'Cilla," Roberta said in a stern voice. "You just watch this. Watch and learn."

The revolting little thing in the sink started to wriggle itself about, looking like a giant caterpillar, both ends turned up at us like a smile without a face.

I don't know who was more shocked, me or 'Cilla. I think we both backed away a little.

"Watch and learn," repeated Roberta.

The worm wriggled a bit more, but one end fell back into the sink. The other was still in the air, pointing at us.

Then it spoke.

"Now you listen to me, Priscilla Abcott," it said in a garbled high-pitched whine of a voice like it had been sucking on a helium balloon. *"You're not the only one around here with talents, you know. And I think it's high time you learned to live with it. If you'd tried a bit more instead of sulking all the while maybe people would've given you a chance in the end. You think about that. You know how long you've got left."*

As this was going on I saw Roberta's lips moving silently. She was staring down at the worm with that same look of concentration on her face that I'd seen outside when we were coming in.

My shock seemed to be nothing compared to Priscilla Abcott's. She wailed and wailed like a siren, it was like a gale going through a museum. When she stopped she looked as though she was about to collapse. Roberta and me grabbed an arm each and led her to her rocking chair in the corner and sat her down.

I stared at 'Cilla then. I couldn't believe the change in her. She was in shock, rocking back and forth, her lips trembling. Roberta gently tugged my arm. "Let's go," she said. "I'll be in tomorrow, 'Cilla," she said over her shoulder, but I doubt 'Cilla heard her.

Before taking the chains off the door, Roberta said: "Apart from my folks no-one knows about – *that,*" she told me, avoiding my gaze. "I'd rather it was kept that way, Ellen, if you don't mind."

"Sure," I replied.

"That's how I put up with her," she said, undoing the chains. "I know exactly what it feels like."

"But you never told her."

"No. In the end I found that I couldn't. Silly huh?" she smiled a humourless smile. "Come on, our public awaits." She opened the door.

I looked down at the step. On the worn mat was the body of the mockingbird, bloated, its feathers ruffled, head bent out of shape and quite dead. "It's a sin, you know," Roberta said, shaking her head when she spotted it. "A damned sin."

On leaving the garden, what seemed like half the neighbourhood rushed forward to ask us what had happened.

In the days that followed, there was lots of talk – but not by me or Roberta. It was soon becoming the stuff of local legend, bits getting added here and there. The people who heard that shriek said it would stay with them for as long as they lived. A few asked if there was another shriek in there – perhaps from me or Roberta. We never heard anything, we told them.

It did work, though – 'Cilla was left pretty much alone after that. Nobody's been over there with a cake or anything like that, but at least she's not being pestered anymore. Even the neighbourhood kids seem to leave her alone now.

What was the significance of the bird? Who can say. Perhaps it was the worst thing her childish mind could dream up. But it served its purpose, that's for sure. I could say 'who knows how their minds work at that age', but that could as easily apply to me.

Yesterday I was walking past her house and looked over at the garden. In amongst all the earth and patches of dying grass I saw a small wooden cross made of two lollipop sticks jutting out of the soil near the window. The wind had blown it off to one side. There was some kind of inscription on the sticks in black felt-tip pen but it was too small to make out.

You think about death a lot at my age. You have to.

And I reckon 'Cilla won't be far behind that bird.

The Cure

Lionel Duxbury felt naked without his watch. It had been the first thing taken from him before he was allowed on the plane.

Looking at his wrist he saw a pale, circular patch of skin where his watch should be. Suddenly, the plane lurched. The pain in his gut flared up and made him wince. He reached into his pocket for the bottle of painkillers but remembered that they'd taken them as well.

They'd taken everything that wasn't cloth or leather: his watch, his pen, his magazine and newspaper, his reading glasses – even a half-eaten packet of mints; for a split second he wondered where his two cases were being stored – he tried not to think about it.

In return for his luggage, he'd been given a detailed inventory by a rather bland-looking man of indeterminate age. Handing Duxbury the receipt, he told him he'd get the items back later.

Taking his seat in the plane, Duxbury saw he had the entire cabin to himself. He took the middle seat in the front row so he had room to stretch out if he wished. Normally he would've taken – demanded – a window seat, but as the windows were blacked out there was no point. Minutes later the plane shuddered and took off. Duxbury felt like a prisoner.

With nobody to talk to and nothing to read or watch, the businessman got bored. When he realised that he was not going to be disturbed he decided to check out the rest of the cabin.

It was a twelve seater. The black leather seats were a decent size but hardly comfortable. When he stood he had to crouch slightly as the roof was low. He wondered if the plane was designed for human or animal cargo – the seats looked somehow incongruous and the whole area had a strange odour about it; he felt like he was flying in a specially upholstered crate. Checking the seams along the walls and ceiling, he found nothing to indicate that communication with the pilot was possible. With a shrug he sat back down.

Once again he began to wonder at the strangeness of the journey he was undertaking: For the first time in decades, Lionel Duxbury found himself at the mercy of complete strangers, and it troubled him more than his illness ever could. Even illness had its purpose, he mused. It was a sobering thought. He was taking a risk. It wasn't the first time and he hoped that it wouldn't be the last. But he'd always had control; and since he'd found out about his illness he'd felt that control slipping away from him. And this was why he was in this ridiculous situation in the first place, giving money to people he didn't know, sitting on a plane with the windows blacked out so he couldn't tell what hour of the day or night it was; because, even in such a bizarre situation with such an exaggerated risk, it meant he at least had *some* control of his situation; without his money *they* wouldn't be doing this – *they* wouldn't exist without *his* illness. *They* were here because of him.

"Whoever *they* are," he mumbled into the stale air of the cabin.

First Day

The first thing Lionel Duxbury did when he got off the plane was shield his eyes against the intense rays of the burning sun. As he squinted at the rest of the Island, the pilot appeared at his side and handed him the case containing his belongings. The other case was nowhere to be seen.

The pilot gestured for him to go ahead. The businessman stepped off the small concrete landing strip and onto a sandy path indistinguishable from the rocks that surrounded him. The pilot walked a few steps behind him.

Ahead, the path wound down between the sand-like boulders. They looked so fragile he could imagine lifting them above his head and crumbling them between his fingers like cinders.

Apart from the sand-like stone, this part of the Island had very little colour; a few emaciated white trees covered with brown blotches poked through the rock in various places, every other one sporting small pink blossoms. The air was heavy with a sweet perfume, presumably from the pink flowers; licking his lips he could taste it. Overhead the sky was almost painfully blue. Despite the vast open space, he felt somehow separated from things, as if he was in a bubble.

He tried in vain to decide where he might be, but without knowing how long they'd been in the air it proved fruitless; it could've been three hours or thirteen; he'd lost all perspective of time.

Passing yet another outcrop of sand-boulders the sea appeared below him, a beautiful shimmering green liquid that only stopped when it threatened to merge with the horizon.

He was still looking at the sea when something white caught his eye. Down and to his left a small figure was shuffling its way up to him. Out of nowhere a childhood memory appeared; in spite of the heat, he found himself smiling.

After a few introductions, Duxbury was shown to his room. Later on in the day he ate the best fish he'd ever tasted in his life.

It had all begun the day he found out he was dying.

When Duxbury went to his private club, it was to get away from people. He wasn't the type of person that poured his heart out, least of all to another man. Even when Ruth died he didn't discuss it with anybody; they'd never been that close, and she'd always been a poor second to the company. He wished he could've felt more when she died but he didn't.

But this was different. He'd been told he had only a few months left to live.

Leaving the hospital, Duxbury had believed half of what the doctor told him; he believed that there was something eating away at him, destroying him; he'd known for months, ignoring the pains that twisted at his innards, refusing to accept that it could be that bad.

But what he couldn't believe was that the situation was lost entirely. He simply *refused* to believe it; doctors weren't infallible. And, that night when he'd gone into his club, he'd gone in with the conviction he could turn the situation around; at every point in his life something had come along to save his neck.

Two double cognacs later, a man with an indistinct face walked past his chair. Duxbury suddenly found that he wanted somebody to talk to – or rather somebody to listen to him.

"Hey – don't go yet," he'd said as the figure moved towards the door. "Let me buy you a drink. I have a story to tell," he'd said, tipping the ash from his cigar into the glass ashtray.

The figure stopped, his back still to Duxbury.

"I thought that would get your attention."

Turning, the stranger faced him. He smiled at Duxbury and sat down, placing his hands in his lap, all the time looking earnestly into the older man's face.

"This afternoon," Duxbury said after taking another swig of cognac, "I was told I only have three months to live. What do you think of that?"

The man nodded, and continued to smile.

Second Day

He awoke that morning with the sun streaming through the window in his small room. After a simple but adequate breakfast he was informed that the sea he'd spoken so warmly of on his arrival would be their destination for the day.

Out on the water, Duxbury stared down into the barely-moving sparkling emerald sea. The air was so still the only sounds he could hear were the water gently lapping the side of the boat and his own laboured breathing.

"So you see Mr Duxbury," the old man said, "that life is in fact never-ending; but at the same time is also a series of 'little deaths' from which we must learn or die once more."

Duxbury looked at the man he'd seen shambling up to meet him a day earlier. It turned out he was in charge. When he'd asked him what he should call him, the other man said he wouldn't have any need to call him anything. It was all a bit melodramatic but the businessman decided to go along with it.

But after twenty-four hours of it, he found himself flagging; he was impatient to get down to the real reason he was here.

"So you see that you have to view this *passage* in your life as simply the end of one phase; like the snake, our paths are sinuous, forever twisting and turning; and, along the way we have to rejuvenate. Once you have undergone the Cure, you will simply begin another chapter of your life."

Duxbury, unused to such sentiments, had to bite his tongue. How much of this new-age claptrap did he have to listen to? But at least the fabled 'Cure' had been mentioned.

As the man continued to drone on about things coming and going around, Duxbury tried to fathom where he was from; he certainly wasn't English because he spoke it perfectly and without accent, foreign or otherwise.

Nodding on cue to a point being made about 'our true natures' he noticed that the man's eyes were almost exactly the same shade of green as the sea that surrounded them.

"Yes," Duxbury replied, nodding passionately, "I agree entirely."

A week later he was walking along a disused path with two suitcases; one containing his luggage for the trip, the other containing money. He thought of the last thing the voice had said on the phone before he left home.

"We understand you have doubts. You would not be human if you did not. However, the amount of money you pay for this service is not beyond your means. You agreed that the amount was reasonable in an earlier conversation."

After an interminable distance he saw something glinting through a gap in the trees ahead. As the path began to ascend the pain flared again. Stopping, he took the pill bottle from his pocket and popped a pill into his mouth.

A few minutes later he reached the top of the slope and found a small plane waiting on a flat patch of ground, with a man standing next to it. Once more his guts squeezed him.

Remembering what he'd been told earlier in the week, he reached into his jacket pocket and again took out the bottle of pills. Approaching the small plane he put the last pill he would ever take in his life into his mouth.

Third Day

After the previous day's boat trip, Duxbury was informed that today he should relax.

"Tomorrow will be a big day for you," the wizened old man informed him.

"You mean my treatment will start tomorrow, do you?"

"The Cure will begin then, yes. So, feel free to spend the time as you please. You will find the kitchen fully stocked. Good day to you."

With that, the old man smiled and shuffled away along a sandy path until he vanished.

For a while Duxbury wondered where he'd gone. Besides the old man, he'd only seen four people on the Island, each one as bland and interchangeable as the last. He'd heard one of them call the old man 'Master'; perhaps they were all going off to pray on a rock somewhere.

After sitting in the sun for as long as he could stand he headed for the kitchen, opening a bottle of wine he found in a stone cupboard. Like the fish, it was superb, the best he'd ever drunk. It was unlike any wine he'd ever tasted, its sweet-heavy taste reminiscent of the Island air, but with something strangely intoxicating underneath it. By the time he finished his meal he was on the second bottle.

Sitting on the small quayside, he found the stillness around him both eerie and calming; he wasn't used to such silence, and would be glad when things got started tomorrow – he also wasn't sure he could stomach another days' quasi-religious philosophising. He imagined what the people under him would have said behind his back – he, master of all he surveyed in the pay of bible-bashers, or whatever they were. But then it occurred to him that they didn't even know he was ill – it had all happened so quickly he hadn't told anybody. Not that it was any of their business.

Before he knew where the time had gone, it was dark and he was tired – all he'd done was stare out at that beautiful green sea but it was as though he'd been hypnotised by it. And the time didn't really matter.

Rising, he felt a pain in his stomach, a different kind of pain to the ones he'd grown accustomed to. He was glad the treatment would begin in the morning.

"Look, is all this cloak-and-dagger stuff really necessary?" Duxbury had asked before getting on the plane, tired of the endless list of instructions. "Why couldn't I have just *written* you a cheque? Why couldn't I have booked the flight myself?"

"Mr Duxbury, I'm sure you can appreciate that everything we do is in the best interest of both parties," the man, presumably the pilot, said. "Our service is an unusual one. Our methods are unorthodox."

"But this is ridiculous! I don't even know where the damned place is."

The man's face bristled behind his sunglasses. "That too is in the best interests of both parties," he replied, his voice now with a slight edge. "As for booking a flight yourself, that is impossible – the Island does not have its own airport. The plane is our own private plane. In fact, we'd be surprised if any airline on earth had ever heard of our Island. We are its sole inhabitants. We are not a holiday camp, Mr Duxbury."

The businessman fumed, unused to being talked to in this way.

"As for being ignorant of our location, that will not change. Even on the Island you will not know where you are. Before you board the plane, you will be relieved of all objects on your person that do not constitute clothing; your watch, for example, could be used to give you ideas regarding our position. You are by your own admission a highly travelled man."

"So you're going to confiscate my watch!" Duxbury found himself almost smiling now. "And what about the tremendous amount of money you are taking from me? That, presumably, is to be confiscated too?"

"That, Mr Duxbury, is payment." The man smiled, his eyes hidden by the sunglasses. "We ask clients to bring cash for two reasons. One, because we do not have bank accounts, and deal only in international currencies. Secondly, a cash transaction is seen by us as an act of faith on your part: you have to trust us implicitly or not at all. We sympathise that this is a risk for you, but as you have pointed out, you are a highly successful man and have built your reputation on risk-taking. And it has been pointed out to you on more than one occasion that the amount of money we ask of our clients is not enough to leave them in financial difficulties; in fact, for the service we provide, it is a small price to pay."

This was true; the money in the case would be a substantial sum to most people, but to the businessman it was a drop in the ocean. And if, as they claimed, they can destroy the disease that was gnawing away at him, then it *was* a small price to pay; on the other hand, if it failed he would still have enough money to see him through – *to the end,* a voice in his head whispered. He had nothing to lose; but everything to gain.

Then he recalled how he'd felt going into his club: and that decided it.

"Okay," Duxbury told the pilot, "let's get on with it."

Fourth Day

He awoke at sunrise to find the 'Master' standing over his bed.

"Do you always watch people in their sleep?" Duxbury grunted, pulling on a shirt.

"I was just about to awaken you. My apologies."

After breakfast, the two men walked for what felt likes hours along dozens of deserted sandy paths fringed with long, sharp grasses at the cliff's edge. Eventually, with the land starting to level out, a small white dome-shaped structure rose above the greenery. As he got closer, Duxbury saw how small it was and could contain himself no longer.

"This is where my Cure is to be administered?" He snorted.

"This," replied the old man, "is the Hermitage. It is the starting point of your Cure. You will spend the day and night here and reflect on your life to this point. It is necessary to think about how you have lived your life."

"I've led a very successful life," Duxbury told him. "And I've no intention of stopping now. But frankly I fail to see how staying in a stone hovel is going to help me."

"We find that concentrating on the past usually brings negative aspects of ourselves into focus. And within these negatives you will find the root of all illness. By thinking these thoughts, you will be bringing your illness to the surface, which will make it easier to remove."

Duxbury had to bite his lip. Was he really paying for this?

"And when will that be?"

"That will be tomorrow."

"So tomorrow you'll start using medicines, things like that?"

"If that's what you want to think of it as, then yes. But remember Mr Duxbury – this is a *very* important part of the process."

With that the 'Master' once more shuffled out of view, leaving Duxbury alone. Staring out over the sea, he saw no ships pass, no birds flying past. It wasn't called the Hermitage for nothing, he thought.

Inside, the Hermitage was surprisingly cool. There was just enough room to stand if he bowed his head slightly. To sleep – again he found himself exhausted, not used to the exertion of the walk – he had to curl up on the floor as there wasn't enough room to stretch out.

He was extremely relieved to find a basket of food and wine against the back wall. He opened the wine immediately. Minutes later he was asleep.

He awoke in darkness to find his limbs aching. Putting it down to the cramped shelter, he went outside and sat on the cliff edge, taking the food and the last of the wine with him. Staring out into the night he began to think of his 'past'. He came to the conclusion that he wouldn't have changed a thing; he'd hurt people over the years, he'd been ruthless at times. His life wasn't blameless. He'd made enemies. He'd made a lot of money too. Smiling, he took another gulp of the sweet wine.

He hadn't liked the 'Master's' insinuation that he'd somehow lived his life badly or wrongly; who was he to judge? He lived his life as he saw fit; if the old fool didn't like it, it was tough – he wasn't paying him so he could be liked. He gulped back the last of the wine, throwing the bottle over the edge of the cliff.

All at once the strange pain he'd felt the day before in his gut began to infect every part of him; he found his arms and legs almost totally seizing up. Sweating, he dragged himself inside the Hermitage; perhaps he could sleep off the cramp. But the cramp got worse; it was as if his blood was solidifying in his veins; his limbs felt like stone, his face locked into an immovable grimace. As his lay immobile on the floor, a gasp of sweet, cloying air escaped him and hung in front of him.

The wine, he realised with sudden certainty. *They've poisoned my wine.*

Outside the night was perfectly still.

"I want to know how you found out about my illness," Duxbury had asked as he was about to board the plane.

"We didn't find out about your illness. You told us. We have representatives all over the world waiting to be found. We don't look for people, we just exist. We didn't come looking for you. You found us. Nobody forced you to tell our representative your life story."

"Rubbish," Duxbury replied. "I've been going to that club for twenty years and I'd never seen that man before in my life."

"He happened to be in the club on that particular night, that was all. He could as easily have missed you. You could have chosen to go home, or to a restaurant, or back to your office. Instead, you went to your club. And, as you could've chosen to have gone anywhere that night, the same is true of our representative."

"So you're saying it was a fluke, then."

"No," The pilot told him, helping Duxbury onto the plane. "What I'm saying is that it was your destiny. *You were destined to become involved with us.*"

Fifth Day

When the old man and a younger man looked inside the Hermitage the next morning they found Lionel Duxbury curled up on the floor, his arms stretched out in front of him, the fingers of both hands curled inwards like claws.

Stepping into the Hermitage, the younger man picked up the body as if it was that of a child. Placing it against the outside wall, the old man stepped forward and looked down at it, its arms raised to the sky.

The old man stared into the face, then nodded.

"I know you can still hear me, Mr Duxbury," he said, crouching down to eye level. "And I daresay you are afraid. But, this is your destiny. Everything we do is a step towards your rejuvenation. *We are going to repair your damage by Curing you of your life.*"

Duxbury's eyes stared back, his lids locked into place.

The younger man stepped forward and picked up Lionel Duxbury once more, putting him across his back and piggybacking him to a part of the Island he'd never seen before. Bobbling along on the young man's back, his all-seeing eyes burned as they moved into a cloud of thick white smoke. Just as it was becoming unbearable he was placed on cobbled stones.

"Mr Duxbury," the old man's voice said somewhere over to his right, "you were anxious for the Cure to begin. It will now begin in earnest."

Despite his physical paralysis, the businessman could feel the sweat running down his face. He was picked up once more and taken further into the smoke, until his lips became coated with it. Through the smoke he could see a large grate set among the cobbles from which the steam was rising. He could still hear the old man's voice but his words were obscured by the steam. As he watched, the grate got closer, until his lifeless body was lying stiffly across it.

His only option was to look down into the grate. Among the great clouds of white rising towards him, he saw welcoming patches of blackness beneath. After a while the blackness increased, until the very steam itself turned black.

In the small dark cabin of the plane, Duxbury opened his eyes, unsure of his surroundings. Evidently he'd found sleep after all.

"Or sleep found me," he grunted into his chest.

Listening, he realised that something was different: The engines had stopped.

The door at the back of the plane opened and the small cabin was filled with bright golden light. When the pilot stepped in front of the doorway, half the cabin was plunged back into darkness.

"We have arrived," he told Duxbury, holding out his hands.

Sixth Day

At sunset, the young man looked up at the great tree and saw that once again the Cure had been successful. To him it was a miracle; but his Master said it was the most natural thing in the world. One day, the younger man had said he hoped to be Cured when he was ready. The older man nodded and smiled.

At dawn, accompanied as always by the Master, he'd removed the body from the steam-grate. As always, he found the partially shrivelled body easier to carry than when he'd removed it from the Hermitage.

"The steam takes a lot of the evil away," His Master had told him. "But it is the sun that helps us the most."

With great care and attention, the body of Lionel Duxbury was then tethered to the branches of the thickest tree the Island possessed. When his Master was satisfied that the body would be in direct contact with the suns' rays, the two men left.

When they returned at dusk, the old man carried a stone bowl in his arms. The younger man walked behind, holding a large rake-like object.

Removing the body from the tree he laid it at the feet of his Master. A small smile spread across his ancient face.

In silent contemplation, both men looked at the blackened and desiccated object before them, its bones poking through the dried-out flesh. After saying a few words over the body the older man informed the younger that it was time.

Dropping to his knees before the body, the younger man placed his left hand on what remained of the corpse's neck. With his right hand, he gripped the bottom of the ribcage and began to pull it up towards him.

Almost immediately, the bones began to separate from the blackened flesh, as if they had never held flesh on them. When the bones were completely free of the body, they were placed against the tree. He repeated the process with the skull and other bones until all that remained was a pile of darkened meat on the ground.

Then, taking the rake-like object in both fists, he ran the tines from head to toe along the desiccated corpse, the meat separating into long shreds. Next he ran the tines across the flesh from left to right until the long strips of flesh became mere chunks.

Together they collected the dried strips of flesh into the stone dish, making their way to the cliffs' edge where they looked out at a beautiful red sunset.

Placing the dish on a rock beside him, the old man took pieces of flesh in each hand. He turned to the young man.

"He is Cured," He told him.

The young man smiled at his Master, watching as He tossed handfuls of flesh down into the sea, repeating the process until the dish was empty. Staring down into the sparkling green sea, they waited.

A few minutes later the beautiful green water began to churn into spume. When they saw the first of the silvery heads break the surface of the water, quickly followed by a second then a third, tears came to both men's eyes.

Ever since childhood, Lionel Duxbury had an image of what God would look like if He existed: He would be small and frail and extremely elderly, with long, white hair and dark, leathery lined skin, probably wearing a white robe. A few seconds after getting from the plane, he found the spitting image of that very man shuffling his way up the sandy path towards him.

But as the man got closer, Duxbury spotted a few differences between his childhood God and the man approaching; this man's eyes were a live and vivid green, totally unlike the dull grey ones he'd imagined. Also, this man wasn't solemn, the way he'd imagined Gods would be – instead, he was smiling, almost grinning from ear to ear.

"Welcome to our Island," the old man said, his green eyes sparkling.

Seventh Day

Rated X

In the middle of the worst storm he'd ever seen, the artist left the city, satisfied that his work there was at an end. His face was covered in the fine white spray blowing in the wind, his feet and ankles covered in the thick white foam running along the pavements, roads and gutters.

But despite the conditions, he couldn't have been happier; large numbers of the statues remained, testaments to his work in the city, subjects made of stronger stuff than anyone but he could possibly imagine. A few of them, oddly luminescent, tried their best to brighten the dreary surroundings of empty shops, broken benches, cracked paving flags and half-eaten food cartons. Wondering what the effect would be from above, he decided that he would find a hill above the city before he moved on.

And so, with a smile on his face, the artist made his way through the blizzard and puddles of white sludge, onto a higher place.

On entering the city, he wandered for several hours, his few possessions carried in a small bundle on his back. As an artist, he had to breathe in and taste the atmosphere of the place chosen to work in. He found that as cities went, it was fairly typical; the only thing that mattered was that this place needed him; he'd known that before he'd arrived.

Trudging through the inevitable sleet, he eventually found somewhere to rest his bones. Instead of investigating further however, he kept walking, knowing that it could wait; before he rested he had to find somewhere to *begin;* and sometimes it could take hours. So, despite the pains in his feet he carried on, knowing that the end result would always be worth the pain he endured.

And then, just as he'd begun to despair, he found it on the far side of the city – a place almost too perfect for words. He felt happier than he had in days, weeks; and when he entered his chosen place of rest and saw that it was perfect too, he felt that his heart would burst with joy.

Later, preparing himself for the work ahead, a ray of moonlight reached him and moved gently across his hand, staining it a brilliant white. It was the sign he'd been waiting for.

He was ready.

Next day, the first of the statues appeared in the local sculpture park.

When it appeared – or rather, *they* appeared, as there were four of them, scattered around the park – it was assumed by the park's patrons that these signature-less icons must have been installed without fanfare to add a sense of mystery to the place; no doubt, they thought, looking at the agony-wracked forms of bone-like material, this masterful artist would be named at some point, once a suitable *furore* had been raised. When the owner of the park professed his ignorance regarding the provenance of the statues and their creator, let alone the fact that they had seemingly 'popped up in the middle of the night', of course nobody believed him.

In a bid to solve the mystery (and also realising the free and much-needed publicity the stunt could provoke), he contacted the local newspaper in the hope that they or their readers could shed some light on the situation.

However, none was forthcoming; the editor, sensing some kind of elaborate scam, decided to ignore the statues. Didn't the sculpture park's owner realise that there were things of *real* importance going on in the city, such as the alarming rise in street crime and violent attacks, the filthy state of the streets, the opening of several 'adult' clubs in the city centre? Why, the editor told the man at the other end of the phone, several people had disappeared in the city in the last twenty-four hours alone. *These* were the things that people wanted to hear about, not 'good news' items, regardless of how strange they might be.

And so the statues, beautiful and mysterious as they were, were largely ignored.

The following day, the owner of the park arrived late and was surprised to find that the mist blanketing the city was, if anything, even worse in the park. It was also the reason he was late getting to the park – his windscreen wipers, ill-equipped to deal with the fine particles, dictated that, like every other car on the road, he had to drive at a reduced speed to avoid accidents.

Getting out of his car, he walked over to the gate and let himself in, removing his spectacles in order to wipe the fine, white spray from the lenses. It was oddly reminiscent of sea mist, but he dismissed that as ridiculous, the city being as far from the sea as it was.

Heading towards the exhibits, he half expected the 'new' statues to have gone. What he hadn't expected was that they would have multiplied.

The owner, perplexed but now also a little afraid, looked long and hard at the *tableau* in his park.

Each statue, evidently cut from a single large block, depicted humanity in the throes of some hideous torment; some stood erect, their blind eyes facing the heavens, while others were curled foetus-like upon the frosted grass as if suddenly struck down by some violent pain.

The owner wished that he could find out who the artist was: Whoever they were, they were supremely talented; the statues were highly unnerving. He was also curious to find out what substance the statues were made of. He was pretty sure it wasn't marble — despite having the same smooth, luxurious feel, it had none of its coldness; in fact the statues were surprisingly warm to the touch, given the dropping temperatures in the area. The whole thing was, to say the least, perplexing.

Shrugging at the mystery, which would no doubt resolve itself in time, he removed his glasses once more to rid them of another coating of the fine spray, wiping it away with a handkerchief. As he was doing this he found himself gazing up at the grey sky, at what appeared to be a face composed of breaks in the cloud. But returning the spectacles to his nose, he found that there wasn't a face there after all.

Over the next forty-eight hours, more statues began appearing across the city in various odd places: At the bus station, near the taxi rank, huddled in alleyways and crouching among piles of rubbish, perched on top of walls outside the shopping arcade; even in the middle of run-down housing estates — over twenty in all. There was only one further addition to the sculpture park.

Nobody who saw these strange, milky-white figures could account for their sudden appearance; it was as if they appeared in the blink of an eye. It was suggested that whoever was responsible was in some way trying to cheer up the city, to divert attention from what looked like an imminent, city-wide gang-war – the past week had seen over a dozen notorious local villains from various factions going missing, with each side blaming the other for the disappearances, and promising revenge.

But to most people the statues were just another element in the city that had to be avoided, along with what came to be known as the freakish 'coastal spray' coating everything and everyone that happened to get in its way.

A few days and several statues later, a scruffy man with long hair and a beard entered the offices of the local newspaper.

"I was wondering," the strange smiling figure said to the young woman on the reception desk, "if you could give this note to your editor as a matter of urgency."

The receptionist stopped chewing her gum for a second, looking the man up and down. "Why, what is it?" she said, suddenly feeling a little queasy.

"It will explain certain recent features of the city and what I am trying to achieve with them."

Before she had a chance to answer, the man turned and walked back out into the mist. Before he had reached the end of the street, she rushed to the nearest sink and vomited, forgetting about the note which remained on her desk for several days.

The artist found the delay in getting back to him inexcusable. Didn't these people *care*? Maybe the additional four dozen statues he'd placed around the city weren't enough. He realised that he'd have to make a statement that would capture the city's imagination:

he knew that another inspirational tour through the streets was in order.

And as he wandered through those shabby streets, he saw what the problem was; people were hanging their heads, looking at the pavements, not at each other or the skies; and it wasn't just to avoid the spray blowing in their faces; no, it was because things were *worsening*: the city was sinking fast. It hurt him to see his work being neglected like this.

However, this disappointment soon turned to resolve – his next work would be something that would *make* people sit up and take notice.

Up a dark, cobbled street rich with the twin odours of vomit and urine, he found just the place; a dingy little establishment with electric blue and blazing pink neon above the door. Despite the weather, a huge man in a bow-tie was stood outside, his bulky arms folded across his massive chest. Making his way past the bouncer, the artist saw a man seated behind a sheet of glass, with a roll of tickets in front of him.

"One, please," said the artist.

It was safe to say that the officer had never seen anything like it in his life.

He'd been wandering the streets for hours, and despite not having encountered any trouble, he found himself on edge. The city was in the grip of a substantial crime-wave – the sudden rash of disappearances in the area was truly alarming – and, he realised as he passed another smooth, white figure in the cobbled alley near the *Logo A-Go-Go* club, these stupid white statues that had started cropping up all over the place weren't helping his mood either. Then he spotted another statue, this time outside the club itself.

Wrinkling his nose against the smell of the alley, he made his way towards it.

It was standing right in front of the door, large as life. It was then he realised that something was wrong; there was no noise coming from inside. Squeezing past the bulky statue, the officer went in to investigate.

A few minutes later he radioed his station.

"Yes sir," he said to the incredulous voice in his ear, "I know how it sounds."

After a short pause, the incredulous voice asked him to repeat something.

"I said," the officer replied, looking around him in disbelief, "that there's even one of them wrapped around the dancer's pole."

The next morning, when the newspaper editor heard about the visit by the strange man and the note he'd left behind, he was not best pleased. The receptionist told him that shortly after the man had left she'd been taken ill, which was why the note had not been passed on.

The editor, waving her apologies aside, grabbed the note and took it back to his office. Reading it through he tutted, then shook his head.

Despite his reluctance, he knew that he'd have to check it out. He grabbed his coat and left. Between the newspaper offices and the disused building, he counted twenty-seven statues.

Looking up into the crumbling face of a gargoyle, he wondered at the lengths some people would go to for publicity.

The note, a sheet of grubby paper covered in tiny handwriting, had informed him that the statues were the work of an artist who signed himself 'Rated X'. He'd had to smile at that. At least whoever he was, he had a sense of humour. It also meant that whoever he was, he knew the area.

The editor was too young to remember the old place as a church – he knew it as a dingy old picture house, a vile-smelling fleapit catering to the worst the city had to offer. Now it was derelict, another eyesore in a town full of eyesores. Oh, yes, someone had a sense of humour all right.

After taking a deep breath, he looked for the gap between the battered old door and the wall that the note had mentioned. Wondering again what he was getting himself into, he managed to squeeze into the gap, feeling like a rat disappearing into a piece of skirting board.

Passing over the threshold, the sounds from the street behind him were shut off immediately. He found himself standing in darkness so complete it was as if he'd never had eyes. Slowly, he began to move forward.

He'd walked only a few steps when a small, lit candle appeared on the floor ahead of him. Guided by its flickering light he made his way towards it, avoiding the broken seats and rubble that littered the floor, trying to make out the blurry figure behind the flame as he went.

"Be seated, please," a voice told him, making him start.

Reluctantly, the journalist sat down. When he asked if he could record the conversation a pale face framed with long straggly hair appeared, the hair almost touching the candle's flame.

"By all means," the face told him, a mouth filled with white teeth appearing through the hair.

"So," the journalist said, clicking on the machine. "You can tell me all about the statues?"

"I can enlighten you as to their origins, yes."

The journalist fired off several questions – why the name, where were the other artists, where did they all come from?

"The name," the artist called 'Rated X' said, "came to me suddenly as I was approaching your city. I knew when I arrived that it was singularly appropriate.

"As for 'others' helping me, I work alone. It merely takes a touch to create, and I work as I go along with the subjects I find. I suppose in that sense it *is* a collaboration. I would not be here were it not for them." The artist paused before resuming his answer. "Am I local? If you consider the world 'local', then, yes."

The journalist wanted to know why his name was 'singularly appropriate'.

"Oh come on," the figure smiled, leaning into the flame again, "this city is a cesspool, you can't *deny* that? It is a city full of people who have seen too much, perhaps in this very building." The journalist felt himself blushing in the darkness.

"They see these things and are not held to account for them. All I do is see these things in people and reflect it back at them. Some people see what they are when the time arrives, but most do not. Some people are affected more than others. It's a matter of degrees."

Such talk meant little to the editor. He decided to try a different tack.

"And what is so dreadfully wrong with our city," he asked of the face beyond the flame, "that means it needs several hundred statues to improve it?"

"Don't get me wrong," the artist replied, "you are not alone. I have been to many places before this and there will be many more when I leave. You are by no means unique. All I can do – that is, all my work can do – is *represent*. The statues in themselves can put nothing right – they are merely one manifestation of the problem."

"But," the journalist said, his voice rising, "*what are they supposed to represent?*"

'Rated X' thought for a while before answering.

"Have you heard of the ancient legend of the Medusa, or more appropriately, the story of the wife of Lot?" he said. When the journalist didn't reply he continued. "Both stories tell basically the same tale, but in different ways. The Medusa was one of the three dreaded Gorgons, and was so hideous to look upon that any who tried were turned to stone. On the other hand there's Lot's wife, who –"

The journalist, hearing enough mumbo-jumbo, rose to leave, his sudden movement blowing out the candle. Before he had a chance to move, a cold hand encircled his ankle.

"The point I was making," the voice said in the blackness, "was that sometimes we have to pay in life for the things we witness. That is all. An 'X' can also denote a mistake, among other things. Now do you understand?"

But 'Rated X' knew that he did not, and let go of him and listened to him stumble blindly out of the building.

The newspaper editor, grateful to be away from the filthy squat and the crackpot who inhabited it, squeezed himself back into the street and looked up into a huge face in the sky made up of clouds. Then a sudden thought popped into his head, which he soon swatted away.

Walking back to work, his body felt cramped, perhaps as a result of being in that damp old building. He wondered about the things the so-called 'artist' had said. Was he suggesting that *he* had something to do with the problems in the city? He swatted that idea aside, just as he'd swatted the face in the clouds aside.

Approaching the office, he saw a dishevelled little man outside, wearing a sandwich board proclaiming that the end was nigh. Shaking his head, he winced at the stiffness in his neck. Dragging his aching body into the lift, he pressed the button to close the door. When the door opened a few seconds later the figure inside stayed where it was.

Sitting there in the dark of the abandoned Church/Cinema, 'Rated X' knew that his work in the city was almost done. He'd lost count of the number of statues in the city and it bothered him slightly, as it always did. If these people had seen too much to begin with, weren't these grotesque parodies of the human form just desensitising them even further? Wasn't he adding to the problem?

But it was a natural reaction to doubt, and he raised himself from the litter-strewn floor to carry out his last task, the one that gave him hope for the world. Leaving the old building behind, he noticed that it had started to rain.

An hour later, with the rain almost torrential and the wind beginning to rise, he found his confidence slipping once more.

He only needed to find one person, that was all; one person to restore his faith in humanity. But so far that person (if they existed in the city) avoided him.

Stopping despite the wind and rain, he looked back at the streets he'd just passed through, every one now devoid of people but filled with statues. He reminded himself that he'd started out from a bad part of town, and set off again, eager to find a worthwhile subject.

But as the storm rose in ferocity the streets began to empty, and everyone he reached out to either slowed to a crawl or froze in agony before his eyes, the transformations taking only a matter of seconds. At the end of another thoroughfare he looked back and saw another nine white figures frozen in the rain. As he watched one of them began to dissolve, white foam dribbling down onto the pavement. A few minutes later, the gutters of the streets he walked were all choked with spume.

And then, his heart was gladdened when he saw a man buckling under the weight of the sandwich board upon his shoulders, his predictions truer than he could ever imagine. Hurrying over to him in the blizzard, 'Rated X' touched the man on the shoulder to say how grateful he was for his presence. But before he had a chance to utter a word the man with the sandwich board fell to the floor, his face a mask of agony.

Then, 'Rated X' heard a frail voice calling to him. *What have you done to him?* The voice asked.

He turned and saw an elderly woman in a raincoat standing next to him, gesticulating. Shaking his head, he reached out and touched the woman lightly on the shoulder.

Instead of keeling over in the road as he'd expected, he saw to his surprise and delight that she remained upright. Licking at the small amount of salt that had formed on her thin lips, she moved away as fast as she could, looking back at him in fear before side-stepping the ever-whitening body lying in the gutter.

Breathing a sigh of relief, 'Rated X' smiled to himself, knowing that his work in the city was complete.

On finding a suitable vantage point, 'Rated X' stopped and washed off the salt that was caked to his feet in a puddle. Then, slicking his hair away from his face, he looked down on the city.

Even through the driving rain he had a good view; scores of white statues glistened in the night, while others collapsed to join the rivers of salty foam sweeping through the streets. A few of the more resilient statues had even begun to crystallise, their jagged lights sparkling like diamonds in the storm. Despite this, and despite knowing how rotten and corrupted such people must have been, he found the sight strangely beautiful. Life, he realised, was full of such contradictions.

He certainly couldn't allow himself to stare for too long, he was sure of that.

Turning from the city and into the rain once more, he set off for the next place that needed his touch.

Networking

I was a silly lad in them days – young, brash, foolish – you know the type. A few years out of school and I knew the lot. Got a job for the council – only sweeping and tidying, mind – but I thought I was the bee's knees.

Aye, it's funny how things sober you up in the end. Here I am, forty years on, and a grandfather! Thomas is a grand lad though; it's just that he makes me feel old. And, like any grandfather I tell him stories. He's only young though and probably forgets most of them. But he remembered *one* I told him a few days ago, my God. I get no pleasure in saying I was drunk when I told him; if I'd been sober he'd have never heard it from me, that's for certain.

I suppose what reminded me of it all was that article I read in the local paper week before last. There's no *definite* connection between the two things, but it set me thinking.

As I said, I worked for the council, a glorified binman, in Whitby. Winters spent clearing the mud, summers spent clearing fish and chip papers, and all the other bumph that the tourists left behind. The money wasn't bad though for a young lad of eighteen, and I can think of worse places to pick rubbish, can't you?

One day, me and another lad called Robert Pickersgill were up at the top of the abbey steps. The 'new' church is situated there with the old ruined abbey behind it and to the right. We stood there catching our breath (for those that don't know, there's a hundred and ninety-nine step walk up there, and even the youngsters get knackered climbing it) and having a fag before tidying up the graveyard.

It never felt like a graveyard to me though, with that view of the sea and town everywhere you looked. A better job than trying to get the muck up from between the cobblestones below! It was just a matter of poking the grass a bit with one of those funny poles with the stabber on the end, and sticking the litter in a sack. It was early morning, nobody else there, and I think we were larking about. I was running among the stones and I tripped over an edging or something, and landed flat on my face on a gravestone. I looked up straight at the inscription on the stone – I'll never forget it to my dying day:

To the Memory of
Frankie Dalton
Departed this life on 21st May 1893 Aged 73 Years
Dearly Missed

In the bottom left-hand corner of the flat stone something else had been inscribed:

614384

"Ey, Bob! Come here a minute!" I shouted to my mate. "What do you reckon this is?"

He came over and looked, frowning at me. "No idea. Not bothered either. Come on, we can't stand around yacking."

And off we went gathering rubbish. I've always been a bit of a sod for remembering things though, and could I get that number

out of my mind? It stuck all day – even through the ruins of
the abbey – and if *they* don't divert your attention, nothing will.
At last the day finished and we went to our gaffer and got our
wages. First stop was the pub. I always loved that first pint of the
weekend. It was particularly sweet that night as I had a win on
the one-arm bandit. Not a fortune, but enough for a good night
out.

At this point things get a bit sketchy. I don't remember going
home to get changed out of my working gear. We stayed in the
pub I suppose, getting legless. By chucking out time we were well
away. So the pair of us staggered through the town (and cobbled
streets don't help) and we ended up at the far end of Whitby near
the abbey. Bob walked into a public phone box. When I'd stopped
laughing I had a *brilliant* idea.

"Hey, Bob! Bob! You 'member that gravestone earlier? One
I tripped on? I must've been drunk then 'an all!" He looked at
me dumbly. "Listen, though, listen. I can't get that number out
me 'ed."

"Cos you're a pillock," he said – or something similar. "I'm
goin' home, see yer."

I stopped him clumsily. "No, no, wait on. I'm gonna 'phone
it. It might be *important*," I added with drunken conviction. I
groped my way to the front of the red box, finding the opening
on something like the third attempt. I grabbed at the mouthpiece
whilst riffling through the winnings in my trouser pocket for the
right money.

Bob pushed in alongside me. "Bloody daft, wasting money.
Be better spent on another pint."

"Aw, shurrup. I've plenty left from the fruit machine," I
replied, jangling my pocket at him. "Anyway, it's my brass, not
yours."

We both started singing as the number and letter dial whirred
back and forth, back and forth. I nudged him in the ribs once I'd
finished and we listened. There was a moment's silence, then it

rang. After a bit more giggling I realised the ringing had stopped. "Bloody hell, Bob! Shush!"

The line crackled. "Nothing there," I mumbled. I'd just started to put the receiver back when a faraway voice spoke. "... *Hello* ..." it said, croaking like a toad.

Heck, it made me jump! Bob started sniggering.

"... *Hello* ..."

"Er, who's this?" I said, trying to sound sober.

"... *Hello* ..."

"Yeah, hello," I said again. "Who is this? Y'see I got this nu –"

The line crackled a bit more. "... *I don't know* ..." the voice rasped.

"You don't know? Bloody hell, you must be in a worse state than I am." I frowned and put the receiver back. I must have gone home after that. I don't remember anything else.

I didn't go out the next night – too hungover probably – but I did on the Sunday, and there was only one topic of conversation that night.

"Aye," an old gent at the bar with a grizzled beard was saying. "She lives two doowers daan. Got a reet scare 'parently, saw it warkin' daan street at two in' morning'. Din't know what it was, but she said it were queer." The old man was a fisherman, and he always had plenty of tall stories to tell so I didn't really take much heed.

The next day we arrived at the depot for instructions and were told to go right up to the abbey – there'd been some trouble up there, apparently.

Two coppers stood at the top of the steps with the vicar, pointing down towards the town. Still panting from the climb, we went over to them.

"What's up then?" asked Bob.

Constable Ellis answered. "Hello lads. Didn't see anything funny up here on Friday, did you?" Bob and I looked at each other. Ellis spoke again.

"See, over there?" he said, pointing to a pile of earth in the middle of the cemetery. "Grave robbers. Some nutter's rifled that grave over there."

Bob and I scowled at each other again. The two of us walked over there with Ellis, the Vicar staying with the other bobby. As we got nearer I saw the stone was tilted back a bit, wind blowing the long grass on either side.

"I mean," said Ellis as we approached, "it's been there over sixty years. Why bother with it now? Just a pile of bones. There's some weird people about."

I was just about to agree when I noticed part of a name through the streaks of mud on the headstone: Fra---- -alton. My heart thudded as I leant over and wiped the rest of the mud away. "Anyway lads, keep your eyes peeled, won't you? Tell us if you see anything peculiar." It's a good job Ellis wasn't the most observant bobby in the world or else he'd have seen my eyes coming out on stalks towards the ex-home of Frankie Dalton. What could I say? I told Bob about it, and I don't think we ever cleared that cemetery so quick as we did that day.

Time's a great healer – you always hear people saying so. And I suppose it's true in a way – especially as we didn't go near the place again for two weeks.

When you're that age, you won't easily admit to being scared, and by then we'd decided that someone had played a cruel joke on us. But, to be on the safe side, we left it at that. No point stirring things up unnecessarily, like.

When we did go back up there – giving Frankie Dalton's place a wide berth – it was to the other side of the church, the right hand side. As I said it's a hell of a walk up those steps (I practically have to be carried up now), so as usual we stopped for a breather, and a nice healthy cig. Now I didn't go looking for numbers, but it's like anything – you try *not* to look, then you *will* look. And sure enough opposite the church and about ten feet away from it, I found some. They were on one of those long flat graves, about two feet high and six feet long – the kind of thing you could sunbathe on if you felt so inclined. I didn't see the name this time, just the numbers – it was as though that's all there was to see. I shook my head violently a few times to shake it out but Bob saw me.

He said I'd been acting weird all day, and went straight home at knocking-off time. I went to a phonebox. If I rang it, it might put my mind at rest.

I let out a sigh before I dialled. There was a long wait before the crackle began. Then a cracked voice spoke.

"... *Thank you* ..." it rasped down the line. I nearly wet myself. I mean, what're the chances of it being a proper number? I slammed the receiver down and shot off home.

I spent that night skulking in the parlour. "Thank you" for what? What had I done to be thanked for? I'd never heard a phone with that amount of crackle on it before, either – not even in those days. You'd have thought I was ringing New Zealand or something.

Eventually I went off to bed, but didn't sleep. I kept on thinking. The speakers had both sounded so *distant*. Later on, though, I'd just about convinced myself it was something and nothing when the silence was shattered by screaming in the street.

I jumped out of bed and ran down the hall to the living room, where both Mum and Dad were at the window looking onto the street. I went to the other window and gawped out too.

The first thing I noticed was that everyone was looking out of their houses up and down the street. Then, I just caught a glimpse – and that's all it was, but it was enough – of what looked like a whitish-grey puppet thing moving awkwardly past a streetlamp.

Someone screamed at an upstairs window, and by the time I'd looked at them and back at the road it had gone.

I didn't wait to see where it had hobbled off to. I went back to my room, grabbed an armful of clothes, and put them on as I ran across town, making my way barefoot up those cold, stone steps in the darkness. I could almost feel my ears popping near the top, my heart blazing in my chest. From the top step to that grave was only a few dozen feet. I stood panting at the moon, as it shone down on the devastation.

The heavy stone lid had been lifted off somehow and was smashed on the floor around the grave like a great black mossy meringue, crumbling pieces everywhere. I looked back towards the town, and all the lights were shining. Others were coming up the steps behind me.

Then I heard a noise at my back. My heart nearly burst as I twisted around.

Old George the town wino stepped out, bottle in hand. I stared at him and then at the grave. He slugged on the bottle before saying anything. "You wouldn't believe me son," he said, shaking his head.

The coppers questioned me but my parents could give me an alibi. What was I doing at the top of the hill at that hour? they asked. I'd heard a scream, I said. A pretty safe answer as George was probably scared out of his wits.

Next morning it was the talk of the town, this thin person *that wasn't a person at all,* shambling around Whitby, terrorising folk. Descriptions of it varied, but all agreed there wasn't a pick on it.

That night I found old George up on the hill as usual, brown paper bag filled with God-knows-what. He was a funny one,

George – nobody ever set eyes on him in daylight, like another that's said to have roamed around here about a century ago.

"Shouldn't joke about such things, son," he told me as we leaned on the fence looking out to sea. "They call me Dracula you know, make jokes 'bout that. They'll make jokes 'o this too."

"But what happened, George?" I asked him.

"Jus' wharra told the Bobbies. I was kipping round yonder again' the church wall an' there's this scrapin' sarnd. Rats! I thought. Weren't rats though. Too much noise. I gorrup an' had a look for me sen." He took a swig from his brown paper. I could hear the drink glooping along the sides of the bottle. "Through gaps in the stones I saw it aye, *pranced* it did, like the ground was wet. Scared me, I don't mind saying. I must've said summat cos for a second it looked like it were gonna turn back, but thank God it din't, it kept on. God knows how it got down them steps in one piece." He shuddered, sucking on the bottle so hard I thought he'd swallow that too. Draining it, he threw it in the direction of the sea, missing by a mile and almost taking a seagull's head off instead.

"And that was all?" I asked.

He squinted at me with leery disgust. "What else d'yer want? A troop a' dancing girls? Not summat you see every day, is it?"

If people don't understand something they tend to ignore it, hoping it will go away. I think most of us in Whitby did that. I tried, but couldn't manage it. Bob phoned in sick all that week. I had to tell someone.

To give my boss his dues, he listened without interrupting me. "So," said Prentash when I'd finished. He carried on picking the muck out of his nails with a penknife without looking up. "Because you find some numbers on a few headstones and decided to ring 'em up, the whole town is plagued with ghosts, is that what you're telling me?"

"It's happened twice!" I told him, as though that might swing it. He looked up at me over his glasses. I could smell his brylcreem, the mug of coffee on his desk. He stared daggers. "Hang on, I've got alibis!" I told him. "Nowt to do with me!"

He arched his fingers. He usually did this to assert his superiority. "Have you considered the possibility that someone's having a joke at your expense?" he said slowly.

"Lot of trouble for one poxy joke," I replied. "The only person who knows anything is Bob – and he was with me the first time."

Prentash said nothing. He seemed to come to a decision, and looked at me slyly. "Okay, then. Let's go up there now."

"Fine," I told him. I'm not sure that's what he wanted to hear.

"Right then! What are we waiting for?" he said, eyeing me with suspicion.

At the top of the hill we passed the first ruined grave (now dug in again, minus corpse). The wind whistled around us. "I don't know if we'll come across any more numbers," I told him, half hoping we would, half hoping we wouldn't. "What are they for anyway?"

"I don't know," he said, kicking at grass with his shiny shoes.

After ferreting around for a few minutes, Prentash called out, "Is this what you mean?"

He was on the left-hand side, towards the back end of the church, a bit away from where I'd spoken to George. I went over and sure enough, there was another – the number in the same bottom left-hand corner.

"Okay, let's ring the bugger up," Prentash said, marching back down the steps to the town. He still thought I was having him on. "I'll phone – just to make sure," he said as we reached the phone box. I shrugged and let him get on with it. "This'll come out of your wages, lad," he told me.

He dialled. Under his breathing I could hear it ringing, and then there was static.

"… *Yes?* …"

"Hello?" said my boss. "Who is this?"

There was a mumble on the line.

"You already said that," Prentash snapped. "Hello? 'yes' what? Who is this?' He got rattled and hung up. "Right. If that grave's been disturbed next morning, *maybe* I'll believe you." And he left me to do my work, alone.

The day passed without incident. I went home and listened to the radio. Around ten o'clock our phone rang. "Hello?"

"It's me," Prentash said, sounding out of breath.

"What's the matter?"

"I was speaking to a mate of mine in the force just now – never mind who – and he says the other night one of the PC's saw something very odd wandering along the main road out of Whitby. Whatever it was got halfway across the road but was run down by a lorry." He paused for a second. I said nothing.

"It was only a pile of bloody bones! Least it was when the copper got there. Meet me at the cemetery in ten minutes."

I dashed out of our back yard, across three gardens and practically flew up those steps. I paid the price for that though, wheezing at the top like an old man. Prentash jumped up and waved at me from behind a cross-shaped stone. George stood near him, swaying and swigging, even further away than usual.

"Now, *listen*," Prentash told me. "I don't have much truck with all this, but I'm here. We'll stay for a bit and if nothing happens, I'll forget it all if you will. Agreed?"

So on a cold January evening we sat huddled on the hill above Whitby, surrounded by dead people, listening to the wind and sea shushing all around us. Occasionally George's bottle sloshed back and forth between us. It was his second.

"Did you ever read *Dracula*?" my boss asked after twenty minutes. I told him I hadn't.

"It's up here that he did some of it, you know. His ... vampiring, or whatever."

"Oh." I looked at the crooked stones in front, glad of this information.

"Aye, someone ran from the Hotel down there because they saw his glowing eyes."

A big fat greasy moon tried shining across the stones, but vanished behind a grimy cloud. Then we heard it.

I don't know about the other two, but at that moment I realised I hadn't expected anything to happen. And as the noise heightened I realised we couldn't get past it because the noise was ahead and we were near the edge of the cliff.

"Where is it?" whispered Prentash.

We couldn't see it as we were crouched to avoid being seen, and it was obscured by other stones in front of it and *it* wasn't that tall. But we heard that noise, and that for me was the worst bit; that almost hollow *scrape* that set your teeth right on edge mingled with what sounded like a bag of sticks clattering around on top of hard stone. Then there was a thump, another rattle. And then its head appeared above a big stone, and it started to move. It was like George said, like the ground was wet, and it pranced away from its unearthed box.

And *still* I couldn't see it properly – someone was looking out for me that night – but I kept hearing it clacking when it passed over a stone, its head coming into view every now and then as it made its way toward the steps. I looked around for the others. Prentash had backed even further up the cemetery; but where was George?

I heard the sound of gravel and then and saw a dark patch on a gravestone ahead. The silly old devil was creeping up on it like a dog, bottle above his head – and it was only a matter of feet from the steps now as its skull appeared above another grave, George about ten feet behind it ...

Then a very odd thing happened, and happened very quickly. George was raising the bottle above his head when there was a sharp noise near the steps. It was still ringing in my ears when the skull dropped vertically to the ground, out of my line of vision, followed by a tinkling noise, then a series of those clacking sounds.

George dropped the bottle he'd been wielding, which also fell to the ground with an almighty crash.

Then George was running through the stones, looking down and pointing. "There 'e is! And there! O'wer there an 'all!" he cackled, his hand swaying all over the place.

As I got nearer I understood. Me and Bob Pickersgill were forever picking up George's discarded empties. I always said someone'd break their neck on one …

I looked up eventually, and for a moment something bothered me. Then I realised what it was – nobody had come up to see what all the fuss was.

Mind you, who in their right mind would want to know?

It all got hushed up, not surprisingly. How, I'm not sure; I've very rarely heard the story around the town – and nobody listened to George much anyway, God bless him.

So, here I am forty years on, never told a soul – until recently. That's the problem.

It started a few weeks ago when people began noticing the cliff was eroding, and consequently some of the graves on the hill were getting closer to the edge. Then a few bones started appearing through the earth – some fell down the cliff, and landed on pavements outside people's houses. It was in all the papers, even in the nationals.

Anyway, it was my fifty-eighth birthday last Tuesday. I'd had a few by the time my grandson came around. I told him a story about a silly young lad who found numbers on the sides of gravestones, and who phoned them up, and how the skeletons started walking around the town. Our Janice doesn't like me telling him things like that – I always said it wouldn't do him any harm.

Yesterday I caught him messing with his dad's mobile phone. I asked him what he was doing. "Trying numbers," he told me. He said a few he'd tried had sounded odd, 'like they'd just woken up', and they wouldn't talk to him.

I had a funny dream last night. I was playing football with the lad in the cemetery, and he kicked the ball at me. I caught it, but it wasn't a football at all. It was a skull. Then it spoke, six digits coming from its jaws before they clamped shut. Those six digits were my phone number.

I've been looking up towards the abbey all day, but it seems normal enough – except for two leg-bones dangling from the side of the eroding cliff, wind blowing them about now and then.

At least I *hope* it's the wind blowing them about.

Cuticles

"When I die, Pete, I want you to read my journal."

That would be a strange request from an old man on his deathbed; to hear it from your best friend who's just turned thirteen is a bit hard to take.

We were sitting at the side of the river the week before school was due to start again, swigging pop from a plastic bottle, pretending it was something stronger. Guy was squinting into the water, chewing the quicks of his nails, looking down at them every few seconds.

"You're not going to die for a while yet," I replied.

"I've just got this feeling, that's all. Everything's changing. It's too fast."

"S'called growing up." I took another gulp from the bottle, sloshed it around. "Bit left if you want it."

Guy took it off me, and meticulously wiped the rim with his sleeve before drinking from it. I'd stopped taking offence ages ago. "Don't want to spread anything," he'd say. Finishing the bottle, he heaved it into the river before turning to me. "You will read it though, won't you?"

I was getting a little spooked by all this. "Yeah, if you like," I said to shut him up.

Guy was odd, there's no other way of putting it. But then again, so was I.

We'd met in school, and I suppose the reason we became mates was because we were shunned by everyone else. He'd moved to the area with his mum about three months after I had in the middle of a school term, when everyone else had made their friends and were reluctant to admit anyone else to their little cliques. Also Guy was called Guy – that meant he must be posh, of course (he wasn't) and my dad was involved with the church, which meant I must be a God-botherer (I'm not). We'd seen each other skulking around at breaks, getting teased or trying to avoid getting teased. It also didn't help that Guy looked and acted differently – he had a skinhead when the rest of us had long hair, and had it cut every two weeks. He also shaved – which at the age of thirteen was amazing. But he *needed* to – whether he started young or just developed quicker than the rest of us I never asked. And then there was the nails.

In the time that I knew him, Guy hardly ever took his fingers from his mouth; which to most people meant he was childish. When asked he said he didn't like nails, that was all.

So there we were, a couple of outsiders together with no other friends, sat by the riverbank on a red hot day in August, talking about Guy dying.

"Just why are we having this conversation?" I asked him after a few minutes silence. "Let's talk about Rachael instead." I probably became all misty-eyed thinking of Rachael; in fact I still do now; I can hear her in the next room, trying to get Davy to sleep, singing him a lullaby. I never imagined I'd end up with her; it was Guy she fancied then.

"She was asking me about you again after school – she says you're cute. And you look manly with your moustache."

"I don't," Guy snapped at me suddenly, covering his face with a hand full of jagged nails, "I look ridiculous. I shouldn't have hair at my age. My mum says my dad was like that, and she calls him a son of a bitch."

It was the first time I'd heard him mention his father. It seemed a funny thing for a mother to say to her child.

"Well, I wish I could grow a moustache. It just means you're growing up quicker than the rest of us, that's all." Guy didn't answer.

Within the school year, Guy died in a private ward, howling in pain.

The school term began again, and we all fell into our old classes, seeing the same people we'd seen two months earlier but with different haircuts and clothes and such. One day we had PE and Guy brought a note in from his mum excusing him. I'd forgotten all about it until I saw his journal last week:

> Sept 8th – A horrible day. Winston said the note I had for PE was 'vague'. He'd been at the pub at lunch – he stank. He dragged me into the store cupboard to ask me what I was playing at. I thought he was going to hit me. He soon changed his mind when I lifted up my shirt. He freaked and let me go home.

In some ways Guy fitted in well; he got good marks in classes (far better than I did). But, being the age we were, it was his peculiarities that stood out.

Like when he started wearing gloves in class.

It didn't matter so much at first; it was a really cold winter that year. Even old Pashley the math's teacher didn't seem to mind that we wore our coats in class. But after a while, everyone noticed that Guy never took his gloves off. He still wasn't doing PE either, which made some kids jealous; they wanted out of orienteering and cross-country too.

The worst of them was Gibson. Gibson made *everyone's* life a misery, except those who toadied around him. He made my life a misery too. He even tried it on with Rachael once, who slapped him across the face. He slapped her back – about half a dozen times.

One breaktime, we were all trying to stay hidden inside as long as possible before a teacher threw us out, when Gibson and his cronies showed up. Guy was standing in the corner and they made a beeline for him.

"Think you're it, don't you Harris, eh? Why don't you take your gloves off? It's not that cold."

"Must be something wrong with him," one of the others said. "Scabby hands."

Guy looked down, hoping they'd go away. Nobody dared cheek Gibson off. The last kid who had never came back. We never found out why.

"Leave me alone. I'm not doing you any harm." Guy's voice quivered.

"Show us what's under the gloves and I will." Guy paled and tried to walk past him. Gibson grabbed his hands.

I'm not sure how they got his gloves off, but they did. One went out of the window and the other ended up under someone's boot. Guy went red in the face and tucked his hands in his pockets. Gibson got angry then, and punched him in the stomach. Guy whined, it was pitiful. Grabbing hold of his hands Gibson stared down at them, shocked.

Half the nails were gone. The skin looked absolutely livid. The nails Guy did have left were scratched to hell. The skin below the nails was full of the same scratch-marks. The woollen gloves must have rubbed them even worse.

"What the bloody hell is going on here?"

Mr. Aveyard, a barrel-chested design teacher who always seemed to scent trouble, homed in on Gibson and started giving him a bollocking, Gibson arguing the toss back in that cocky way he had. As Aveyard marched him off to the staffroom, the other kids following for the fun, I heard a horrible whine coming from deep within a pile of coats. Moving them aside, I saw Guy sitting there, crying, tucking his hands as far into his pockets as they would go, his face streaming. I was nearly crying myself – the noise had been so pitiful. I moved reluctantly to put a hand on his shoulder when I became aware of people walking past. A girl smiled at me, a girl I liked. I didn't want her seeing me put my arm round my best mate ...

With a mixture of anger and embarrassment I stormed out of the cloakroom and looked for Guy's missing glove.

The next day, Guy didn't turn up for the first lesson (English, I think). I never asked him why. He was there for Maths though and asked to borrow my compass.

"Where's yours? You always have a compass."

"I don't anymore." That was all he'd say.

A couple of weekends later, we were walking along the canal path when Guy broke the silence in that way of his which meant he had something important to say.

"Me and Rachael went out the other night."

I remember that moment like it was yesterday; I felt weird, lots of emotions at once – happy for him for getting a date, particularly with Rachael, who was gorgeous – but also envious because it was him and not me. I also felt like I'd been left behind: everyone had girlfriends – or so they said. I doubt it now, but it doesn't make you feel any better at the time.

"What happened?" I asked, trying to sound casual.

He looked like he regretted mentioning it now. "Nothing really. She said I was really cute."

There was a long pause. "And?"

"And ..." he paused again. We'd stopped walking by then. A few crows squawked in the distance, a dog barked. "And we kissed, and ..."

"*And?*" I was getting impatient.

"It was a disaster. I stopped it." I'm not sure how he wanted me to react but I said nothing for a long time. "Why?"

"Because ... it would've got out of hand. It felt weird, Pete. I would've ended up ..."

"Well, who wouldn't?" I said with a cockiness I didn't possess.

"No, I don't mean that. I mean it was ..." He looked at me, appealing for me to tell him how he felt. I'd no idea what he was talking about. Suddenly he picked up a stick and flung it angrily into the river.

"I've been seeing a ... doctor. In school, I mean."

When he said that I knew what kind of doctor he meant; my head was full of horrible thoughts and I got scared. I said the first thing that came into my head. "Did your Dad ... hit you and things?"

He turned to me, startled. "My Dad? I've never met my Dad." I didn't know what to say. "You know I've been using your compass the past few weeks? It's to do with that."

I'd no idea what he meant but didn't ask. Then I got hold of the journal:

Nov 15th Miss Bigelow says not to have sharp objects for lessons. When she asked me why I did it I told her I was bored. She's spoken to my mum too but she knows the real reason. Mum says she wished she'd never mentioned that stupid story now.

Nov 29th Hung around town with Rachael. Said she liked my moustache (I keep shaving it off!) and tried to touch it. I backed off. Later we kissed. I felt strange. It was as though I'd bitten my cheek or something. I could taste blood in my mouth. I was nearly sick. I wanted to kiss her back but it didn't feel right. I felt angry.

Got Mum to tell me a bit more tonight. She seemed
to sense that something was wrong. She said that I'm more
sensitive than he was. She said the story came from Dad –
he had weird nails too.

A couple of weeks later, Christmas was nearly upon us and we were
doing less and less work, skiving off, hanging around the town.

Then Gibson went missing.

Nobody was especially bothered by that except his parents,
who were on TV saying how much they loved their son – which
was a joke as he lived with his grandmother because he couldn't
stand their rows. Besides, he'd vanished before, once sloping off to
a music festival and not going home for a month.

The police found the bits stuck under a hedge.

According to the local rag, they couldn't even call it a body
anymore; it had to be identified by dental records.

Nobody could stand the bastard but it was terrible way to go.
The police were quite cagey about the whole thing, never said if
they had a definite suspect.

Christmas came and went, and Guy was hardly ever in school.
I used to go round and take him the work we'd done in class. I
rarely saw him – his mother usually said he was at the doctor's, or
away visiting relatives. On one such day, I was walking away back
down the path. Being the over-sensitive child I was, I wondered
if I'd said something to offend him; had we fallen out and I hadn't
even noticed? I was trying to think when I heard a tapping behind
me. I looked up.

I wondered at first what it was, behind the nets. It moved
slightly to one side and I saw it was Guy. He looked dreadful,
haunted; the look on his face was one of terror. I marched back up

to the door, knocked again. Loudly. "I've just seen him upstairs," I said as his mum opened the door. "What's the matter with him?"

"He's got an iron deficiency," she said, "he's not been eating enough meat." She smiled bitterly. "Okay?" Before I had a chance to answer she closed the door.

I'll never forget the look in both their eyes.

By March Guy's attendance record was really poor and the teachers kept asking me where he was. "He's not got some kind of odd religion, has he?" asked Mr. Marsh one day, a teacher who considered himself something of a wit. "Because it's always the same times he has off. Must be his time of the month," he quipped, to the amusement of the rest of the class.

On the occasions I did see Guy, he looked really awful; his face was all sucked in, and he wasn't shaving as much anymore, his beard was patchy. His hair, also longer now, was stuck up at odd angles, like he had about three partings at once. He got a lot of hassle when he did turn up. He'd also started wearing polo necks all the time, which were about as unfashionable as you could get in those days. His hands were still covered.

Rachael had gone off him of course; when I mentioned this to Guy one day he actually smiled. "Yes," he'd said. "Good for her." I think one of the reasons we got on so well was that we never seemed to talk about girls much, not like the other lads in the school. I was slightly more up front than he was, but Guy … he seemed to lack that predatory edge that growing up gives you when desire rears its ugly head.

Now I see that I was only half right.

The next few months are a kind of blur to me, lightened only by the journal. A close relative of mine died and I was inconsolable; then my Dad lost his job and it looked like we were going to have to move again, this time down south. The only thing I really remember of that period was that there seemed to be a local crimewave going on; a lot of shops were looted, violence in the town. I had a fair bit of time off school myself as we looked for houses around London. In the end though, Dad got another job up here and we were safe.

As I started to feel better I wondered about Guy, who I hadn't seen in about two months. I phoned him up one night after school. His mother answered.

"He's not in," she said down the phone in a loud voice. "No, I don't know where. Bye, Peter." The phone was slammed down hard. Just before we were cut off I heard another noise in the background. The next time I saw Guy I'd ask him about it.

The next time I saw him was three days before he died.

I'd managed to get myself a girlfriend; don't ask me how, it's still a mystery to me. God knows what she saw in me. I was in my room with her listening to records (among other things) when my mum knocked on the door. "Peter," she said, popping her head round, her eyes red and wet, "I think it's about time Dawn went home."

Saying my goodbyes to Dawn on the step, I dreaded the lecture I thought I was going to get. But she didn't mention me and Dawn. "I've just had Guy's mother on the phone. He's in the hospital."

As we drove along in silence, I realized that something was wrong. We'd just driven past the hospital. I was about to say something when I realized we were going to the *other* hospital. At that moment it crashed in on me how sick Guy must be.

It was a depressing place – the most depressing place I've ever seen. Within a year it would close. Most of the corridors and wards were empty as we walked through.

Guy was in a room by himself, which had to be unlocked by a nurse, making my mum gasp. Inside, Guy was strapped to the bed; his mother, standing next to him, looked dazed. "I want to speak with Pete. Alone," Guy whispered. Both the adults left.

"Hi," Guy said. I was speechless. "My journal … you will still read it?"

"Yes," I replied. I could barely look at him.

"I told you I was changing, didn't I?" he said, his voice a paper-like rasp. "Growing up, eh? They never tell you what into though." He started to laugh but ended up coughing.

I tried to change the subject. "I didn't know you had a dog," I said. "I heard it when I phoned you a while ago." For a moment he looked confused. "No, we don't have a dog," he said, looking down at the sheets.

At that point a nurse walked in and I was shunted from the room. It was the last thing he said to me.

I was in such a daze at the time, but looking back now I realize the funeral was late in coming. Nearly two weeks passed before we were told when it was to be.

I still didn't know how it had happened. I tried to contact Guy's mum but with no luck.

Going through the journal, I saw an entry that hit me in the gut – it was made just after I'd left the hospital and was the last thing Guy had written, barely legible:

Pete's just gone. I could see from his face he was wondering what was wrong with me. But I couldn't tell him. I can't even write it down. IT DISGUSTS ME. 'Do I have a dog?'!!!! No, I don't *have* a dog!

The funeral itself was a strange affair. Guy's mum was dressed head to foot in black and covered in jewellery, standing over to one side with what must've been Guy's aunts, uncles and cousins and a few other people. I was just about to go over when mum stopped me. "That's not Reverend Good," she said.

Standing near the grave was a man who didn't look like a vicar or a priest to me, but he was wearing the outfit. He was quite young and looked more like a film star, his long black hair, greying at the sides, swaying around in the wind as he stared down into the grave. Guy's mum saw him and went over. Taking off a lot of her jewellery, she handed it to him. He kissed her forehead tenderly.

The service started, and at that moment the clouds broke and the sun shone, the clergy's hair flying wildly about in the wind as he shouted above it. I couldn't place his accent; it had a thick resonance to it that made me think he must be extremely clever. I realized that I was squinting; something shone brightly near me.

It was the coffin. The nails, plaque and handles were of highly-polished silver and shining in my eyes. Then, a little later when the coffin was lowered into the hole, Guy's mother and several other relatives started removing the silver rings from their fingers and throwing them onto the lid, the glare even brighter in the seconds before the coffin disappeared into the ground.

The whole thing went by like I wasn't there. I couldn't believe it was happening.

After the service, we were invited back to the house. The walls were full of silver ornaments, some looking more expensive than others, many of them religious. "It looks better here than it did at ours," I heard one woman say to a man at her side, pointing at what looked like a large silver pellet crowned on a pedestal.

I was stood in the kitchen on my own, not knowing what to do or say when Guy's mother came in, a sad smile on her face. It was the bravest thing I'd ever seen. "Guy told me he wanted you to have something of his – the journal." I nodded. "When you're old enough," she said, patting me on the shoulder, "when you're old enough." I was totally confused. I felt like I should say something, but couldn't. Suddenly there was a lot of shouting from the hallway followed by a door slamming. Leaving the kitchen, I went with Guy's mum to the hall, picking up on her anxiety. "That was him, wasn't it?" she said to the people crowded there.

"Don't worry Pat, we got rid of him," a heavily-built man told her. Looking through the glass in the door, I saw what looked like an old tramp shambling away down the street. I couldn't tell if the blackness about him was a hood, or hair, or both.

Last week a package arrived for me. The postmark was smudged, but judging by the state of the paper, it had come a long way. I was just setting off for work, but curiosity got the better of me and I opened it up anyway.

Guy's journal.

I knew that if I started to read it I'd never go to work, so with a great effort I put it on the table and left. I got nothing done that day, I was so eager to get home and read it.

After we'd put the baby to bed Rachael went to see the neighbours, so I sat down and read. Guy's mum had put a note at the front: *Peter, I've moved back to live with my family – I don't have long. Here is the journal. Remember this – it wasn't his fault. He was too sensitive for the changes.*

A lot of it was the usual teenage scribble – his moods, feelings. But certain paragraphs jumped out at me:

-First shave today. I know it's too early but I needed to. Cut myself several times.

-Asked mum about dad. She said it ran in the family and hoped I wouldn't turn into him. She said I was at a funny age, when you start changing. Asked about nails again. She said it was just a silly story that the half-moons on certain peoples' nails became full as the real moon changed. I said it sounded cool. She shouted at me, said that it wasn't.

-Saw a programme on TV about a farm. Sight of animals made me feel weird. I was sick.

-Nails changed. Not half anymore. It's horrible. Started biting them.

-Had odd dream, that I was chasing a rabbit. The bed was covered in mud when I woke up.

-Woke up feeling like I'd just eaten a huge meal. Room smelled of metal. Turned light on and was sick. Mum came in and cried, kept screaming "the son of a bitch!" over and over again. Then she told me. It happened at the same age with him. Mum's keeping me out of school at danger times. I hope I die soon.

-Saw paper. I can't remember any of it! I CAN'T REMEMBER!

-On way home from school a dog crossed the road and jumped at me, licked my hands. It nearly got knocked down. It bit a kid at school last week.

-Police at door today, doing inquiries about the attacks and break-ins. Mum says she'll lock me in at night and board up the windows. I won't be able to see the sky.

-Mum thinks I'll get used to it but I know I won't. This is what I am. I can't stay a child forever. But I don't want to grow up, go to that next stage.

There's a lot more. Not for the first time, I don't know what to think or do.

At the back of the book is a sheet of paper – a copy of Guy's death certificate. Guy's mother had crossed out the given cause of death and put another word in its place:

"Adolescence".

Whenever I think of Guy now, I try to be positive – remember the good times we had. But it always seems to come back to one image – him with his fingers in his mouth chewing his nails, removing the cuticles and stripping away the protective layer to reveal the raw flesh underneath, and the changes that Guy couldn't endure.

King of the Maggots

The time had come for a new King to be crowned as the old one had almost rotted away.

A meeting was hastily arranged, and possible candidates put forward. This was merely tradition, as they all knew who the next King would be. The King, whether he was aware of it or not, usually chose himself.

At least he did in this Kingdom.

Instead of wiping his feet on the WELCOME mat, Maddox saw he was wiping them on another petition against him. Removing his boots, he bent to pick up the two sheets of unlined paper.

Mr Maddox (the first sheet began), we realise that you appear to work unsociable hours and that taking care of your property is not important to YOU, but the fact that various forms of parasite have been seen scuttling through your garden is plainly unacceptable. It would be greatly appreciated if you could rectify this situation. Please find listed below the names of local people who agree.

Maddox gave a quick glance to the names on the list, most of which he'd never heard of. Kicking his boots into the kitchen, they collided with a cardboard box full of empty liquor bottles. With the bottles still chiming on the floor, he followed his boots in, opened one of his cupboards and carefully placed a small package behind a couple of jars containing mouldy condiments. Closing the cupboard door, he shuffled his way through the half-eaten meals, dog-eared magazines and lopsided furniture that was his (aptly-named) living room, and went into his bedroom, where he flopped down on the bed, wondering why his name on the first page of the petition was blurred when nothing else was.

Our story begins many years ago, on the day that an elderly housewife awoke from a deep sleep to find that her husband had vanished. She wasn't unduly worried to begin with, as he'd vanished several times before. His illness, she told herself, always his illness.

Only this time, he didn't come back.

Calling the police, the old lady found them as sympathetic as ever, already aware of her husband's increasing mental frailty. They assured her, as usual, that he would probably return, safe and sound, in a few hours like he always did. But for some reason, the old lady felt that this time was different.

Plop.

After the fourth one dropped on the bed, he found that blinking made them go away.

It'd started a couple of minutes earlier, while he'd been thinking about that awful man and his brat of a child –

"Maggots? Did you say 'Mr Maggots'?"

"*Maddox.* I'm here to give your son his piano lesson."

The door had opened a crack. "Oh. Well you should speak more clearly. I suppose you'd better come in."

It was the third time in the past week people had misheard his name. No wonder things like –

Plop.

were happening to him, the people he had to deal with just to keep up a 'good front'. It sometimes surprised him that people let him into their homes at all; they certainly wouldn't if they knew what his *main* source of income was. He suspected the only reason he got any piano work at all was because he was so cheap.

Plop.

"Are you always so pale, Mr Maggots?" the boy had asked as he sat down at the keyboard. "I can only see your fingers when you touch the black keys."

Plop.

And then, lying on the bed, he'd spotted it out of the corner of one eye.

Wriggle. Shiver. Wriggle. *Plop.*

He'd never really paid the curtain rail much attention before. But he certainly did when the maggots starting dropping off the end of it, wriggling their way towards him.

Plop.

They weren't really maggots, of course; the curtain rail just had too many hooks attached to it, more than was needed to support the curtain – perhaps his mother had put them up years ago as spares. A current of air (or possibly a draught through the rotted window frames) must've got into the room somehow because the little hooks on the curtain track appeared to be gently pulsing across it, looking like overgrown –

Plop.

Maggots.

Raising his head slightly so he could better watch the latest hook/maggot slowly top-and-bottom its way across the bed towards him, Maddox wondered what would happen if he didn't blink. But he never found out, because his eyelids began to droop naturally and he fell asleep.

Plop.

A few hours turned into a few days, a few days into a few months.

During that time, the bungalow and garden were thoroughly searched, but nothing was found. There was no evidence to suggest that the old man had been forcibly removed from his home, or even that he had planned to take himself away. Conducting her own search of the premises, the old lady said she didn't see anything amiss, although she did mention that she hadn't seen her husband's collection of terracotta soldiers for a while. But that in itself wasn't strange as her husband cared for them himself; she was strictly forbidden to dust them (not that she would've wanted to interfere with them — she hated them nearly as much as Marcus did). Her husband loved those terracotta figures, though. His 'brave little soldiers'.

As the search for her husband went beyond the house and onto the neighbouring streets and estates, she did find some comfort in the fact that their son, Marcus, evidently disturbed by the disappearance, had decided to move back home to be with his mother in her hour of need. If it hadn't been for Marcus, she sometimes mused, heaven knows what kind of thoughts she'd entertain.

He awoke in the middle of the night, smiling. For some reason he'd just had the most wonderful dream of his life.

He wasn't sure what he'd done to deserve the honour, but in the dream Maddox was carried shoulder high along the street by a group of determined-looking revellers who were chanting something over and over; so loudly in fact that he couldn't make out a word of what was being chanted. A shame, as presumably it had something to do with why he was being carried aloft in the first place.

Putting that detail aside, Maddox, exhilarated by this unexpected boost to his ego, sat up in bed and found that he was parched. Wading through the wreckage on the floor of the cramped bungalow in the darkness, he made his way to the kitchen to get the one bottle of milk in the fridge that he hoped wasn't on the turn.

Opening the fridge door was like opening a portal leading out into the great whiteness of space. When his eyes adjusted to the sudden brightness inside, he reached for the bottle. But as well as not being able to locate the bottle, he found that due to the blinding whiteness he was also having trouble trying to locate his arm.

A stark panic gripped him before he took a deep breath, reached further inside the fridge and found the bottle. Unfortunately, the comforting coldness of the glass was soon replaced by a soft clamminess as it began to soften and squirm in his grip, squishing between his fingers like glue. Repulsed, he dropped the bottle.

What he did next surprised him.

Bending slightly, Maddox crawled inside the cramped space of the fridge as if looking for some secret compartment or room. As he crawled further in – a seemingly impossible distance – he lost sight of himself altogether, until only his clothes were visible to him. Undeterred, he kept on crawling.

Then, ahead of him, something took shape in the whiteness. He could make out features; yes, it was a face, *there was somebody already in there –*

When Maddox awoke – really awoke – it was daylight and he was not smiling. Above him, the hooks on the curtain rail quivered.

Quicker than usual, he got out of bed.

The old lady, who felt she had nowhere else to go, stayed in the bungalow with her son and hoped that her husband would return as if nothing had happened, completely oblivious to the trouble he had caused. She knew that Marcus hadn't always seen eye to eye with his stepfather (even she had to admit that he had not been very attentive to Marcus as a boy), but had he been able to see the concern he showed now, he would surely have been quite touched. Although probably not quite so touched by Marcus's complete lack of interest in the garden, which was rapidly going to seed. Indeed, one neighbour had even suggested that such an untidy garden was bound to attract unwelcome visitors.

Two years came and went, then four, and her sense of helplessness grew. Her hopes for her husband's return faded a little more every day. In the sixth year, she knew that another twelve months would see her husband declared legally dead.

That year was the longest of her life and when it passed, the old lady, unable to stand the place and its associations any longer, left it – and virtually all her possessions and a fair sum of cash – to her son. Over the years since his stepfather's disappearance, Marcus had seemed to develop an attachment to the place that he'd never possessed as a child. That, at least, was a comforting thought for the old lady as she moved into the rest home to end her days.

After shaking the last of the nightmare from his brain, Maddox changed his dirty clothes for some more dirty clothes and stood in front of the mirror to comb his fingers through his hair.

As he smoothed down the tufts he noticed with some anxiety that even by his standards he was unusually pale. Memories of the nightmare came back to him. Trembling, he watched the glass as his curd-like hand rose against the check of his shirt and inched slowly towards his throat.

There was a violent braying at the door.

"Maggots! We know you're in there Maggots," a harsh voice called through the letterbox. "Just to let you know we've called the environmental health people and they'll be paying you a visit soon. Have you any idea how much you're lowering property values for the rest of us? Your mother – God rest her soul – must be spinning in her grave knowing what you've done to this place." The letterbox snapped shut and silence descended once more.

Going through to the spare room (the state of which was more appalling than any other room in the house – so bad that Maddox wouldn't even leave his merchandise in there), he pried the damp curtain from the wall and watched the neighbour stride back to his house. Maddox remembered the man when he'd been growing up – an interfering busybody even then. Though his stepfather hadn't seen that, of course. They'd got on like a house on fire. Sticking the curtain back to the wall, something clattered beneath his feet. One of the floorboards, no doubt. He glanced down.

He wasn't sorry, he realised.

Moving away and standing by the door, he looked at the spot again. A slight smile touched his eyes.

No, not sorry at all.

The old lady had only been in the nursing home for three weeks when she died in the middle of a nightmare.

The three of them – Marcus, her husband and herself – had just moved into the corner bungalow at the end of the street. Marcus was in a sulk again because his new stepfather wouldn't play with him. "He cares more about those soldiers than he cares about me," the boy was saying.

Suddenly there was a shout from the spare room. "Come here, both of you. Look what I've found."

Dutifully, she and Marcus went through to the spare room. There was a hole in the middle of the floor, and Marcus's stepfather was standing in it up to his waist. "Look! It's a sub-basement, or something like that. The builders must've changed their minds." He turned to the boy. "Perhaps, Marcus, we could turn it into a secret playroom. What do you say?"

His mother smiled as Marcus's face brightened at the idea.

She awoke with a start. The last thing she thought before her heart gave out was: The sub-basement – I'd forgotten all about it until now. And so, she realised now, had her husband.

But not her son.

And it was on that day, all those years ago, that the King was born.

As he often did in times of stress, Maddox took his frustrations out on the piano. *The neighbours can knock all they like,* he thought. He was amazed that they hadn't. How long had he been playing? It'd been broad daylight when he'd started, and he sat virtually in the dark now. Feeling slightly better, he continued to pound the keys.

As the room grew dimmer, he became aware of something small and white wriggling across the top of the piano. The keys felt oddly pliable, as if he was kneading dough.

He wasn't unduly concerned by the thing on top of the piano. It was just another hallucination, like the things on the curtain rail … the keys softening beneath his fingers was a hallucination too, and the milk bottle and the fridge. Blinking, the maggot vanished from the piano.

He realised that the sensation of kneading dough was wrong. It was more like marshmallow, a gooey warmth that was taking all the feeling from his fingers. There was also a faint clicking sound as he struck one of the keys.

After another minute of decreasing sensation, he found that he couldn't resist a look down. As he did he knew that he didn't have to worry about his hands being too white for the keyboard any more.

Seeing all that blood smeared across the keys immediately brought sensation back into his fingers, a stinging pain that came from bashing the keys so long and hard that he had virtually mashed them to a pulp. And then came the realisation that the clicking noise he'd been hearing hadn't come from one of the keys but from one of his fingers. Through the blood a white shard of bone was plainly visible, peeking through the ragged flesh.

Years went by and the boy grew, as did the hatred inside him. And although his stepfather's 'brave little soldiers' didn't grow, the man's admiration for them did.

The boy decided something had to be done.

His stepfather never called him 'brave'; he never spent that much time with him. No, the soldiers always came first, sitting there on their own shelf in the spare room, the place that should've been his secret playroom.

So one night, the boy went to work.

When Marcus's stepfather awoke in the middle of the night he thought there was an intruder in the bungalow. Getting out of bed quietly so as not to wake his wife, he took a torch and crept to the door of the spare room, which was slightly ajar.

Inside he saw Marcus on his knees, beside a hole in the floor. Marvelling at what he was seeing he knew that somehow, with a mixture of strength, ingenuity and planning, Marcus had not only pulled up the carpet himself but had even levered up the floorboards. But why?

"Marcus, what on earth are you doing in here?" his stepfather said, stepping into the room. "And what's that you're holding?"

Shining the torch onto Marcus's hands he saw two of his beloved terracotta soldiers. And he was astonished to see that the sub-basement was half full of them.

"We won't tell your mother about this," Marcus's stepfather said once he'd caught his breath. He began removing the warriors from the hole. "Least said, soonest mended. Now help me to clear up this mess."

Quickly and quietly they removed the soldiers, replaced the floorboards and flattened out the carpet.

Back in bed, his wife thankfully unaware of the night's events, Marcus's stepfather wondered if the boy needed a hobby. That was a strange thing he had just done. He seemed to remember a few weeks ago the boy's mother mentioning piano lessons.

Yes, that was it.

Piano lessons.

It was a dark and stormy night.

Because he didn't have any first aid equipment in the house, Maddox reluctantly went out to seek some. Walking to the nearest chemists (his hands were too battered to drive), he picked up some cream and bandages and fended off suspicious questions from the woman behind the counter.

As he was painfully fumbling for his house key in his pocket, a gang of teenagers slunk past his gate wearing silly paper hats from a fast-food restaurant. The wind rose and blew one of the hats into the overgrown garden.

As Maddox found his key, one of the youths muttered something about 'catching something if he went in there', and the others laughed. Maddox unlocked the door, stepped inside and kicked it shut behind him. In his rush to apply the cream and bandages to his throbbing hands, he forgot to lock the door.

Before the King could live he first had to die. It was then and only then that his wealth could be shared among the Kingdom.

The King-in-waiting to the King-in-waiting was getting impatient. How much longer, he wondered, could the old man live? It was obvious the man's mind was as good as dead, but his body kept going, on and on. It wasn't as if he needed the money, either. The only thing that concerned him was that blasted army of his, and they certainly didn't need it. And whenever Marcus broached the subject he always got the same answer: "Not until you change your wicked ways." It made his blood boil.

One day, the King-in-waiting to the King-in-waiting found he could wait no longer.

The old man was in one of his smaller rooms, fretting over his army when he heard footsteps behind him. Without turning he knew who it was. The old man was asked a question which he answered, and then he died.

And so it was for a number of years: the dead King lived. Long Live The King. But it wasn't long before his loyal subjects grew tired of him, and a new King had to be crowned.

Maddox had a bad feeling as he unwrapped the bandages. It was the colour; it reminded him of the maggots he thought he'd seen. Everything seemed to revolve around maggots lately …

And it was at that moment he experienced one of the few instances of clarity in his life, a clarity which enabled him to see what was really going on, going on beneath

the floor

the strange happenings of the past few days.

And all at once he was like a child again, in the spare room removing the clutter from the floor and peeling back the carpet to reveal the loosely arranged and badly-fitted boards, and he was grabbing one and pulling it back –

With a huge effort he managed to stop himself, retreating to the dingy living room. He hoped that the sting of the ointment on his hands would take these thoughts away. But despite the pain of the cream as it cut into his wounds the memories kept coming, hurtling towards him like a train without brakes.

Marcus didn't go home very often as he sensed their disapproval, although they hadn't had to bail him out of trouble for a long time because he'd been careful. But that night his mother had asked him to stay as she wasn't very well. She could normally manage the old man herself, but on this day she was too weak to cope with him alone. At first he'd resisted, but then he thought that perhaps he could use the opportunity to persuade his stepfather to at least give him a loan. He was that desperate.

He'd arrived late to find his mother already fast asleep and his stepfather – surprise-surprise – in the spare room talking to his soldiers, the only light coming from a small lamp on the desk.

Unable to stop himself, he'd come straight out and asked the old man. The old clown, who was unusually lucid that night, had replied that every time he came here it was for the same thing, and that he knew what he really needed the money for and the kind of people it would be going to, and that he wasn't about to give his hard-earned life-savings to villains like that ... especially now. He needed his money for a private collection that had finally come on the market. These brave soldiers, he'd informed his step-son without even turning round, they didn't come cheap ...

At that moment, all Maddox's carefully rehearsed phrases counted for nothing. He lost his temper, and grabbing one of the soldiers, he raised it above his head and brought it down, raised it and brought it down, raised it and brought it down ... then the carpet was raised but he didn't remember doing that. But he did remember removing the boards from the floor

I'll show him brave

and suddenly the old man was in the hole and the soldiers were raining down on top of him, dozens of them all over the old man's body, which thanks to the light from the small lamp was sickly pale like the colour of bandages and maggots and things gone bad. And then he was replacing the floorboards and the carpet was back down.

Breathing heavily, he went into his mother's room, expecting her to be wide awake and terrified. But he saw the sleeping tablets on the bedside table and realised that she was fast asleep.

And on that night, as on this, he did two things:

He went into the living room and hit the piano, making his hands bleed. And he removed a bottle of scotch from a cupboard and quickly snapped off its seal.

He couldn't face wearing those bandages, not now. He decided that the whisky could take care of the pain for him.

And he took a long slug from the bottle.

The King Was Dead. Long Live The King.

It was a dark and stormy night and a new King was about to be crowned. A great wind whipped around the palace, blowing dirt and rubbish across the courtyard. One gust was so powerful that it managed to blow open the door to the palace, carrying some of the rubbish inside …

Opening his eyes, he had the sensation that something had just landed on his head.

After a few seconds he realised he was lying on the living room floor, and the pain he was now experiencing in his head was nearly as bad as the pain in his hands. Beside him, an old friend lay empty on the carpet.

Despite his inebriation he was freezing. Turning his head to the left he saw that the door was wide open and a gale was blowing into the room. Trying in vain to rise he found his body was heavier than lead, and that it was much easier to stay where he was. Dropping his head back to the cold floor with a thud, something slipped down over his forehead.

He closed his eyes for a few seconds, then opened them again. What he saw straight ahead convinced him that he wasn't on the living room floor at all; he was in his bed, fast asleep. He knew this to be true, because earlier in the evening he had been in some kind of mad trance and had gone into the spare room and lifted the carpet. But then he'd shaken himself out of the trance and gone *back* into the living room to tend to his wounds. He had definitely *not* raised the floorboards; but here they were in his dream, all lined up against the wall under the window, large as life, like a row of

brave little

soldiers.

And then, despite the gale blowing through the room and the intense cold, he saw that his view of the boards lined up against the wall was distorted by an apparent heat-haze rising from the floor. The whole floor ahead was shimmering. It was almost hypnotic.

When he blinked this time, nothing happened. The shimmering heat-haze inched ever closer, until he saw that it wasn't a heat-haze at all. It had a solid form, like the movement of thousands of tiny limbless bodies pulsing their way towards him. Like a sea of maggots. On and on they marched, to his left and right, before going around him. He could feel them beneath him, shivering against his skin.

Then, as if an inaudible order had been given, he became aware of a slight tension in his back. It felt like he was being raised slightly from the floor …

With a start he knew that either the clutter in the room was moving or he was, because here was the fireplace, and it hadn't been there a minute ago. Then to his left a chair moved away from him, as did the piano. To his right was a picture on the floor that had been there so long he'd forgotten all about it. He could see something in the glass, a ghastly pale figure being carried horizontally across the floor by unseen agents, an ill-fitting golden paper crown wobbling back and forth on its head. It revived the memory of a dream in which people were chanting something he couldn't quite

Long Live The King

make out.

And at that moment, the chilly realisation came that he wasn't dreaming at all. But he was powerless as the procession went on and on, out through the living room and into the hall and then the spare room, where suddenly he was falling and it was raining, large shivering droplets hitting his face and body, eventually covering him until their soft plopping sound was all he could hear.

Several days of silence followed, which were only broken when, as promised, an emissary of the Kingdom went to the palace to check that everything was well with the King.

On entering the courtyard the emissary saw that the door to the palace was wide open, and that a terrible smell was coming from within.

What the emissary found inside was almost beyond belief. There was rubbish all across the floors, empty bottles everywhere and packets of strange white powder had been secreted into hidden nooks and cupboards. There was even dried blood on a piano. The palace had gone to rack and ruin.

But it was in a small room away from the main hall that the worst atrocities were found. It was at this point that higher authorities were called in to deal with things.

Once the Kingdom had been cleared and only the most important people remained, the small room was examined in detail. It was agreed by all who entered it that what they found there was beyond any of their experience.

In the centre of that cramped, smelly and decaying room was a large hole. In the hole lay the rapidly decomposing body of the King, his body ripe (and to some, it seemed, almost alive) with the larva inching across it. Bizarrely, the golden paper crown perched on the King's head was completely untainted by decay ... Slowly and very carefully, the decomposing body was removed from the hole.

But that was not the end of the horrors.

Because underneath the slime and putrefaction left behind by the crowned figure, an even more bizarre sight was uncovered. The remains of a broken skeleton littered the dirt floor, and among the bones lay hundreds of terracotta soldiers, their lifeless faces caked with earth and slime. These too were eventually lifted from the hole, and the palace was shut up indefinitely.

It is sad to note that nobody ever missed the King. He was never mourned, and nobody in the Kingdom ever spoke his name again.
     Yes, happily, nobody lived ever after.

- For Peter Straub

Reflections from a Broken Lamp

The Victim:

How it all happened is immaterial – how can I think about that when they won't let me shine or function? If they gave me it back though, I could explain. Will you ask them for me, will you?

Ask them to give me back the light of my life?

The Eyewitness:

Martin was close to the edge before Veronica; when she … wasn't there anymore he got worse, cut himself off from everyone. He should have made a fresh start instead of brooding in that big house by himself. He used to read all day I think, read and brood about it all. That night was the first time I'd been in the house for nearly three years. He wouldn't allow visitors.

The Burglar:

Of course I know it's serious – I've never seen anything like it before. Don't want to neither. He was a fruitcake. I mean, I'd heard he'd gotten a bit eccentric ...

Look. Pinning the robbery on me is one thing. I can hardly deny it. But I had nothing to do with the rest of it.

The Policeman:

Mr. Verrell informed us some time ago of a prowler around his property and insisted they were 'going to get him'. Nobody else saw anything, but as his house is within walking distance of the station it was easy to keep a check on it.

Around 3.15 am I heard noise in that general direction. As I made my way over there, a man I recognized as a neighbour was entering the house, apparently through a smashed doorframe.

The Victim:

I hadn't been able to sleep as usual. I hear every noise and see every thing. I'd been waiting for it to happen so long it was second nature to me, having an eye and an ear open.

The Burglar:

At about three in the morning I decided I'd waited long enough. The upstairs room was lit up purple the way it always was – he was watching the telly with the lights off, I reckoned. All the valuables would be downstairs anyway. If he did disturb me I could easily scare him a bit and get out. And I had my mask on too. Marilyn Monroe.

166

The Victim:

There was a scrabbling noise downstairs, very faint. At first I just thought it was the wind against the back door; the trees needed cutting.

The Burglar:

Picking the lock was easy, and he didn't have an alarm – some big houses don't. It'd been three years since I'd been in last. It didn't seem to look any different: wood panel walls, shelves full of books, drinks cabinet over by the bay window, maroon leather chairs … very tasteful. I used to work there, as a gardener. Then all that happened with his wife and he fired everyone. He was a bit odd in those days, too. Anyway, I remembered the layout and started to look around. Wherever I swung the torch I kept seeing pictures of her, Mrs. Verrell. They looked odd somehow.

The Victim:

I turned the television off, a murder mystery or something. As I got back into bed there was a creak downstairs. Two steps from the front of the bureau there's a loose floorboard. I heard it, as clear as I can hear myself now.

That's when I knew.

The Burglar:

The bureau was up against the staircase wall. I knew there was a fake drawer in the bureau, and that the safe behind it actually belonged in the cupboard under the stairs and the bureau covered it up. The light from the torch landed on one of those photos of

Mrs. Verrell. The glass was missing from the frame and the picture was covered in scratches, and some of it had been torn away. A few other pictures were the same. I stepped back to look at the drawer when a floorboard creaked. I waited a few seconds, heard nothing, so crouched down to the bureau.

The Victim:

I knew it was her. But the thought occurred to me – what if it isn't? I stood in the bedroom for a few minutes, thinking what to do.

Then I remembered the safe.

The Burglar:

I swear I never heard him coming. I'd removed the drawer and sure enough there was the safe. I wondered if I could get into it any easier from under the stairs in the cupboard. I went round to the right but there wasn't a door there anymore. It'd been sealed up, like a fake wall. I went back to the bureau.

The Victim:

Never heard me? I'm not surprised! I know where to tread. I hung over the top of the balcony and saw a small patch of light near the bureau. I took my time going down the stairs. At the bottom, all I could see was a black mass crouched on the floor. I was virtually on it when she looked up.

The Burglar:

I remembered his wife years ago talking about a safe. It wasn't really a safe, she said, just a small cubbyhole that they'd built into the cupboard and put a door on. I guess she trusted me. It wasn't even locked.

I had my head inside the bureau. It was full of dust – I was glad I was wearing a mask. I shone the torch around but there didn't seem to be anything of value, just a load of old clippings from the papers. I thought I saw a picture of his wife on one of them.

Then I noticed the smell to the right of the safe. It was foul, made me uneasy … I thought I was going to be sick. When I jerked my head back out he was there. I moved away from him.

The Victim:

She turned to face me. Neither of us spoke … I was frozen to the spot. Her face was … it was greasy in the moonlight but I could see she was grinning. She fell backwards into the freestanding ashtray. I lunged at her.

It was her or me, you see.

The Burglar:

He was really quick. I took a swing at him and missed and fell backwards, landed funny. He jumped on my chest. I could just make out his face. He looked haggard, like an old man, but with a young man's strength. He started strangling me, and banging my head against the floor. There was saliva flying out of his mouth. He started shrieking in a funny voice as he shook me. Then my mask fell off and his eyes glazed over.

The Victim:
I shook her but she kept grinning; her hair even stayed in place. I looked for the mark on the side of her head but it wasn't there; I couldn't make out her eyes either. I shook her harder, harder, and – her face came away in my hands. I … I can't remember anymore.

The Burglar:
It was like he wasn't looking at me anymore. I wondered if maybe he'd recognized me. He kept saying his wife's name over and over. He was still on top of me. There was a table nearby with a shadeless lamp on it. I made a grab for it, but then he got off me and started throwing furniture around – he smashed a glass door at the side of the house when he hurled a chair at it. He went over to the wall next to the bureau, the sealed bit, and started pounding his hands against it, screaming "Why are you doing this to me! Why can't you leave me alone?" I started to back away.

The Eyewitness:
I heard glass smash next door, someone screaming. We were used to the shouting and yelling. When Veronica disappeared he blamed himself and shouted and cried a lot. If you tried to pacify him he laughed at you.

I went into his garden and saw the glass door was shattered enough for me to get through the frame. There was a man dressed in black in the centre of the room. Martin was over by the wall next to the bureau, yelling.

The Burglar:
It was hard to make it out but it sounded like he was apologizing. It was like *he* was the intruder! There was a noise behind me and someone climbed in through the broken door. I turned back and saw Verrell looking at something on the floor. He was crying. He picked up the shadeless lamp and stared at it. He was talking to himself.

The Eyewitness:
I was trying to think what to do when Martin picked up the lamp. There's a lamp in his house that got broken a few years ago and he never replaced the shade on it, so it was just a bare bulb. He said it was Veronica's. He was staring into space and rolling the lamp through his hands. "You want it, do you?" he said in a quiet voice. "Do you?" Then he started striking himself over the head with it.

The Burglar:
It was bizarre, like a nightmare. He kept bashing himself with it over and over again, there was blood pouring out of the side of his head. "Is this what you want?" he shouted. "Even the score?" Then the copper turned up.

The Policeman:
As I ran towards the house I heard somebody yelling but I couldn't make out what. I radioed for help. Then another voice shouted "No".

The Burglar:

When he stopped hitting himself with the lamp he had that strange look on his face again. He started grinning and mumbling, but I don't know what.

The Eyewitness:

He stopped hitting himself. There was a lot of blood. He looked down at the lamp and unscrewed the bulb. He let go of the lamp but kept the bulb in his hand. He laughed and began mumbling as he looked at it, the same phrase over and over. "Light of my life, light of my life". Later on I remembered the typewritten note Veronica had left him before she disappeared. That's what it said on the bottom. Then he – no, I can't, I'm sorry.

The Burglar:

He was going on and on while he looked at it. Then he stopped. The bulb was in the palm of his hand, and the cap was pointed at his face.

When he stuck it into his eye he was still grinning. I swear it.

The Policeman:

He was trying to screw the bulb in with his left hand, and with the other he was pointing over near the bureau. He fell heavily against a chair and landed on the floor. The bulb stayed in his left eye socket.

The Victim:

I loved her, you see. I even kept the house exactly as she had it except for the cupboard under the stairs. That had to change, of course. We all need somewhere to sleep.

But she'd committed a sin. It'd been going on behind my back for years. She denied it of course, but I *knew*. When they found her she was still wearing my last gift to her, so for a short while we were one again. Fitting, really. But I don't have it anymore. I don't even have somewhere to sit. I wish they'd give me it back.

I feel naked in the darkness.

Less Ahead Than Behind

1

They were nothing like caterpillars, Joe thought as another one slid past inches away. *They were more like carriages if anything.*

Later, the image shocked him nearly as much as finding himself there in the first place; soaked through to the skin without his hat and coat, his slippers no protection against the puddle he'd stepped in a few minutes earlier. Perhaps they'd saved him – maybe it was stepping in the puddle that had brought him to his senses for a second or two, and made him stop at the lights instead of stepping straight out into the oncoming traffic.

The last thing he remembered was being in his living room. He'd been nodding off on the sofa, and remembered thinking that the room was uncomfortably hot, even for him, and that he should get up and turn down the heating. Instead, he was standing at the bottom of a hill next to a set of traffic lights, watching helplessly as dozens of cars, lorries and buses hurtled down towards him, each close enough to touch before they turned sharply away to his left, bumping over a loose drain cover as they went with a rattling clank.

He had to get home as soon as possible, before anyone saw him. Stepping onto the road he was stopped almost immediately, immobilized by the blare of a car horn to his right. Looking in that direction, it took him a few seconds to realise; the reason the traffic had stopped coming down the hill was to let the traffic in this lane go. As he stood there he saw the man that'd presumably blown the horn punch it again. As if feeling the blows directly, Joe moved back onto the kerb.

"Use the lights you stupid old fool," the man shouted out of his window before speeding past.

Reaching to touch the cold silver button, he blinked at the bright headlights as the wave of garishly-coloured metal slid by on the left, the constant procession making his eyes cross so that the cars crashed into each other as they passed. By the time he'd blinked the last of them from his vision, the traffic had stopped on the right and was replaced once more by a succession of rain-smeared faces hurtling down the hill towards him, acutely aware that the only thing between him and them was the drivers' ability to keep their vehicles under control and a slightly raised kerb.

As the traffic swept away from him, several faces turned to watch him as he stood there. Doing the same thing, Joe saw that the road branched off into three lanes but the cars all stayed together, bumper to bumper, oozing away from him like an enormous multicoloured caterpillar as they snaked round towards the roundabout. Momentarily, the illusion was broken when one of the cars moved away to join another lane, but the gap it left was filled up almost immediately.

Turning his attention back to the oncoming traffic, he saw a huge lorry heading towards him, its driver wearing a blue smock, putting him in mind of a guards' uniform. As the lorry passed and its lights dazzled him, it must've nudged the drain cover out a bit more because the clanking sound was twice as loud as before; even when a small car passed over it a few seconds later it wasn't much quieter.

Despite the increasing number of headlights shining in his face, Joe couldn't look away. Two more cars went over the drain cover in quick succession, followed by two more: *clank-clank, clank-clank,* as if they were all parts of a bigger machine, its rhythm becoming unbearable. But still he couldn't turn his attention from it, or the metal carriages coming towards him. Yes, carriages, that was it – why had he thought the cars looked like caterpillars? If they looked like anything it was a long set of carriages –

"Uncle Joe? What are you doing here?"

Turning, it took Joe a moment to realise who was under the hood.

"Steven?" he said, squinting at him through the deluge. "I – I was at home, and –" He stopped, shaking his head in disgust, rainwater flying from his straggly hair.

"It's happened again, hasn't it," Steven said quietly. "Well, we'd better get you home." Removing his coat, he put it round his uncle's shoulders, both crossing the road before the lights changed again.

"It was like I was being hypnotized," Joe said as they waited for the next set of lights to turn green. After that, neither of them spoke until they were back indoors.

"It was sheer chance I was there," Joe heard his nephew say in the kitchen above the noise from the extractor fan. "Nina, I know we will, but it's difficult. I don't want to be the one who –" Steven lowered his voice. Even when the fan clicked off, all Joe could hear for a while was the rattle of cups and spoons. "The third, I think," he heard Steven say after a cupboard door closed. "At least that's all he remembers, poor devil. Anyway, I'll speak to you later." As the kitchen door began to open, Joe went back to his chair and sat down, the wet towel still hanging over his shoulders.

"There you go," Steven said, coming in with two mugs. "Warm you up a bit."

Looking down at the hot milk, Joe pulled a face. "Put some rum in it. There's a bottle in the sideboard there."

"Good idea," Steven said, sliding open the door. "Might help you sleep."

"I don't want to sleep," Joe mumbled, shifting uncomfortably in his seat.

They'd almost finished their drinks before Steven spoke. "Look, Uncle Joe –"

"I know what you're going to say, so don't," Joe interrupted him. "It can't carry on like this, I know that. Just … just give me a couple of days. I'm not sleeping well, I told you that. Decent sleep and I'll be fine. If it happens again you can call the doctor and have them lock me away."

"You know it's not like that," Steven chided.

"It's this town," Joe snapped, not hearing him. "I don't recognise it any more. It's not the place me and your auntie lived in. I probably just lost my way, that's all."

Steven drained his cup and made his way to the door. "I'll be in touch," he said. "Look after yourself."

Without replying, Joe locked the door. *It's this town; I don't recognise it any more.* After putting the chain on – *and it's come to something when you've got to barricade yourself in your own home during the day* – he went back into the living room and over to the sideboard. Taking the pen and pad of paper from the top, he sat down in his armchair and started to write:

Dear Sir,

I'm writing to express my concern about the state of the roads in this town, along with the people who are allowed to drive on them. Earlier today whilst doing my shopping, the clanking noise coming from a loose drain cover was so loud that I forgot to press the button for the crossing. I'd barely stepped a foot onto the road when a driver in an oncoming car called me something that I'd rather not repeat before telling me to get back on the pavement. Is it any wonder the town is the way it is today, with people like that driving about?

- Joe Wanless

After addressing the envelope – at least that was something he never forgot, the amount of letters he sent them – not that they ever did any good – Joe turned on the television. After watching the rubbish he had to pay a license for for as long as he could stomach, he switched it off, checked everything else was switched off, and decided to have an early night.

In the hall, he looked up at the flight of stairs and sighed, knowing that getting up there was going to be an effort. Maybe he should think over what Steven said (or rather as he suspected, what Nina told him to say), and look around that new block of sheltered flats that had gone up near the town centre – it'd save him crawling up the stairs to go to bed every night like he'd been doing lately.

He'd barely begun the long trek upwards when something different caught his attention. His second pair of shoes, which were normally on the second stair, were now on the third. He'd obviously done it himself, but like so many things lately he couldn't remember. At least Bertha wasn't around anymore to see him like this.

"I wish you wouldn't leave your shoes there, Joe, it's an accident waiting to happen," she'd say, taking her own shoes off the stairs and placing them beside the front door. "That's if the smell doesn't get them first. I'm half expecting them to walk up the stairs on their own one of these days. It'd be better than them cluttering up the place. Somebody's bound to trip over them."

That was in the days when there were seven or eight pairs of shoes in the house – it didn't matter how tight the money was, Bertha liked her shoes. But he could never see the problem; as long as each pair was flush with the wall, with his, bigger, shoes on the bottom steps, and Bertha's smaller ones on the steps above, also flush with the wall, who was going to trip over them? Then, after she died and there were just his two pairs to worry about, he'd kept doing it. So why were his second pair now on the third step?

Grabbing hold of the errant footwear, he put the shoes back on the second step where they belonged.

After cleaning his teeth and getting into his pyjamas, he got into bed and turned out the bedside lamp. Yawning in the darkness, it still took him several hours to nod off – after what had happened earlier, he kept thinking about trains for some reason, which was silly, because there hadn't been a train line in the town for years – but mainly it was because he was afraid where he might find himself when he opened his eyes.

Screwing the lid back on the urn, he leaned against the railing of the bridge in the darkness and looked into the thick, black water at the large, almost circular scattering of ashes rippling on the water's unbroken surface.

For some reason he'd expected them to scatter, but instead they all clung together.

He was just starting to wonder why when he noticed movement within the circle, two ragged holes appearing side by side at the top. Then beneath this, another slightly smaller hole started to appear; and beneath that, a long, ugly horizontal split opened up along the bottom, leering at him like some huge, toothless mouth.

Reluctantly he looked back at the top holes – just pools of water appearing among the ashes, he told himself – but he couldn't escape the feeling that he was looking down into a huge, warped face; or the certainty that the face was looking back up at him.

A few seconds later, as it opened its mouth to speak, Joe woke up.

2

"Another yellow notice up on the lamppost, Joe," his neighbour said over the hedge that morning.

"Who now?"

"Number twenty-six. Wants to build a conservatory. Wouldn't think they had room for one."

"No," Joe said, locking the door after him. Putting the key in his pocket, he looked down at his shopping list to make sure he'd remembered everything: bread, milk, can of polish, rum –

"What's that, a Christmas list?"

Looking up from the sheet of paper, Joe wondered if Paul was joking – it wasn't even December for another week. But apparently he was serious. He mumbled back a reply.

"Well, you can't start too early," Paul said. "We've already got Paul junior his train set." Joe froze on the step, giving his neighbour a strained look.

"You remember dad was a driver?" Paul said, feeling he needed to clarify his remark.

"Yes," Joe said quietly, looking back at the sheet he'd torn from the notepad. "I – I don't know what I was thinking."

"Aye, you can't start for Christmas too early," Paul repeated. "Anyway, I'll let you go."

"Can't start too early," Joe muttered as he headed for the post-box. What was wrong with everybody? All that fuss for a couple of days – it wasn't even as if anyone was any happier at the end of it all.

After posting his letter, he stopped level with the lamppost to look at the NOTICE OF PROPOSED DEVELOPMENT sign fastened around the pole and shook his head. People just couldn't leave anything alone anymore, especially buildings. As far as he could see, all they did was make them uglier, like that new block of so-called 'Luxury' apartments that had gone up in the town – he'd never seen such a sterile-looking building in his life. 'Cronenberg Towers' Steven called it, whatever that meant. Mind you, if they weren't building things they were pulling them down – the whole area was like a building site now, rubbish everywhere.

Apart from the rubbish, walking into town Joe felt he had the streets to himself, as the few people who passed him were either talking into their phones or listening to music; one man he saw was apparently so lonely he appeared to be having a conversation with himself. But by the time he reached town, the pavements were choked solid with mothers and toddlers and students sitting on the cathedral walls, smoking. Seeing one of them tapping ash onto the wall brought back the dream. It seemed vaguely familiar – then again it would, having been the third or fourth time he'd dreamt it. But something about it nagged at him. What it was about, he had no idea – the best he'd been able to come up with was that Bertha's ashes had been scattered in the Dales last year, but it hadn't been done at night and certainly not in a filthy river –

"Morning. Bit brighter today, isn't it?"

"What?"

Looking round, he saw a girl standing beside him. "I'm sorry to bother you," she said, smiling, "I'm from the college –" a small plastic identification card appeared in her hand and was whipped away before he had a chance to look at it "– and I'm doing a project for my Sociology course about how the town has changed over the years. Can I ask how long you've lived here?"

"All my life."

"Really?" the girl said, sounding surprised. "I imagine that it's changed quite a lot, then?"

"More than I would've believed it could. They're destroying the character of the place."

"But maybe the character's just developing?" the girl said. "Being improved? Nothing stays the same forever, does it?"

Tutting, Joe pointed towards the bottom of the hill. "I'll give you an example. See down there? There's a subway round that corner, and I keep reading in the local paper that it's full of druggies and weirdoes. It's got so people are afraid to go in there. Is that an improvement? And what about him, standing over there?" he pointed towards an obese man in a suit with stuck-up hair, standing far too close to a nervous-looking woman. "He was here on Friday. Do you know what he does? He stops people and asks them if they've had an accident and would they like to sue someone. I always thought that an accident meant it was nobody's fault."

Looking to the girl for agreement, she smiled back at him uneasily.

"Look, love," he said. "You don't mind me calling you love, do you? I mean, you can't even do that anymore without causing offence."

"Er, no," she said, surprised. "Whatever."

"It's not you. But you asked if the town's changed much over the years. Well, I'd say it has. And not for the better, either. Put that in your report."

"Project," she told him.

"Project then." He started to walk away.

"If you could just answer my questions –" she called out.

But he didn't hear her; he was thinking about what he'd just said. *An accident meant it was nobody's fault.* It reminded him of something, but he didn't know what it was.

Back at home, he dumped the shopping in the kitchen and went into the hall to take off his shoes. Sitting on the stairs, he removed them with a grunt and placed them on the first step, below his second pair.

Only his second pair weren't there.

God, I'm getting worse, he thought as he crawled up the stairs to get them, certain that he'd moved them back yesterday – it seemed he couldn't keep anything in his head longer than a few seconds these days. But as he reached them and was about to head back down, he stopped – he *had* put the shoes back yesterday; he was certain, because he hadn't had to crawl up to get them: they'd only been on the third step. Looking down, he counted eight stairs below him. Why on earth would he put his second pair of shoes halfway up the stairs?

Going back down, he tried to think. How come he hadn't noticed them there when he'd come down this morning? Because he'd had another bad night, that was why; he hadn't been in a frame of mind to notice anything. If it came to that, he didn't feel much better now; it seemed like every time he left the house these days there was some new thing to annoy him.

Angrily dropping the shoes on the correct step, he went into the living room and over to his armchair, grabbing the pen and writing pad off the sideboard on the way. Not that it would do any good, of course.

Sir,

       Aside from what appears to be a deliberate attempt to make everyone's life a misery with the noise and inconvenience, can I ask why there's so much building work going on in the town lately? It seems like there's hardly a house in the whole area now that hasn't been altered in some way, with extensions and conservatories and whatnot. As far as I can see, all these changes do is make perfectly good houses look ugly.

And while I'm on the subject of unwarranted intrusions, why are there so many people in the town square armed with clipboards these days? I can't remember the last time I got my shopping finished without first being asked to fill in some survey or give to a charity I've never heard of.

One final point. Does the local council really feel that it's necessary to put Christmas decorations up in the precinct before we're actually in December?

- J. Wanless

In bed that night he was still having trouble getting to sleep, which was daft because it was only a dream, after all, and always the same dream at that. But later, when he awoke in the middle of the night covered in sweat as he had on previous occasions, he realised that this time the dream had been different: this time, when the mouth opened, it spoke to him.

"*Help me, Joe*" it said.

And although he hadn't been able to place it, he was sure he'd seen that face before.

3

Posting his letter the next morning, Joe wondered what he was going to do next. He'd already been up for several hours, and try as he might he couldn't think of a single thing he needed to do. In fact, he was able to think of little else but the dream.

The face wasn't Bertha's, he was sure of that; it looked nothing like her, and the voice hadn't sounded like her. And those words – he couldn't be completely sure, but he was pretty certain she'd never said anything like that before she died. So who the hell was it?

Walking aimlessly and further than he realised, he found himself down at the bottom end of town half an hour later and still none the wiser. His legs were on fire, but he was determined to walk home even if it took all day. Passing the bus stop, he weakened for a second – maybe just this once it wouldn't hurt to take it easy – but soon changed his mind as the bus pulled in, full to bursting with people half his age and twice his weight: he might be a lot of things, he thought as he walked on, but lazy wasn't one of them.

A few minutes later, he was back at the traffic lights where Steven had found him and his face flushed. He still had no memory of leaving the house that day, nor of the other times it had happened. On those occasions he hadn't got so far – the first time he'd ended up in the corner shop; the second time Paul had pulled up alongside him in his car at the end of the street. But that last time … it could've ended badly. So where had he been?

He tried to reason it through. He'd been standing next to the traffic lights, as if about to cross the road. Had he been going back home? If he was, where had he been first? Perhaps he'd been walking round the town the way he was now, and got lost. Somehow, that didn't seem right; the town might have changed almost beyond recognition but he wouldn't have got lost, no matter what he'd told Steven. So if he *hadn't* come his usual route then he must've come along the road next to the roundabout and up through the subway. But why would he have done that? If he did, it was a wonder he'd got out in one piece, according to the paper.

As he looked in that direction, a couple roughly his age were coming up the ramp from the subway itself, neither looking particularly ruffled. How long was it since *he'd* been down there? Not since the articles started appearing in the paper, anyway.

"Excuse me," Joe asked the old man, "it is safe down there, is it?"

"It is when I've got him with me," the woman said, tightening her grip on the man's arm.

"Well we've just been in and there was nobody there," the man said, smiling at his wife's remark. "I think it's safe enough during the day."

"And you can't spend your whole life being frightened, can you?" the woman added.

"No," Joe said as they walked past, "that's true enough."

With her words still fresh in his mind, Joe headed down the ramp, with only a slight feeling of apprehension as it fed into the tunnel. Its walls were daubed with graffiti, which thankfully he couldn't read in the greying light, and the ground was strewn with lager cans and chewed-up food wrappers. Stepping into the daylight provided by the hollowed-out stone circle at the centre of the subway, the realisation that the road above would be full of cars proved of little comfort; here, the silence was eerie. No wonder people were afraid to come down.

Before his misgivings gave way to something stronger, he made his way across the circle, passing the two darkened exits on his left and on towards the one ahead, squinting into its gloom to see if anybody was lurking inside. About ten feet from the tunnel entrance his heart thudded, spotting what looked like someone curled up in a sleeping bag just inside the entrance; getting closer, he was both relieved and annoyed to find it was only a black bin liner, filled to the top with rubbish.

At the other side of the tunnel, the murk only lifted slightly. Ahead of him, a slimy-looking wall gave the impression of being propped up by the stairs that led off left and right. Knowing that if he had been along here yesterday he must have come past the river, he took the stairs on the right.

Halfway up he saw another black rubbish bag, its ragged mouth flapping down at him near the top of the stairs. Level with it, he spotted a yellow bin attached to a pole behind the bag, also stuffed to bursting; he realised then what the bags were doing there in the first place. But why not just empty the bins?

"Because that would be too straightforward," Joe muttered to himself, passing the council offices on his left.

Crossing at the next set of traffic lights, he made his way towards the river and another example of the towns' so-called rejuvenation – a former builder's yard reduced to a pile of fenced-in rubble, soon to be replaced by another block of yuppie flats. According to Steven, the ones in town were going for a quarter of a million. How anyone could pay that sort of money for a view of a polluted river was beyond him. They must have more money than sense.

Standing by the railing, he looked down into the thick, dark, oily water. They reckoned it'd been cleaned up over the years, but to Joe it didn't look much different to the last time he'd been here, whenever that was. Shivering, he wondered if that had been the day before last, because all of a sudden it seemed so familiar to him. But he wasn't sure why – even as a child he hadn't spent much time along here, not after his father had said the river was full of rats. He'd told him that when a friend of his had fallen in, the rats had got hold of him and dragged him under. A few days later, when the boy's body washed up there'd been nothing left of him but his skeleton – according to his father, the rats had picked his bones clean. Strange, the things you believed at that age. Still, he hadn't been the only one – Bobby had believed it too when he'd told him. In fact, it was after he'd told him that they'd changed their minds about the river and gone over to the railway line instead –

Bobby – he hadn't thought about Bobby for decades. He and Bertha never spoke about him. It seemed to be the best way of dealing with what happened –

A chill ran through his body as he remembered the dream and where it came from, what had triggered it. Then, looking down at the water, he realised where he was – it might not be dark and there wasn't a face there, but it was here that he'd told Bobby about the rats.

And as he stood there shaking, still looking down into the water, he realised with shame that he'd never told Bertha the truth about what happened.

Well, maybe it wasn't too late, he thought, turning his back on the water. Perhaps if he told her now she'd forgive him. His head a jumble of remembered thoughts, he somehow managed to hobble home without being struck by traffic.

Unlocking the door, he barged through the kitchen into the living room. The house felt empty; she must've gone to bed again. Standing in the hall he shouted up the stairs, knowing she wouldn't be asleep.

"Bertha? Bertha, I need to talk to you."

No answer – maybe she was asleep after all. He was just about to shout again when he saw something that didn't make sense – half a dozen pairs of shoes, Bertha's shoes, were missing from the stairs. His were there; the pair he kept on the bottom step he was wearing, but the other pair that should've been on the step above were only a few feet from the top of the landing – she'd go spare if she saw them, but he had to speak with her first. Crawling up past them, he straightened himself out at the top of the stairs and walked into the bedroom.

"Bertha, love. There's something I have to tell you –"

The left side of the bed wasn't just empty; it looked like it hadn't been slept in for months. Confused, he shuffled back out into the hall, wondering where she could've gone. It was only when he spotted the shoes a matter of feet away on the stairs a minute or so later that memory and grief returned. Dropping down on the top step with his head in his hands, the shoes a few feet below him, he didn't know which was worse.

The dream had started a few days after Bobby died, Joe remembered now, pouring himself another rum.

It was the same time of year too; it must've been, because it was dark early. They'd been throwing stones down at the moon's reflection in the water when he told Bobby about the river rats.

"Ugh. That's horrible," he'd said. "Let's go somewhere else." So they'd ended up at the railway line.

It was easy to get onto the tracks in those days – none of the mollycoddling fences or signs they have now; the assumption was that you knew it was dangerous. But they'd been in a devilish mood that night, and had started playing on the line.

It'd been funny at first, when Bobby got stuck in the rails; it was like something out of one of those silent films, where the girl is tied to the train tracks by the villain but gets rescued in the nick of time. At first, Joe had thought he was messing about; but then he saw that he wasn't. They'd just started to wonder what to do when they heard the train coming, *Clank-clank, clank-clank* in the distance.

Bobby hadn't panicked at first, he remembered; he reckoned he'd plenty of time to get his legs free. But Joe had panicked right from the start, and the rumble of the train became like a second heartbeat, pulsing in his chest.

Then the lights appeared and the train came around a bend behind them, closer than they realised. And Bobby started screaming.

"*Help me, Joe!*" he yelled as he tried to free himself. But Joe froze, staring into the light as if hypnotised, the clanking getting louder. Then he could see past the lights and into the windows, saw the face of the driver and his look of horror as he realised what was about to happen.

A second before the whistle blew, Bobby screamed again; but Joe couldn't take his eyes off the driver, thinking about the trouble he was going to be in if he was seen. But he didn't think the driver hadn't spotted him. Before he got the chance, Joe hid behind one of the trees lining the edge of the track.

"*Joe, please!*" Bobby screamed, still trying desperately to free himself.

Tearing his gaze from the driver, Joe looked at his friend. In the lights from the oncoming train Bobby's face was bleached white like the moon, his mouth a large black hole. He screamed a final time, but the noise was cut off by the shrieking of the whistle and the train as it thundered along the track. But Joe didn't need to hear the words to know what they were – "*Help me, Joe –*"

Gulping the neat rum, he shivered. Strange, how he could remember all the details now, after not thinking about them for over fifty years; the squealing of the train's brakes as he ran home, crying, wondering if anybody had seen him; letting himself into the empty house, his father at work and his mother out visiting a friend in hospital, sitting in the darkness, ashamed of what he'd done; his father the next morning telling him what had happened, asking him if he knew anything about it, then the look from his father that said he didn't believe him – maybe if he'd told him what he wanted to hear he'd have let Joe go to the funeral service and crematorium. "No place for a *child*," his father had said before he and his mother left for the church that day. That night he'd started having the dream that would torment him for years, right up until he and Bertha had started courting all those years later.

He'd thought it strange at first, them getting together like that. They'd met at the factory one day, and seemed to get on. For a while he'd wondered if she was going out with him because he'd been so close to her brother, but when he'd tried to talk to her about him one day she'd changed the subject; people didn't talk about things like that in his experience. After that, she never mentioned him. He'd thought that she wanted to put it all behind her as much as he did. And now Bertha wasn't here anymore it was coming back to haunt him –

Bloody hell, that was the kind of nonsense his father would have come out with. "You're not here to enjoy yourself lad, you'll do well to remember that," he'd said when they'd started going out. "God watches our every move and knows all our secrets. Profit by someone else's misfortune, you'll get your comeuppance in the end. You don't get something for nothing in this life." Maybe his father had been right – he'd had a good life, up until Bertha died. And ever since then everything had gone downhill.

"Oh for God's sake," he muttered, tipping the last of the rum into his glass. Hadn't he been scared enough lately with what was happening to him without frightening himself even more with his father's prophecies of doom? It was a long time ago and it'd been an accident, and an accident meant that it was nobody's fault – he was sure he'd heard that before, and recently, but couldn't recall where. But it didn't matter – what did matter was that it was true.

Draining the rum in his glass, he went over to the sideboard to get the fresh bottle. Seeing the paper and pen, he picked them up too and returned to his seat.

Well, he was sick of being frightened; it would get to the point where he'd be afraid to leave the house; he'd had to think twice before going in that subway. Nobody said anything anymore, that was the trouble. Well, not him. The town might be a filthy tip these days, but it was all he had left.

He'd barely got a few lines down when a knock at the door made him jump. Cursing under his breath, he answered it.

"Just thought I'd come round and see how you were," Steven said, following his uncle into the living room.

"Fine," Joe said, picking up the bottle.

"I see you're keeping yourself busy," Steven said as he sat down.

"Nothing wrong with having a drink during the day," Joe said as the rum slopped into his glass. "I'm a grown man, you know."

"I didn't mean that. I meant the letter."

Joe looked down at the notepad. "Oh. That."

"What's it about this time?"

"Not that *you'd* understand," Joe said, capping the pen, "I'm writing to the paper to complain about the filth and rubbish all over the place and the kind of people who drop it. It's no wonder people are afraid to go out anymore."

"But you're not. Are you? I mean, after what happened the other day."

Steven tried to hold his uncle's gaze but Joe was having none of it. "I just got lost, I told you that."

Steven sighed. "Oh come on, we both know that's not true –"

Joe stood up, knocking his knees against the coffee table. "So I'm a liar now am I, as well as senile? Go on, get out. I'm sick of listening to people giving me advice today."

"Why, who's been giving you advice?"

"Nobody," Joe said, confused for a minute. "Look, Steven. Just go. Please."

Standing beside the net curtain, Joe watched Steven get into his car and start talking on his mobile phone, certain that he saw his nephew mouth the word "help". Moving from the window as the car pulled away, Joe wished everybody would stop treating him like a child. So angry was he that when he went to the toilet he didn't crawl up the stairs; this time, he marched.

It wasn't until he came out of the bathroom a few minutes later that he noticed the shoes outside the door, facing him toe to toe. Why had he started leaving them out like this? Kicking them as hard as he could, the shoes clattered down the stairs before smacking against the front door. Following them down, he put them back in their rightful place, then went into the living room to continue writing his letter.

> Having just walked from town, I find myself stunned at the vast amounts of rubbish on our streets. For example, going into the subway today, I had to make my way past several unsealed rubbish bags dumped there presumably because the bins were full. One of them was even on the stairs! Supposing I'd had an accident, and tripped over it? No doubt that would have been my fault!
>
> But that seems to be how things are going now. Is it any wonder that the rivers and streets are full of rats these days –

Joe stopped writing, unsure what to put next and unable to remember what he'd just written. Reading it back, it didn't make a lot of sense – maybe the rum was clouding his thoughts. He could finish the letter in the morning; it was still early but he'd had enough for today. Pouring himself a nightcap, he took it up to bed with him.

Finishing the rum, he turned off the light and waited for sleep along with the now-familiar dream. Only it didn't come.

At least not at first.

He was in bed and his mother popped her head round the door and told him to come downstairs: his father had something he wanted to tell him.

He was sitting in the armchair next to the fire as usual, with his pipe in his hand.

"Joe, I'm afraid something happened last night to your friend Bobby. We don't know why, but he was out on the railway line and he got hit by a train." His father eyed him carefully. "You don't happen to know why he was there, do you?"

194

Before he had a chance to speak his mother butted in. "Of course he doesn't! He stayed in last night like we told him to, didn't you, Joe?"

Slowly, Joe nodded.

"Well, I hope so, for his sake," his father said quietly, the pipe now in his mouth, his eyes never leaving Joe's. "Because Bobby wasn't just hit by a train, you know. He lost so much blood that it killed him."

"There's no need to tell him any more Arthur," his mother put in.

"And the reason he lost so much blood," his father said, ignoring her, "was because the train hit him so hard it cut his feet off –"

"*Arthur, that's enough!*" his mother shrieked.

"No! The boy has to be taught right from wrong. His feet were cut off and they found them on the other side of the tracks, twenty feet from his body, still inside his shoes. Because he'd been somewhere that he shouldn't have been."

Cut his feet off … twenty feet from his body … still inside his shoes … The image had stuck in his head for years … then he was back at the river, looking down at the face in the thick, black water.

"*Help me, Joe!*" it said –

"Bobby!"

Sitting upright in the bed, Joe looked around the room. For some reason he was in a double bed, but his parents weren't there. They couldn't have come back home yet.

Horrified, Joe realised he'd left Bobby alone at the railway line and run home.

He had to go and help him.

4

"Help me, Joe!"

Looking around, Joe couldn't believe the amount of rubbish lying about. Was it any wonder the town was full of rats? A cold breeze blew around his ankles. Looking down, he wondered why he was wearing his slippers and pyjamas. Hadn't he'd been writing a letter when –

"Help me, Joe!"

That was right – he was going to help Bobby. It was a good thing his parents weren't back yet – he'd promised them he'd stay inside.

Peering into the darkness around him, he tried to figure out where he was. It looked like the subway, but why come here? He'd left Bobby at the railway line, which was the other side of town.

"Joe, please!"

But he sounded close – he must've got free after all. As long as he followed his voice he'd be okay.

"I'm coming, Bobby!" he called out.

He'd barely started walking through the subways' huge open circle when he remembered it was dangerous – people had been mugged down here; he remembered Bertha telling him about it. He couldn't see anybody, but to be on the safe side he walked along the wall as it curved round towards the nearest exit.

He was only a few feet from it when he stopped. Just inside the entrance, it looked like a tramp was sleeping in a black bag. Holding his breath, he watched it for a few moments before realising that it was just a black bin liner, full of rubbish. Why didn't the council come and pick it up? Their offices were only just above him. Maybe a letter to the paper would spur them into action.

Stepping carefully past the bag for fear of what might emerge, he muttered to himself. All this rubbish everywhere, it wasn't healthy. It'd attract rats. They were already in the river as it was –

Halfway through the tunnel he stopped. Bobby – they'd been at the river earlier; he'd told him about the rats. He sounded quite close now – was he at the river? He must be, because the train line was miles away. Lifting his feet, he set off once more.

Leaving the tunnel, he was standing between two flights of steps when he heard a faint rustling behind him. At first he thought it was just the wind, but then realised it could've been Bobby, hiding in the rubbish bag trying to scare him; but the voice was ahead of him, over towards the river, not behind him.

Making his way up the stairs on the right, he spotted another rubbish bag. Below, he was sure he heard the rustling sound again. Bobby? No – Bobby was up ahead.

Which meant that somebody else could've been hiding in the rubbish bag.

His heart slammed in his chest, a warning not to look. He'd heard about the muggings down there, the drug dealers. They had to creep out of somewhere – was that how they did it? Before the thought had sunk in, he became aware of other noises – a dragging sound, followed by an irregular hopping. He forced himself to look back for a second but saw nothing; hearing the noise again, he looked away.

He couldn't turn back now he realised, even if he'd wanted to. Instead he had to get up the stairs and past the second bag, no matter what was inside. Drawing level with it, he looked intently but could see nothing except rubbish. But why leave a rubbish bag on the stairs? Things like that were a breeding ground for rats – he half expected something to crawl out of it and start following him, like Bertha said his shoes would when he left them on the stairs –

"Oh my God," Joe said, still looking down at the bag.

Bertha was dead. How had he forgotten that? He'd forgotten earlier too, when he'd seen his other pair of shoes on the stairs, and the way he'd had to keep taking them back down because they –

Had started walking upstairs on their own.

After laughing uneasily, Joe took a deep breath. Utterly ridiculous! He just kept forgetting he'd moved them, that was all. He kept forgetting lots of things lately; like the other day when Steven had found him in his slippers by the traffic lights –

Below him, something was hopping towards the stairs. He had to keep moving. Quick as he could, he moved past the rubbish bag, breathing heavily. Through his gasps, he heard whatever was there coming up the stairs behind him.

"Joe, please!"

Whatever it was, he could think about it later – right now he had to help Bobby, who had somehow managed to crawl away from the railway line and back towards the river. At the top of the stairs, he gulped in the cool night air. In the silence, he could clearly hear the hopping below him, quickly followed by another sound, even closer – a slithery, rustling sound, as if something was trying to crawl its way out of the second rubbish bag only a few paces behind him.

Despite the pain in his legs – nothing compared to the pain Bobby must've felt if his father was right, he told himself – he hobbled on even faster, even more afraid to look back and see what was following him, trying to quieten his breathing so he could judge how close the noises were behind.

He was almost past the council offices when he realised that the noise had changed. The hopping was still there, but the slithery noise had gone, as if whatever had been in the rubbish bag had crawled up onto the level ground to join it, creating an awkward, double-hopping sound; by the time Joe was almost at the traffic lights, both were in step, resulting in an urgent *clip-clop clip-clop*, like a pair of heavy-soled shoes coming up behind him.

Well, they weren't going to frighten him. His father would sort them out, once he'd got over the shock of his son being out in the middle of the night. In the meantime he had to help poor Bobby, who he could hear quite clearly now over at the river – God knows how much blood he must've lost getting there. Images of his father and Bobby welled up in his mind; his father giving him the bad news, followed by Bobby at the river, bleeding all over the pavement. And of course he'd have to break the news to Bertha –

Clank-clank, clank-clank, the sound of the train approaching.

Cut his feet off … twenty feet from his body … still inside his shoes …

"I'm half expecting them to walk up the stairs on their own one of these days."

Clip-clop, clip-clop. Clip-clop, clip-clop, the noise getting louder, speeding up behind him.

"Help me, Joe!"

The road thankfully empty, Joe scuttled across without waiting for the lights, realising how angry Bobby must be to be doing this to him. His father had been right – he was being punished for leaving Bobby at the railway line like that. But maybe he could at least save him now, do what he hadn't been able to do before –

Clip-clop, clip-clop.

He wasn't even halfway across when he saw the lights of the train ahead on the road. Letting out a little squeal of panic, he tried to get to the other side. He'd just about made it when he realised the squeal wasn't coming from him now, but from the brakes of the train as it slammed to a halt in front of him. But as its lights were shining in his face, he knew it couldn't be a train because the line wasn't there anymore. The lights were coming from a car instead.

"Are you all right?" a voice said from behind the twin beams.

"He's in his pyjamas," another voice said. "He must be freezing."

Without replying, Joe moved out of the light and across the road towards the river.

"You better follow him," one of the voices said. "I'll wait here." Letting out a cry of frustration, Joe hobbled on towards the river.

Looking around he couldn't see Bobby, but he could hear him yelling on the other side of the bridge. Dragging himself to the railing, Joe looked down into the darkness, where he saw Bobby's huge, white face mouthing up at him from the water.

"I'm coming Bobby!" Joe yelled, scrambling up onto the top of the railing, ignoring the voices behind him.

"Hey, what are you doing?"

"Stop him, for God's sake!"

Even above the sound of rushing water, Joe could hear the footsteps, louder and quicker than before. Experiencing a moment of almost unbearable panic, he looked down into the water, at his friend's agonised face imploring him to help.

But there was no decision to make. Doing what he should've done last time, Joe let go of the railing, and jumped.

5

A few months later when they took the ashes up to the Dales, Steven recalled his uncle's words the last time they'd been there.

"When I'm gone, you can bring me up here," he'd said as he scattered Bertha's ashes. "It's a bit of a tourist trap now, of course, but it's still nice. We've always liked it anyway."

Standing on the same spot, Steven let out a noisy sigh. "Maybe if I'd listened to you sooner about getting him into a home –" he said quietly.

"You did what you thought was right," Nina said, giving his shoulders a squeeze. "We couldn't have known he was so far gone. I mean, did he ever mention a Bobby to you?"

"Never. Maybe they misheard him over the sound of the water and everything. Aunt Bertha did have a brother called Bobby, but he died when she was a child."

"You've never mentioned him before," Nina said.

"Nothing to mention. Aunt Bertha refused to talk about him. They were as bad as each other sometimes." Steven shifted uncomfortably. "I don't understand how he went downhill so quickly. He was fine up until last year."

"I know. I think it was Bertha that killed him in the end. Her dying, I mean."

"Maybe," Steven replied.

As he unscrewed the lid of the urn, Steven looked at the view, the beautiful hills with their thick, green carpet of grass running down to the river. Scattering the ashes, they both closed their eyes and thought about Joe. Then, as the last of the ashes spilled towards the river, the peace was shattered by the blast of a whistle from an old steam engine as it pulled onto the platform, just like it had the day they'd scattered Bertha. With sad smiles on their faces, Steven and Nina linked arms and walked back up the slope in time to catch the train.

Links Ain't What
They Used To Be

The bus – like all buses – was late. Very late. And I hate hanging around that station longer than is necessary, but on a Saturday night you really are taking a chance. And then there's the usual dilemma to deal with at bus stations. And sure enough, along he came.

For some reason these people always hang around public transport, especially bus terminals. Maybe it's because they're the most affordable; if you're going to be strange for a living, I suppose you've got to keep to a budget. That last pound coin in the threadbare trousers pocket could prove vital; you never know who you'll have to follow home if the fancy takes you.

So I stood there, impatiently waiting for the forty-seven when over he shambles, on a warm August evening with a heavy coat and a thick blue and white scarf wrapped between his shoulders and head. What should I do? I did think about pre-empting him; I haven't got any cigarettes, my watch has stopped, that kind of thing – when I saw he wasn't looking at me at all, but was messing with his scarf.

You always end up being on your own at these times; over a dozen platforms, and all of them empty on a Saturday night. I tried to bide my time; looking at the surroundings through the 'glass' of the shelter, with the three-foot-high vomit up it (how do they manage that, incidentally?), over at the pirouetting crisp packets and footprint-ragged old timetables, the clogged drains, the fading painted zebra crossing and 'slow' messages on the road. The highlight of the station was quite surreal; a slice of bread which had been buttered and then stuck on the wall. Amazingly it'd been there three weeks earlier, too.

Frustrated, I started tapping my fingers on the bits of the shelter that I dared, and wished for a bus – any bus – to take me home. Then, a bull-necked beetroot-headed driver in a grimy, off-green outfit came clumping up from the depot itself. My bus, I thought at last – but he walked straight past. As he did, I noted with disgust that he seemed to look at me with more disdain than he did at Mr. Scarf nearby. I let out an almighty sigh. It was halfway out before I realised Scarfman might take this as a cue to unmeaningful conversation.

He was as good as my word. "I expect you're wondering why I'm wearing this scarf," he said, giving me a sideways glance.

I told him I hadn't noticed, looking away.

"You must have," he said in surprise. "Everybody else has. I don't usually go around like this you know. You wouldn't believe the day I've had. I'm going to the hospital."

Oh God, I remember thinking at the time. Not just a serial bus nutter, but a serial bus nutter with an ailment.

I couldn't get away now; it was too far to walk. "Oh, really," I said, deciding it best to respond. "Why's that?"

"It's what's under this scarf," he replied, fidgeting. "I'm not even sure how I'm going to explain it."

At this point I thought maybe I'd been a little harsh. He seemed normal enough, and perhaps the scarf was covering some kind of burn or unsightly growth.

"Try and explain it to me first," I told him. "It can't be as bad as all that. I imagine the doctors have seen everything up there."

He eyed me up as though checking whether I could be trusted or not. "It started about lunchtime," he said a little loudly, his voice echoing around the station before he lowered the volume. "I love Saturday lunchtimes, don't you? Just finished the week's final shift, few beers the night before. Magic. I got up late, watched a bit of telly, and my belly started rumbling. Lunchtime. So I got out the pan and stuck a block of fat in. The wife says 'You'd better use them sausages, they go off soon. Do me a couple while you're at it.'"

"So I got a string of them from the freezer – they weighed a ton! Must be all the ice, I thought – and I ran 'em under the tap to get all the ice off. Managed that bit easy enough – but could I separate 'em? Could I hell. They were solid. The pan's big though so I wound the sausages all round it.

"Of course by that time the fat was too hot, and it sprayed everywhere. I turned the gas down and went back into the living room to watch the football while they cooked. After a while, I heard the squealing."

At this point I wondered if the man worked on a farm or something; his face was bright red, like all farmworkers seem to be. Then again, it could've been sunburn, or maybe he'd scalded himself with the fat later on. I nodded at him stupidly as I thought about it, realising that I'd missed part of his speech.

"... in the pan, sizzling away. I've heard sausages make noise before, but that was like someone letting the air out of a balloon, you know?

"So I turned them over, and I swore they were bigger. Not ready to burst, but just that they'd somehow grown – in the pan. My mind was playing tricks, must be. So I went back in to watch the telly. Ooh, bloody hell," he said suddenly, mouth in an 'O', tugging at the scarf. "Nips like crazy. I don't mind telling you, I'll be glad when this is sorted out."

He was pulling on the scarf so fiercely that I thought he might throttle himself. I got a bit embarrassed, and looked over his shoulder, as though for the bus. All I saw was an old man peeing up a wall at the other side of the depot. I was pretty sure he farted as well, as the wind carried some odd sound over to me. I prayed that would be all it carried over. I turned back to the man garrotting himself with a scarf. After a few more tugs, he stopped.

"That's better. It twitched about, you know. Terrible. Anyway, a few minutes later I went back in the kitchen. The sausages looked brown enough, and I'd just started draping the bacon over the pan when I noticed how much the sausages were sizzling. You ever noticed that? The way they kind of dance in the pan? It seemed to mesmerize me for some reason.

"So I watched for a few seconds. But then, *then*," his eyes stared eerily at me, and I was worried again. "*Then*, they started to *really* move about. It looked like they were breakdancing – remember that? And they started to jump a bit, higher and higher, and eventually *leaped* out of the pan at me, and coiled themselves around my neck! All still in a link! My God, I nearly jumped as high as they had!

"After a few seconds though I got my breath back, and tried to grab 'em and stick 'em in the bin. I didn't wanna eat 'em now. If they'd fallen on the floor, maybe. But I'd just come off a long shift – I was filthy.

"But as I grabbed them, they started to dance again, and wrapped themselves round my bloody throat! It was like a python or something, coiling itself round and round – and they were bigger, remember. I couldn't even shout out – they were wound tight and getting tighter all the while. I tried throwing them off but they wouldn't budge. I tried breaking one off at a time, but the link was too strong – like it was a cheese wire. Thankfully my wife came in, and after she'd finished screaming she grabbed one end and pulled. It's a good job our kitchen's big, as I was pulled back and forth all over the damn place. At last they came loose, and I was sent spinning like a top and crashed against the brekkie bar."

He stopped and looked at me. He was panting with fear. I wondered how fast he could run. If I dashed off suddenly, would I get a clear distance before he stopped me? It was knocking on a bit by this time, the hooligans would be wandering about the town soon and here I was, stood next to a day release case who says he's been molested by his lunch. I mumbled something about his neck getting better and that I'd better be off. There was a taxi rank three miles away.

He looked even more frightened, and gripped my arm. "Please. I'm not finished yet," he panted. His grip was vice-like, his eyes positively maniacal. He looked so far round the twist he was nearly as sane as I was.

"No," he said, adjusting his scarf and wincing. "I've got to tell someone. My wife slung them in the bin while I sat down in the living room. The football had finished by then unfortunately. I asked where she'd got them. She didn't answer, just looked away. I asked again. 'A little guy near the market, dark glasses. He was practically giving them away, and – *oh my God, the mince! I'd better see if mum's alright!*' and she dashed out of the house.

"I certainly wasn't hungry anymore. I doubt I could've swallowed anything anyway, my throat was that bad. I took a can from the fridge instead and decided to have a drink – a few beers might help. I don't know whether they did or not, as I fell asleep. Just before that though, I heard rustling at the back door. The wife coming back for something, I thought. Then I passed out.

"I woke up a bit later. I felt thick, warm arms round me – the wife, just back from her mother's, I thought. But when I stood up to ask how she was, and she answered me from the hall, just coming in, like – I looked down and saw what was really there – *it was these!*"

As he moved the scarf away and unzipped his coat, I saw the long, pink-brown monstrosity wriggling around his neck, looped round twice, and dangling down to his navel. Some of them had split open, the meat sticking to his T-shirt like mushed-up flesh. Which of course is what it was. He called after me when I ran, and maybe I heard a cut off scream behind me, I'm not certain. I didn't turn around to look. I was too busy trying to avoid running into the number forty-seven bus which had just arrived. I ran and kept on running – I needed the exercise. I had to burn off my lunchtime fry-up somehow.

The Tobacconist's Concession

It was the end of the world again, which meant the hotel was busier than usual.

Not that it made any difference to Leo – the outside world could take care of itself; the hotel and the concession could not. They needed his careful attention, like they'd needed his father's before that. Leo had learned the basic workings of the place from him as a boy, on weekends when he should have been doing schoolwork – watching his father, he learned the art of how to deal with people, how to sell. Then, when his father died (his death was peaceful, for which Leo would always be grateful) and Leo took over the business, he knew that he had to learn how to deal with the other things too, because someone had to. This part wasn't always easy.

But, as his father had told him just before he died, he had been born to the job: Leo was a natural who took everything in his stride. Over the years he'd seen most things, standing behind the counter of that small and cramped kiosk – Births. Deaths. Marriages.

Giants covered in birdshit who looked like they'd just seen a ghost.

1. The Abduction of the Penguin

"That's him," George said, squinting into the sunlight.

"You sure?"

"Course I'm sure. Fancy dress. Take a look at him."

Artie did: Crisp white shirt, immaculately pressed black pants, liquorice black top hat, gleaming black cane. He looked down at his boss. "What's he come as?"

"The Penguin, how should I know? Who cares, it's fancy dress, right? The perfect cover."

The two men were parked at the side of the long, grassy road leading up to the hotel, its gleaming white castle-like structure a mile ahead. As the man, the Penguin, got closer to the car, Artie noticed the expression on the man's face, a mixture of anxiety and pain which he could empathise with. Suddenly, the man glanced quickly up at the car. Putting his head back down on his chest, he kept walking.

"What's he doing?" George said, watching as the man walked past the side of the car.

And kept walking.

"Maybe he wants us to follow him," Artie suggested hopefully.

And walking.

"Why?" George snapped. "We're a good mile from the hotel here. Nobody's going to see us. What the hell's the matter with him?" with a grunt the little man got out of the vehicle, his short salt-and-pepper hair lifted into tufts by the stiff wind. "Hey!" he shouted to the retreating figure, "where do you think *you're* going?"

Stopping, the man turned on his heel. "Excuse me?"

"I said," George shouted, his voice now a sandpapery growl, "where do you think you're going?"

Pulling a face as though he couldn't hear for the wind, the man made his way back towards the car.

As he did George began tapping on its side. He was still tapping as Artie kicked his door open, its hinges groaning. With all the elegance of a giraffe exiting a photo booth, Artie prised his six feet eleven frame out from the tiny car's confines. As he unfolded himself back to his proper shape, the man in the costume spoke.

"I'm sorry, I couldn't hear what you said. What did –"

"Just hand it over for Christ's sake," George said, a trace of disgust in his tone.

The Penguin looked perplexed. "I'm sorry, but I've no idea –"

"Artie," George said in a voice that was slowly losing patience, "If you'd be so kind …" Rolling up his sleeves, Artie eyeballed the Penguin. In turn the Penguin began to nervously fiddle with his cane.

"Listen, I don't know what it is you think I've got, but –"

"Artie," George said quietly, "fetch."

Artie bent down and grabbed one of the man's ankles so quickly he didn't have time to protest. With barely a breath of effort Artie upended him, holding him upside down at arm's length as if he were contagious. Grabbing the man's other ankle, Artie shook him like a branch. Apart from a few coins and bills dropping to the ground, nothing much happened. Still holding the man upside down, Artie shrugged at his boss.

"Okay," George said. "Get him on his feet." The disoriented man was then placed right way up. Stepping forward, George stared up into his frightened eyes.

"Okay. Powder. *Now.*"

"I – I don't have any powder," he said, unable to back away with Artie standing behind him, "Listen, I don't know who you think I am, but – I'm at the hotel, and –"

Punching him in the gut, George expected him to fall to the floor, and he did; but he hadn't expected the man's chest to erupt in a wild bouquet of whirring feathers.

"What the –"

The ten seconds it took for all the terrified birds to fly past were among the longest in George's life – they flapped into him, into Artie, into each other – the air became unbreathable for feathers and birdshit. When he looked down at his suit, George saw it wasn't just salt-and-pepper hair he had any more; it was salt-and-pepper everything. Trying to maintain a semblance of dignity, he went over to the man clutching his belly on the ground.

"I don't have time to ask you what just happened there," George said, flicking at his suit, trying to keep as much dignity in his voice as he could, "I just want what's mine. Then we can –"

"Boss."

Following Artie's gaze he spotted the top hat and cane in the grass. Before he could issue the command, Artie brought them over.

"Nothing in the hat boss," he said, punching a hole through it.

Remembering the Penguin's nervous gesture earlier he instructed Artie to try the cane. Unscrewing it, he looked down its long thin barrel before tapping it with the flat of his hand. Finally he blew down it. "Nothing, boss."

George was fuming. "Put him in the trunk. We'll take him with us."

"Where we going?" Artie asked, bending down to pick up the Penguin. He knew fine well where they were going.

"The Sprawl. I knew that louse would welch on the deal. A few hours down there, this guy'll tell us anything."

When Artie opened the trunk the man began to scream. Knocking his head against the side of the car, the big man bundled the limp body into the trunk before folding himself back into the driver's seat. Taking a deep breath, he started the car and drove as slowly as possible. Artie didn't like the hotel.

From a distance it looked beautiful – a huge shining fairytale castle perched on the cliffside, its rock caressed by the foam of the North Atlantic far below, as white-breasted gulls painted invisible pictures in the air above. But Artie, whose mother had always told him he was a sensitive soul, saw how the view altered the closer you got; perhaps it was a trick of the light or something, or just his overly vivid imagination, but he always felt there was a moment when the glistening white structure ahead went from a fairytale tower into something resembling an ugly, squat prison; a grey, flat-roofed monstrosity encircled not by a graceful parade of gulls but by a vile squadron of vultures. As the car chugged forward he watched for it happening, as it always did, usually just before they reached the hotel's large sandy parking lot.

Suddenly a figure appeared to their left among the long grass, a young woman with a thick crop of shaggy hair, seemingly making her way towards the hotel. As Artie watched her, a solitary gull broke free from the others above the hotel and glided towards her, then around her several times as if binding her with an invisible thread. Appearing to tire of her, it started to fly away, only to turn back suddenly and fly straight for her. Straight *at* her.

Straight *through* her.

Artie stamped on the brake pedal.

"Did – did you see that?" he said, trying to sound calm.

"I saw that." George tried to sound even calmer.

"But she's not there now. The gull – went straight through her, and she –"

"She vanished," George replied quietly, matter-of-factly, slowly removing a cigar from its wrapper, lighting it. "I know."

"Boss, she had –"

"Pink hair, I know." Puffing out thick cigar smoke helped to obscure his shaking hand. "Artie," George said, his voice not quite under control, "this is my last cigar. We'll have to go to the hotel and get some."

"Do we really have to go down there, boss?" Artie pleaded. "And the hotel as well? After *that?*" he pointed out of the window. George didn't answer.

Artie had quite forgotten about the view of the hotel as he pulled up among a hundred other cars in the quiet lot. Going round to the trunk, he listened but heard nothing. With a sigh of relief he went to get George's cigars.

In the hotel's glass doors Artie saw his dishevelled reflection – a big man in a shabby suit splattered with bird droppings – he thought he looked like a ghost in waiting. He shuddered at the idea. Crossing the threshold into the hotel lobby he shuddered again, as he always did.

Seeing Leo at the kiosk didn't make him shudder but it didn't make him feel any better either. He'd been buying George's cigars here for years, and despite Leo always being friendly and courteous towards him, there was something about the little man that always threw him a little off balance.

"Hello, Leo," he said glumly as Leo got the cigars.

"How are we today, Artie?"

As usual the big man felt that Leo was actually saying more than came out of his mouth. "Huh? Oh. Yeah. I'm er –" looking down at his bespattered suit, he waved a shovel-like hand at it, taking the cigars with the other. "Yeah. Fine. Er, I gotta go, we –"

Awkwardly, Artie spun himself round until he was roughly pointed at the exit. Before he got there he saw the damndest thing coming towards him. Moving away from the kiosk as quickly as he could, he decided today was going to be one of those days.

Watching Artie leave, Leo sensed the real reason behind his discomfort – it wasn't the fact his expensive suit was covered in filth, or the unusual costume of the man coming towards the kiosk. No, he knew what had turned the giant as white as a sheet: things were about to change. Obvious.

As obvious in fact as his next customer's reason for buying Leo's most expensive penknife.

"Hotel's busy today," the man in the costume said breezily.

"Yes it is," Leo replied. "As well as the End of the World party there's a conjurer's convention on this weekend. Been booked for months. They decided to go ahead with it, end of the world or not. I mean, look at the number of times we've been told this time it was going to happen – it's like crying wolf, isn't it? Still, I suppose they've got to be right some time. And it's bound to be the end of the world for somebody today, right?"

As Leo smiled the man gave a small laugh, followed by a cough. "Well," he said, waving the penknife in reply to Leo's unwavering gaze, "I guess I'll go open that bottle of wine now."

"Yes," Leo said as the man headed for room 1127. "Yes. You do that, sir." He had no doubt that the man was going to 1127 – there was a thing about knives in that room. With a loud sigh he began to tidy his counter until the next customer came by.

2. A Rash of Stabbings

"There's a door at the door," the Devil said to the Insect on the bed.

"Tell it we've got one. Hasn't it got eyes?"

The Devil looked exasperated. "*It's a door!*" it said.

"Well," the Insect replied, scratching a mandible, "show it in."

With not inconsiderable difficulty, the Door forced itself through the door. It spoke:

"What have you two come as?"

The Devil and the Insect cracked up.

"What have *we* come as?" the Insect laughed, pointing at the six-feet high oblong of cardboard in front of them. "Geez. Davy here's Lucifer and I'm a Locust. *It's an end of the world party.* Which begs the question," the Locust looked the cardboard figure up and down, frowning. "What the hell *have* you come as?"

The Door shook itself indignantly, like it was ruffling feathers. "I've come as The Door," it said huffily. "The one to *The Other Side?*" It glanced at the wall behind the Insect.

"Oh, well in that case," it said, "I hope you've brought something with you to help us get these beauties open."

With a papery rustle, the Locust, also known as Louis Sansano, got up off the bed and looked at the wall he'd been leaning against, slowly shaking his head in admiration.

"A masterstroke," he said to his two companions. "An absolute masterstroke."

For reasons unknown to most of the patrons of room 1127, twelve small and badly painted cupboard doors of varying sizes covered the entire space of one wall, with each door containing a small keyhole.

216

"If you ask at reception they'll tell you they're full of linen or cleaning equipment," Sansano told his colleagues, still admiring the wall. "An absolute masterstroke," he said again. "Okay," he turned to the Door. "What did you get?"

"This." Taking the penknife from one of its recesses, the Door looked at each of them in turn. "Pretty inconspicuous, huh? The guy down there said it was the best penknife he had – it's got a corkscrew, half a dozen blades, toenail clippers –"

Sansano waved a pincer in the Door's general direction, a signal to stop.

"Oh – and while I was down there I saw Artie."

The heavy silence that followed was eventually broken by the Devil. "I told you we shouldn't have come here," he hissed.

Sansano turned to the Door. "Did he recognise you?"

"Not in this outfit. And there's –"

"Exactly," Sansano interrupted. "We're *all* dressed like this. All George knows is that we'll be here in fancy dress, with his merchandise. Only we have his money but don't *have* his merchandise and he's expecting us to meet him to complete the deal. But we can't. Luckily for us, by the time George realises we aren't coming and he's gone through the hundreds of people here in fancy dress trying to find us, we'll have got one of these doors open –" he pointed at the wall, "and be in The Sprawl. Which means that George and his oversized goon can't get at us."

"There's a magician's conference here this weekend too," the Door added. "The guy downstairs said so. They'll all be dressed up too."

The Devil thought about it. "What if George knows how to get down to The Sprawl?"

"He won't, he's too dumb," Sansano told him. "Snap that knife open and start opening doors."

The Door, bending over the bed, began trying various blades on the small cupboards. When the first door swung inward, a stale blast of air rushed into the room.

"Nothing but pipes," the Door said, looking inside.

"Try the next."

It wasn't long before two more doors were open – one leading to a linen cupboard, the other into another maze of blackened piping. As the Door pried at the next cupboard, the Devil spoke.

"How do you know about this place?" he asked Sansano.

"From someone who used to work here. This place was built way back, when people lived in castles and were into hidden rooms and concealed entrances, that kind of stuff. In that it's like the cliffside, which is supposed to be full of caves. But go far enough down and the whole cliff is hollow for miles and miles; it was used by smugglers at one time. Anyway, they built one of the rooms, *this* room, with a secret door so you could go right down there through all these secret passageways. The perfect place to hide."

The Devil stroked his chin. "And if the big one does go off in the next couple of days, we can escape the blast."

"Exactly. It's been used every time we've had a warning – people have died in fights to get down there. Remember that Nuclear Crisis a few years ago? Two parties double-booked this room for the same weekend. It ended up with six people being stabbed to death and nobody even got down there. And after all that they averted the crisis. But this time, I don't know. I've got a bad feeling about this time. How you doing?" he asked the Door.

"Three more," the Door said, wiping a hand against its cardboard.

"Well, hurry it up. George is probably looking for us now."

Ten minutes later only one door remained. Sansano started to sweat. It had to be this one, and it had to work. As the Door cracked it open, another rush of freezing air came into the room. Only this time there were no pipes or towels. Instead there were steps.

Sansano rose to his feet. "Thank Christ for that. Right, let's go."

Before any of them had a chance to move, the steps appeared to waver, obscured by bulks of greying darkness which began to bundle into the room like clouds of cotton. As the clouds started to form into shapes, the room turned to ice. In the ice, limbs and faces began to appear. Angry faces.

Had the room on the tenth floor been occupied, it would have sounded like three heavy statues had toppled in the room above. But even had someone been in that room they'd never have heard the faint scratching at the door as rapidly stiffening fingers struggled to prise it open.

It was a while before Leo had another customer. And he wasn't a customer at all.

"So you haven't seen him?" the magician asked. "Dressed the same as me. He did say he felt a bit sick and was going out for a breath of fresh air, but that was ages ago."

Leo shook his head, smiling sadly.

Suddenly the man shivered. "Maybe it's the air conditioning in here or something. You know, I haven't felt right myself for a while." Leaning over the counter, the magician lowered his voice. "It's a strange place this, isn't it?" he said conspiratorially.

"I suppose so," Leo answered in his normal voice, the trace of a smile still on his lips, "but I suppose all hotels are strange to some degree."

The magician gave Leo a funny look. Thanking him, he went back towards the elevator. But Leo didn't notice.

He was too busy thinking.

3. Smoke and Mirrors, Piss and Wind

"Nobody's seen him," Nick said above the furious splashing of water coming from the bathroom. "I've looked everywhere." Thirty seconds later the steady rush of water showed no sign of stopping. "What are you doing in there, taking a leak or drawing a bath?"

"I expect he's – hang on, here comes another one –" the sound of Jerry's urine was momentarily cancelled out as his sphincter got in on the act, emitting a long, loud rasp. "– got the same thing I have. My guts haven't been right since we arrived. I wonder if I'm going down with something. Is it me or has it turned cold in here? Hang on, here's the sequel –" a quieter but no less noxious emission began to drift through the open door as the tinkling water stopped. "Whew! Not bad as sequels go," Jerry said cheerfully, moving the smell around artfully with his hands, "a *Jaws 2*, I reckon."

"Maybe it's as well I couldn't find him," Nick said, turning his face away. "That doesn't even *smell* like a fart. What have you been eating? Sewage?"

"I agree with you on that," Jerry said as he closed the bathroom door, "about Ray not coming back. We both know he lets the act down. It'd be no great loss if he didn't show. Which reminds me – there's something wrong with the cabinet. When he went in before he left, he was still there when I opened the door. The catch must be jammed or something. So," Jerry said, making elaborate gestures towards the cabinet, "if you'd be so kind ..."

Nick folded his arms and stared at Jerry. "You know I don't go in the cabinet."

Jerry sneered. "Listen, Nicky boy – whoever heard of a *claustrophobic* magician? Did Houdini try and worm his way out of stepping into the sack and chains? No, he didn't. If Ray was

220

here he could do it but he isn't. So, if you want to go down there with any kind of act, get in."

"A minute," Nick said, walking towards the black box, "a minute and no longer."

"Perhaps Ray has vanished after all," Jerry said, closing the door behind Nick. Tapping various panels of the box, he spoke again. "He wouldn't be the first in this place – it's supposed to be honeycombed with secret rooms and shit. Maybe he's wandered off into one. That's what happened to that girl. Did you hear about that?" Inside the cabinet, a small muffled voice spoke. "No? Well, some girl found out how to get into the passageways and got lost in there for a while. She made the mistake of opening a secret door that led into the room of some *very* heavy gentleman who weren't too pleased to see her. I don't know the exact details, but she ended up getting stabbed and they shoved her back in." *Tap Tap Tap.* "Anyway, she was crawling about in those passageways for ages – they found blood all over the place. When she eventually did find a way out it was up through somebody's closet or something, just as they were reaching in for a suit. And the crooks got off scot-free because of their expensive lawyer. Typical, huh? I'm done," he called to Nick, "coming ready or not." With a hearty tug, Jerry opened the door. "Ta-DA!"

As it should be, the black interior of the box was empty.

"Nicky boy, we have lift-off. I'll have you out in a second." Closing the door again, he quickly reopened it.

"Oh."

Nicky boy wasn't there.

"Er, having a few problems out here my friend," Jerry called out. "Nicky? Nick?"

No answer.

"Listen," Jerry said, his voice higher than usual. "Third time lucky, okay? There's no need to panic." Once again he closed the door. Then opened it again.

Something came out of the cabinet this time, but it wasn't Nick. The something walked past him, a translucent body beneath a shock of pink hair. As it approached the wall, the outline of the body vanished completely; only the hair stood out temporarily against the burgundy wallpaper like a stain. Then it too disappeared. Jerry gulped noisily.

In a kind of frenzied calm, Jerry went back to the cabinet and closed the door. Then he opened it again. Closed it. Opened it again, closed it again.

He was still doing this an hour later when he heard the sirens outside.

In that time nothing else came out.

Hotels were strange places all right. Like well-upholstered dumping grounds. This was because people didn't respect them. The idea that people just 'pass through' a hotel was nonsense – they always left something behind, no matter whether they stayed a month or a night. There was the baggage people brought with them, both physical and mental – their quirks, their suppressed energies and extremes of behaviour; away from home people became more playful, outlandish, took more risks, became increasingly desperate because the chances were they weren't coming back.

People die in hotels. All the time.

Sometimes naturally, other times not. Sometimes they died for the silliest of reasons. And that creates ghosts, whether you can see them or not. And this was an old hotel, with a lot of ghosts. And unlike the paying customer the ghost remains. But they needed to move on like the rest of us. Ghosts were like small children that don't know how to behave properly. Sometimes they're shy and keep out of the grown-ups' way; but sometimes they demand attention and explode into violent rages. And ghosts don't always discriminate.

Usually, when a ghost got the chance to move on, it had to take it.

Leo hoped that was about to happen. Because it was getting pretty crowded down there.

4. The Magic in Old Hotels / Loose Ends

"I don't like it down here, Boss," Artie said, un-crumpling himself from the car once more, "it gives me the creeps."

George shielded his eyes from the sun's reflection off the sea, the white glare of the arcing gulls. "Don't you ever give it a rest? She's dead, she can't hurt us. Now get that idiot out of the trunk."

Artie hadn't just meant the girl and he suspected George knew that. He'd seen things down here, unfriendly things. Opening the trunk, he pulled the semiconscious man from within, standing him up as George came forward.

"Hey!" George prodded him in the ribs. A pair of woozy eyes snapped fully open. "Now. It's nice and quiet down here, we won't be disturbed. So you can either tell me where my goddamned powder is, or you can tell me where Sansano is. I don't mind which. But whichever you choose you do it quickly, because –" he curled his hand into a fist.

"Boss, wait." Artie's voice sounded puzzled, frightened.

"What now?" George snapped. He was still looking up into the man's eyes.

Artie's voice dropped, mingled with the cawing of the gulls. "That – that isn't him, George."

"What?"

"That's a different man to the one I shoved in the trunk. I mean, the clothes are the same, but –"

Instead of just the eyes, George looked at the whole face. Slowly, a look of utter disbelief spread across his own. Artie was right: it wasn't the same man.

"What the *hell* is going on today?" George shouted up at the gulls.

There were three main ways to get into The Sprawl.

There was the smugglers' route (the one Leo knew George sometimes used), which was little more than a narrow crack in the cliffside down on the beach.

The second was through one of the doors in room 1127.

The third way was to walk through the walls and keep heading downwards.

All that energy. All those ghosts.

The Sprawl wasn't just the ultimate dumping ground for secret things; it was also the ultimate hiding place. All that energy ... but ultimately all that energy had to be released. It needed a catalyst.

Unwittingly, Leo provided it.

"I should tell you," George said, chewing on his cigar as he followed Artie and the quivering figure through the gap in the cave wall, "I don't really care about what happened earlier – with the birds, I mean. Or the fact you seem to have grown a new face. I just want what's mine. Then we can all leave."

Nick began fidgeting with his collar. "I – I don't know how this happened. I – I was in this cabinet in our room, and the door closed, and it went cold, and – I've – I've got to get out of here," sweat was running from Nick's brow into his eyes, "I don't like closed-in spaces."

"Oh, that's okay," George told him, his voice equal parts reassurance and sarcasm. "This place isn't closed in at all. See?"

Following George's hand, Nick looked up into the clammy darkness. Wherever he was, it had the damp atmosphere of a cave; only he couldn't see its roof. It was even colder than in the cabinet; his freezing breath jumped out of him in nervous puffs of smoke. Somewhere in the murk, small drops of moisture fell into invisible pools. It was like the atmosphere in the hotel. Only much, much worse.

"Look," Nick told them, "I really have to get out this place –"

"*JUST-TELL-ME-WHERE-THE-POWDER-IS!*" George screamed, slapping his hands against his legs after each word like a petulant child, "*JUST TELL ME!*"

It took almost a minute for his voice to stop rebounding off the cave walls, by which time Artie knew that George was at least as scared as he was. The three men looked at each other, unsure what was supposed to happen next. Finally, George spoke.

"Okay," he said, barely above a whisper. "Okay. Then where is Sansano? I'll speak to him."

"Sansano?" Nick whispered back. "I don't know any Sansano."

"Boss," Artie whispered.

George looked round and saw Sansano and two other men standing a matter of feet away.

"Talk of the devil," George said, eyeing one of the costumes. But his usual cockiness had gone: something was very wrong here. Then he saw the pink-haired girl next to them. Behind her there were others – dozens of them coming forward, circling him. Stepping backwards, Nick managed to move away without being noticed.

He was only a few feet from them when the whole cave became a huge screaming echo chamber, each scream louder than the one before.

Disoriented by panic, Nick stumbled through the cave looking for the exit, his hands clamped over his ears. When he eventually found the way out he was too frightened to notice that the cave wasn't freezing any more, or that the screams at his back were fading out.

As his eyes readjusted to the sunlight he staggered along the beach, his brain trying to comprehend what had happened. Above him and to his left he saw the hotel.

At least he thought that's what it was – only its shape kept altering somehow; it was as if another building was vying for position with it. Later he'd say it was like making yourself cross-eyed as a child, so that one landscape imposed itself over another; only Nick knew that there wasn't another building up there, just the hotel.

Despite the heat from the sun, Nick was shivering again. Walking along the beach, he prayed a road would appear out of nowhere, away from the cliffs and the hotel.

Miki, she'd been called. She'd shown up at the hotel one day, looking for work, pink hair all over the place like a badly-made nest. She was funny, bright, lively. And unfortunately adventurous. Leo thought she could start a conversation in an empty room. And she probably had. Many times.

He'd managed to get her a job in the kitchens – she said she was so grateful that she'd do him a favour in return someday, even if it took her the rest of her life to do it. He didn't see a lot of her after that but she seemed happy enough. One day in a lull she'd asked him about The Sprawl. Where was it, How do you get in? I don't know how you get in, he lied. Besides, he told her, it was supposed to be dangerous down there.

Then one day she didn't show up for her shift.

How she found her way in, he never knew. He only knew one thing for certain – the day she'd turned up at his kiosk, he should have sent her packing.

Later, when Pestilence came out of his room on the eleventh floor, he didn't feel particularly refreshed by the short nap he'd had. Perhaps it was all this talk of the end of the world, or even the lurid costume he was wearing (his *papier-mâché* sores looked especially revolting under the hotel's sharp lights). There was an eerie atmosphere about the place, as if it was waiting for something to happen. This thought didn't make a lot of sense to him. Going back to his room after the buffet, the first thing he'd done was throw the whole lot back up into the bathroom sink; but the sudden purge had made him feel even worse. Laying on the bed, he closed his stinging eyes. For a second he thought he heard frantic cries close by, but he was suddenly too tired to care.

Pestilence dreamed. He was in the belly of a vast and diseased animal, and the stink of it was slowly killing him. He had to escape. But each turn he took, every new cavern he entered only led him further into the animal's stomach. The dream ended just as a gigantic rushing *whoosh* came down one of the glistening tubes towards him.

Waking up, Pestilence decided he was going to leave the hotel before the weekend was over: he'd face the end of the world at home. But first he'd have a drink downstairs and let everyone know he was going.

He was passing the room next to his, room 1127, when he saw the door was slightly ajar. It was propped open by a hand, its stiff, unreal fingers beckoning him. Recalling the cries he'd heard before he fell asleep, he moved closer.

The hand belonged to what appeared to be a man in a devil's costume sleeping on the floor. But then he spotted the knife stuck in the man's chest, and the blood. And then there was the smell. And through the crack in the door he saw another two men who weren't sleeping either.

The end of the world was making everybody crazy, Pestilence decided.

He went back to his room to pack.

Normally, the sight of someone leaving the hotel without paying would have roused him into some kind of action, but Leo knew this time was different. Perhaps it was the costume the man was wearing. He knew something was about to happen. Folding his arms, he waited.

It didn't take long. The other people in the lobby had barely had time to notice the strange whooshing sound building around them when the glass doors leading to the ground floor rooms shattered under the force of countless frantic, flapping wings; and by the time everyone had dropped to the floor to avoid being beaten by them the lobby was empty again. There were still people on the ground when someone came running through what remained of the lobby doors and started shouting about dead bodies on the eleventh floor.

In his mind's eye, Leo was sure that the first bird to break through those doors had a shock of pink feathers.

She never did do him that favour, he thought sadly.

Picking up the phone on the kiosk counter, he called the Police.

Hearing the sirens, Jerry had the terrifying idea that they must be for him. First Ray had gone missing, then Nick. This hotel had a terrible history. Strange things happened here, people died horribly.

Men went into magic cabinets and never came out again.

He opened, closed and opened the black lacquered door again but nothing happened. He had to get Nick back before the police came up. He grasped the cabinet door again.

For a brief moment, sanity returned. He was being stupid. Whatever it was that was going on here, it had nothing to do with him. Ray and Nick were probably just playing a trick on him, that was all – they'd be hiding in some hidden part of the room right now, laughing at him. But he realised that couldn't be true either – he'd known Nick all his life and he was definitely claustrophobic. He really hadn't wanted to get into the cabinet. And as for Ray, he was the most humourless man that ever walked the earth; he wouldn't know a joke if it came up and introduced itself. So, closing the door once more, Jerry tried the cabinet again.

Open, close. Open, close. Open. Still nobody appeared. He slammed the door shut.

He couldn't carry on like this. There were police downstairs. He'd get them to come up and have a go. If he looked foolish, he looked foolish. So be it. But before he went he'd try it again, one last time.

Open. Close. Open –

Standing inside the box, a look of pure astonishment on his face, Ray looked like he'd been dragged through a hedge backwards. He stared at Jerry with large, haunted eyes.

Jerry did two things.

One: he turned as white as a sheet.

Two: he produced a sequel to *Jaws 2* even better than *Jaws 1*.

Later, after things had calmed down and the police had taken statements from bewildered customers, he closed up the kiosk and went to the manager's office.

"Quite a day, all in all," he said to the secretary.

She looked at him strangely, although not unkindly.

"I don't know how you can be so calm about it," she told him. "The whole thing's been horrible."

"Well," he told her, sitting down at his desk, putting his feet on the edge, "the end of the world. It's bound to make people do silly things."

"It won't be *the end of the world*," she said scornfully. "It never is. They get people all worked up for nothing, is all."

"Maybe," Leo replied. "But maybe the hotel needed it to happen."

She looked over the top of her glasses at him. "Not for the first time Leo, you've lost me. Doesn't it bother you, all that damage, the cost to the hotel's reputation? Your father must be spinning in his grave! I don't know why you keep that kiosk going anyway – being out there didn't stop what happened today, did it? There's more important things –"

"I know, I know," he interrupted. "But I've told you before, I promised him. He said there was more to running a hotel than hiding away at the back – you needed to be out there, at the front, keeping a real eye on things. I happen to think he was right." His expression changed. "There's more to running a hotel than the people, you know."

He sat in silence for a few moments, tapping a cigar on his desk. After a while his secretary spoke. "Cheer up, Leo," she said, half laughing. "It's not the end of –"

Looking up at her he smiled. "No," he conceded. "No, I don't suppose it is."

A minute later, there was a knock at the door.

Leaving the hotel, Pestilence had wondered if the funny little guy at the kiosk would report him for not paying his bill. But how could he know? For all he knew he was going out for a breath of fresh air – heaven knows he needed it – his senses had been that badly shaken that he couldn't even remember where he'd parked his car.

It was as he was walking around the parking lot searching that he saw his reflection in a car window and saw that in his hurry to leave he'd forgotten to take his costume off, it was so comfy. No wonder the guy was giving him funny looks – Pestilence didn't pay his bill!

As he continued to look for his car he wondered if perhaps he *should* go back and pay, but then remembered that wasn't the only thing he hadn't done – he hadn't reported the bodies he'd seen in 1127 either; if he went back now it'd look bad. No, screw it – why should he pay his bill after witnessing something like that? The whole place was a madhouse –

Hearing what sounded like a hundred windows breaking, he turned back towards the hotel. At least he thought he had – when he looked up at it, it seemed to resemble some kind of ugly gothic prison rather than the place he'd just marched out of. Still, it wasn't his problem anymore. Turning away, he focused his attention once more on the parking lot, and the certainty that wherever his car was now, it wasn't there. Because now, none of the cars were in the parking lot – it was just a wide-open concrete expanse of nothingness.

Before he got the chance to swear and wonder what was happening, he heard a huge whooshing noise in the sky, like the one he'd heard in his dream, coming towards him. Blocking out the sky, a great squadron of birds descended on him, flapping around him, pecking at his clothes. He managed to bat most of them away but a pink one refused to move, no matter how many times he managed to hit it, its beak jabbing first at his chest, then his legs. Then, after what seemed an age, it too finally flapped away.

Letting out a great breath, he looked down at himself. No real damage had been done – his clothes were badly torn and his turned-out pockets were full of holes, but other than that –

That didn't make sense. But looking down at the concrete he saw nothing but tar, feathers and bird droppings; no coins, no notes.

"Hey! Bring back my money!" Pestilence shouted after the bird as it flew over towards the beach.

Hearing the shout in the distance, Nick looked up from the sand but there was nobody there.

This wasn't right, he thought again. This wasn't right at all. How long had he been walking along this beach? It'd got so he daren't even look at his watch to find out. It felt like he was going to be stuck here forever.

Then, with the echo of the voice he'd heard still hanging in the air, Nick saw a bird with pink feathers floating down towards him, lower and lower. *It's going to crap on me, I know it,* he thought, a split second before it all came hurtling at him. Hunching himself against the impact, he waited for the rain to stop.

When several drops of it hurt, he realised it couldn't be what he thought it was. Looking down at the sand, he picked up the several coins and notes he found there, along with a huge pink feather. Running it between his fingers, it suddenly occurred to him that he should go back to the hotel. Jerry and Ray would be wondering where he was.

To his surprise, he found his way back there quickly, and found himself standing outside the manager's office. Knocking on the door, a part of him rebelled against what he was about to do, he wasn't usually so public-spirited.

"Yes?" the man now standing in the doorway said.

"Er, I found this outside," Nick said. "Thought it must belong to someone at the hotel."

But the manager wasn't looking at the money; he seemed more interested in the feather.

"Ah," he said, smiling, "she managed it after all, then."

"Pardon?" Nick said, handing everything over.

"Oh, nothing," Leo beamed. "Just someone doing me a favour."

Shaking his head, Nick walked away.

- For Donna Thornhill

In Bleed

He renamed it Bleed on account of the massacre.

On his travels back and forth across the land, he'd been close to the small town of Goldstone many times but never passed through, never needed to. He was a *mestizo,* and he knew from bitter experience there'd be someone in the town ready to preach how a half-breed was a half-breed and therefore not welcome. So, Kaw-Liga kept his distance.

That was until he heard the screaming.

He'd been about five miles out at the time, and the people passing the other way on the dirt track in their wagon must have wondered what he'd been listening to; they certainly wouldn't have heard it. Nobody would.

For a few minutes he'd kept walking along the path away from Goldstone but the screams got louder; and those screaming sensed there was someone nearby to hear their screams.

Turning, he shielded his eyes with a leathery brown hand and looked back. From this distance the town was no bigger than his thumbnail. But still the screaming rang in his ears.

He knew he had to go. He couldn't leave them to scream like that. Nobody else could help them.

Sitting up in the bed, he left a sweaty imprint of himself on the sheet. His eyes searched blindly in the darkness but found nothing.

It was the fourth time in two nights, and he put it down to not enough drink, not because he was the only one left. He felt no guilt about that.

It was just a silly nightmare, that was all.

Each time the same; the Sheriff's face grinning at him with the bullet there in his temple, a small black hole among the wrinkles on his brow. Grinning, just grinning with his fine white teeth, arms folded across his chest.

"Why don't you come and finish what you started, brave man?" the Sheriff always said just before he woke up. "Come back and finish the job properly."

He turned over and tried to sleep.

When he was within a mile of the town, Kaw-Liga put his hands over his ears, but it never did any good. The screams and screeches were pitched like taught wires in his head, so many of them, each trying to yell over the others, struggling to be heard.

Rays from the sun flashed in his eyes. Looking up he watched as vultures, dozens of them, soared overhead soundlessly. The town's welcome sign was streaked with crimson fingerprints. Further patches zigzagged across the empty street. His stomach turned over.

Shielding his eyes again, he realised something had changed. The screaming had stopped.

"Well," said the doctor sitting back at his desk, "I can't see anything in there."

"I tell you, it's there all the time, a kind of screaming, like a boiling kettle."

The doctor looked across at him. He didn't like this man at all. He'd pushed his way in demanding to be seen because of the noises in his head and the crazy dream that taunted him. When he asked why the man was holding his side, he got no answer. A thoroughly bad lot, the doctor decided. Nothing wrong with this man but a guilty conscience for some misdemeanour or other.

"There's nothing wrong with your ears that I can see," he said again. "As to your dream, if it's scaring you that much —"

"Did I say it was scaring me?" the man snarled.

"All I was going to say was maybe you should think about what it means. Maybe the dream means something," the doctor said, trying to humour him.

The man muttered something under his breath and left the surgery.

As he stared, a huge cloud passed over the sun and blanketed the town, bringing the dark splashes on the cabins into relief. He was looking at a body slumped over a balcony, a ragged hole in the back of its head. Below the window, two small bodies one on top of the other, their blood boiling on the ground nearby. Kaw-Liga moved forward as a ball of tumbleweed cartwheeled past him. Stepping into the saloon he almost tripped over a man on the floor, half his face missing.

It was the smell that got him first. A mixture of blood and raw liquor running down the walls, tables and chairs. Limbs and chair-legs littered the sawdust floor like twisted branches, broken glass crunched and squeaked beneath his boots. He felt the skin on his arms pucker with the cold and the silence. It was just like – he closed the thought off from his mind.

It was as he turned to leave that he saw the first of them running through a wall out into the street, a man with a thick moustache who blended momentarily with the wood as he passed through it then was gone, like a wind-blown cloud. Looking back into the saloon again, he saw several shapeless patches of haze trying to rise from the body-strewn floor, the energy boiling the clotted blood that surrounded them. This was the worst – the second worst – he'd ever seen. They couldn't even move now after all the screaming they'd done. Most of them would be like this for a while.

He found the same thing in nearly every building and alley in Goldstone; broken and burst corpses with their rippling hazes hovering close by, shimmering piles of vague, washed-out colour with a metallic odour, mixing into the blood that congealed around them: a man in a tub whose bathwater had turned pink, his spirit dipping in and out of the cloudy water as it tried to free itself. A family parlour with its lights smashed out, four children shot in the back, along with their mother and father. In several rooms he tripped over them, and the contact he'd deliberately avoided up till then brought disjointed, unconnected images of what had happened into his head, each one clashing like a hammer on an anvil; in the jailhouse he found that two of the men on the floor were part of the gang. Another four had fallen in the bank, the safe door in the backroom swinging to and fro, covered in bloody fingerprints. From time to time he'd see one of the spirits run in blind panic through a wall or a table, sometimes through their own bodies. And he knew suddenly that it wasn't about money, this massacre, not really; it was the sport. If things had been taken it was because it was expected.

Back outside, the clouds had thickened and the wind whipped Kaw-Liga's hair across his face. Going into his pocket for a piece of string to tie it back, he looked up into the sky and saw the vultures still circling above. *They're afraid to come down,* he realised. *The ghosts.*

Through the wind he heard another noise.

He found him in the backroom of the barbershop, fading in and out of view next to a cupboard. The boy's mouth worked open and closed. "What was it?" he said eventually in a thin, barely audible whisper.

Kneeling before the boy's ghost, like he had so many others in the past, men and women, children and animals, Kaw-Liga stared straight into the boy's eyes and he told the boy about himself. He then told the boy what *he* was, what they all were. His eyes were the only things about him that seemed to stay in focus, almost growing brighter with distress.

"I need you to tell me everything you know," Kaw-Liga told him.

And as the boy told him he felt a cold slab of ice pierce his stomach. And he knew. He couldn't see him in his mind, but he knew.

He dreamed again.

He didn't recognise it at first; it was something that happened many years earlier which he'd forgotten about, a small settlement somewhere long ago. It had been the same as the other jobs he'd run but he remembered that, as they'd been riding out, they'd found a wagon on the road nearby, and they couldn't take any chances that they'd been seen. They'd broken into the wagon and found an Indian there. A damned Indian, with a white *woman! And such a pretty one too ...*

The Indian had struggled until the bullet in his chest silenced him. It didn't kill him so he had to watch and listen, which served him right. She'd struggled too, until they'd broken her arms and legs to stop her thrashing about.

By the time they left she was dead, and the Indian wasn't far off.

He remembered that part of the dream. That happened. But the next part was new.

As they left the wagon, the Sheriff of Goldstone was outside waiting for them, still with his arms folded, still with the bullet hole in his forehead, still grinning.

"What a cowardly man you are," he said, smiling at him. "No man at all."

Laying there in the darkness, he wondered again at what the doctor had said. Maybe it did all mean something.

For the best part of two days he dug holes for the bodies, stopping every once in a while to wipe either tears or sweat from his face as the ghosts watched nearby with frightened eyes as their bodies were lowered into the holes. He was oblivious to their injuries, unless they had broken arms or legs. Then the tears would start again.

He'd been playing in the hills that day when he heard the gunfire. He'd been with a prairie dog, 'talking' to it his father would have said, just looking into its eyes and learning its ways, it learning his. Hearing the gunfire he saw the fur of the animal stiffen, its eyes staring into his, holding him back. It could sense it too. There was nothing he could do there. He had to wait.

Then the pictures started in his head, what had happened, what *was* happening, and he ran screaming down through the hills which seemed to take forever, emerging just in time to see the last of the gang ride away into the heat haze, too far away to see faces.

240

When he got there his mother was dead, his father barely alive. Tears streamed down his father's face as he tried to speak.

"They made me watch," his father said. Then, with a wheeze, his father said the words that were imprinted on his brain forever.

"You are special, you know that. You have gifts within you, special gifts. Use them wisely. Try to help those you can with their torments. Try and still their ghosts." Kaw-Liga had nodded. He started to say he would avenge them both but saw his father couldn't hear him now.

And all his life he'd done that; help other people still their ghosts.

Now he had a chance to still his own.

All the bodies were in the graves, except one. Kaw-Liga picked it up and carried it into the saloon. The ghost of the Sheriff's son watched as his father's legs swung over the big man's arms.

After six days of calling, Kaw-Liga knew the man was close. He'd been sleeping in one of the few barns without blood on the floor. The effort of calling and sending the dreams for so long had made him weary.

He sensed the man's anxiety, and his feelings of irrationality; the obsessive way the thoughts intruded upon him, the overwhelming need to come back, to see if doing so would stop him from going crazy.

Not for the first time Kaw-Liga wondered if this was the best way. But it wasn't just his parents that had to be avenged. There were probably hundreds all over the country that the gang had killed. They had to be thought of too. There was just the one left now, but he was the leader. Talking to the boy, he'd discovered that he even shot two of his own gang in the jailhouse to escape capture. He'd been shot in the side too but somehow had got away.

Leaving the barn, he crossed to the saloon and knelt before the body of the Sheriff. Taking a small knife from his side, he turned the Sheriff's wrists to the sky and cut into the rigid, unbleeding flesh, his lips moving quickly. Then he cut deeply into his own wrists, barely flinching as the red crescents ran either side like bracelets. Raising them above the wrists of the dead man, he balled his hands into fists and squeezed hard, the blood dripping down onto the dry veins of the Sheriff. Kaw-Liga's lips quivered with the burble of sounds that broke from them, their pitch rising and falling like some peculiar singsong melody.

As he watched and sang, the blood began to run into the dead man's veins almost as if pulled there by a magnetic current. A few minutes passed and a slight colour returned to the face, the eyes lost some of their glassiness. It wasn't a true life, but it was life of sorts. It wouldn't last long, but it would last long enough. Kaw-Liga muttered something to the Sheriff.

The Sheriff answered in a language that had never passed his lips before. Then he spoke in English.

"Are ... are my family ... On no. Oh Jesus no," he pleaded.

Kaw-Liga explained quickly what had happened and what was about to happen. The lawman didn't object. Kaw-Liga handed him a gun he'd found in the jailhouse and the Sheriff took it, rising on unsteady feet.

He arrived when the sun was at its highest in the sky.

The place looked empty as he approached, but he knew it wasn't. Now he was close to it again, he knew his dreams hadn't lied. The air was charged, it was all wrong. He had to get these feelings out of himself and leave them here.

Putting his hand up to his face, he squinted at the town sign. WELCOME TO BLEED it said in red, over the original letters.

Suddenly he saw something flicker close by, next to the saloon wall. Grabbing his gun from his holster, he fired at the wall. There was nothing there. Nothing his eyes could see. But there *was* something.

The saloon door creaked open.

The man watched in amazement as he saw the Sheriff appear, his skin grey like paste, his clothes smeared with dirt and blood as he'd seen them before; even the hole in his head was there, just as it was in his dreams.

"Welcome to Bleed," the Sheriff said, his voice deep and unnatural.

The man looked at this abomination, feeling his skin tighten on his bones. "I – I stuck a bullet into your skull," he said, his voice unsteady. "I can see it from here."

"It's called Bleed because that's what you're going to do," the Sheriff said, ignoring the comment. "You have a lot of blood to spill." The voice now was a hybrid mixture of his own and the Indian's.

Then, as he opened his mouth again, two other voices spoke, a man and a woman, screaming, begging for their lives. Then there were other voices, begging, pleading, screaming, quickly followed by the sounds of gunfire, splintering wood, breaking glass, frightened horses. Then just as suddenly it all stopped, and the man stood looking at the Sheriff in stunned silence.

"You killed my family too," the Sheriff said in his own voice.

Shaking, the man raised his gun and fired at the Sheriff, both bullets hitting their target and landing in his chest with a dull thud. The lawman rocked back on his heels, blinked. But that was all. Then he started to move towards the man jerkily, his legs rigid, arms limply at his sides like branches trailing towards a stream, fingers splayed around the gun.

The man moved back several paces and fired again, this time into the Sheriff's face, crying out when he saw the bullets pass through his cheeks with a noise like shredding paper. Still the lawman moved forward, his feet slapping on the ground. The man was about to turn and run when he saw a *mestizo* standing behind the Sheriff, his eyes like daggers.

"You killed my family," he said in a low voice. "You broke her arms and legs you filthy bastard." Kaw-Liga saw the panic in the man's eyes, who in turn saw the concentration on the face of the Indian. He could hear the Sheriff getting closer still. He looked at the ragged mess of his face, then at the Indian, then back at the Sheriff. He fired another bullet into him, but still the Sheriff kept coming. He tried again but his pistol clicked empty. He turned and ran.

Narrowing his eyes, Kaw-Liga began to mutter and burble, as he had earlier in the saloon. The Sheriff, raising his gun, fired two bullets, one into the man's right leg, the other into his left arm. Half falling to the ground, the man somehow managed to scramble to his feet, shrieking as he tried to escape; but as further bullets dug into his other arm and leg, he fell face first into the dust, squirming in his own blood.

Kaw-Liga turned to the Sheriff.

"Thank you," he said.

Muttering a final time, Kaw-Liga watched as the body of the Sheriff crumpled to the floor, the remaining light draining from his eyes. Picking up the body, he slumped it over his broad shoulders and carried it to the grave of his wife and son before turning his attention to burying him beside them.

It wasn't until he was flattening the earth down that he became vaguely aware of the screams of the injured man.

Turning slowly, he watched the pitiful worm squirming in the dirt. Seconds later, he saw the black shapes in front of the sun swooping lower and lower. Kaw-Liga smiled.

Finally, the vultures were coming.

Gaseous Clay

As I had done on the previous four evenings since the dream, I waited until Kirsten had gone to bed before burying the gnomes. But the second I heard our bedroom curtains sliding across the wooden rods upstairs, I finished my drink, got the shovel out of the garage, and dug the holes as quickly and quietly as I could in the far corner of the garden. Then, with each hole dug to a depth of perhaps two feet or more, I grabbed the gnomes and placed each one in a hole and filled in the soil. This evening, as an added safeguard, I sank spare paving stones on top of the refilled holes, even though I knew fine well that neither they nor the gnomes would still be there in the morning. At least when I looked over the fence into the next street, nothing appeared to have changed. My work completed, I went back inside and slipped into bed beside my wife of a few months, my back turned against her, hoping against hope that the night wouldn't bring a recurrence of the terrifying dream (for dream is what it must have been) that I'd had at the beginning of the week ...

"Will you take me there or not?"

"Yes, of course I'll take you, Annie. It's just that –"

She looked daggers at me, her head slightly to one side. "Yes?"

"I was just wondering if it was a good idea, that's all. After the flower arranging and the French lessons, what makes you think you'll like pottery classes any more?"

"I'm not asking you to come with me if that's what you're worried about. I saw the way things were going after I bought those binoculars. If you want a separate life, then that's fine by me. But I'm not going anywhere. Unless it's to a different house, of course. But that's something else you won't discuss either, is it?"

"What time does the class start?" I sighed.

Things had been like this for longer than I cared to admit. But how could it be any different, I wondered at the time, after thirty years together? Especially when you hitch up with each other at school.

We weren't alike even then – she, always the practical one, able to cope with a world I found impossible, even at that age; me, the idealist who always had his head in a book and kept, in Annie's words, 'coming out with things'. But when you're young, you like what's different: opposites attract. Then, eventually, they start to grow up. Finally, they grow apart. It takes a while, but you get there in the end. And when you do, you wonder what you ever saw in them in the first place. I know I did. Frequently. And I shudder to think what Annie thought of me. When we argued I saw flashes of it in her eyes, but it wasn't until later that I saw the *real* fury.

It's hard to say when the rot set in exactly, or if anything could have been done about it. Of course there were little signs, such as suddenly finding Annie's practical nature stifling, or the fact that when I 'came out with things' they never got a giggle any more, but you learn to live with things like that. What I can say is that I didn't do enough to head things off; I can see that now. Annie, always the pragmatist, did at least try in her own misguided way, suggesting that we 'did things together'. This in turn led to the vicious altercation which I think heralded the *real* rot, the *there's-no-way-back-now-and-we-both-know-it* kind of rot.

Bird watching.

Needless to say, the idea of sitting in a freezing hide looking at sparrows didn't appeal to me at all. In my defence, I would say that I was pretty sure – and I knew Annie better than anyone else – that the suggestion was largely talk. If I had by some miracle turned around and said 'Yes, that sounds wonderful', I'm fairly certain she'd have found some way to wriggle out of it. Anyway, she'd convinced herself that we could go bird watching together, one day presenting me with an expensive bird-watching book and an even more expensive pair of top-of-the-range binoculars, the kind that cost about a month's wages. My shock at such a colossal extravagance was so great that I couldn't speak for a moment, unable to 'come out with something' before Annie stopped me in my tracks.

"Oh I see, it's like that, is it?" she said, her eyes boring into mine like heated pennies, "even the suggestion that we do something together is so awful you can't bring yourself to answer."

"It's got nothing to do with being together," I said, looking at the receipt she'd 'neglected' to take from the box. "It's about finances. How much do you think I earn in a year?" Amazingly for once she had no comeback, no tart reply. Unable to remember the last time I'd had such an advantage, I decided to go in for the kill. "You don't want to go bird watching any more than I do, admit it! I can't believe that you'd go to such lengths just to try and score a point! If you hate me so much, why don't you divorce me? I certainly wouldn't stop you."

I didn't mean it; it was heat-of-the-moment stuff, anything to stop the argument. But as I should've realised that she would, Annie took my words literally.

"*Divorce*? Is that what you think of me? You think I'm the kind of person who gets *divorced*? Oh, no. That might be what you want, so you can get another woman, but it's *never* been what I wanted. When I got married it was *for life* – 'in sickness and in health', remember that? Naturally, I had hoped that we might have had a few children as well along the way, which is what married people do, isn't it? But oh no, not you."

"Over the years I've made it quite clear I wasn't interested –"

"You made nothing clear. Why did you think I was marrying you? But I'll tell you this: if I *ever* catch you so much as looking at another woman, I'll –" screwing up her face, she walked away.

As well as not finishing her own sentence, she hadn't let me finish mine. If she had, she'd have heard me say that I'd never been interested in looking for another woman. And I hadn't. Deep down, I think she knew this was true. As for children, it had just never happened. I was surprised to hear it mentioned now. Anyway, putting this big argument to one side, we stuck to the little niggles after that – why didn't I do anything around the garden, the area was going downhill, why couldn't we move house, that kind of thing, and we muddled on. We let things fester. We – or at least I – headed for the path of least resistance.

And I took my wife to her pottery class.

So on a blustery evening in early April, I drove Annie to her class, half expecting there to be a message waiting for me on the answerphone when I got home. Instead, the only thing waiting for me was the sound of the wind, howling through a gap in one of the seals on the windows as I opened the back door, just as it had when I'd opened it on our way out.

"You could at least have a look at that while I'm gone," Annie had said as I reversed the car out of the drive. "If we ever *did* move —"

"Which do you want me to do more?" I snapped. "The garden or the window? It's only a couple of hours before I pick you back up." *Unless you happen to fall out with someone there first,* I refrained from saying.

"I'll leave that important decision to you," she said simply.

Having had a quick look at the window the week before despite having no idea what I was looking for, I decided to tackle the garden, leaving the back door open so I could hear the phone. After replacing a few of the empty fat-balls for the birds, I grabbed a brush from the garage, and moved a few broken twigs and bits of rubbish from one side of the garden to the other for half an hour or so. It was now eight o'clock, which meant she'd outlasted the flower arranging class, where she'd phoned early for me to come and get her after picking fault with the tutor: "Phillip, the woman had *three* earrings in both ears and a *stud* in her nose. And I'll bet you she was our age!"

"Which is only forty-five," I reminded her. "That's quite young these days, believe it or not." *Or at least it should be,* I thought.

"Well, I think it's silly. Who does she think she is, some young thing on a night out?"

By twenty-five past eight she'd broken another record, that of the failed attempt at Mediterranean cookery: "Phillip, there was a man on that course who swore like a docker. I heard him. *Twice.*"

By the time it came round to quarter to nine, the garden looked tidy (to my eyes at least) and still no call. Getting the car keys from the kitchen, I wondered if the building she was in didn't have a payphone.

On the short drive there I realised that I was being unfair. She'd stuck the French class for two weeks before deciding she was never going to go again, and besides she didn't much care for the French anyway. Maybe, just maybe, this one wasn't going to be a flash in the pan after all. But it didn't look good when I pulled up at nine on the dot and she was already waiting for me at the kerb.

"Well, how did it go?" I asked, my innards clenching.

"Yes, very good," she said, climbing in the passenger seat. "Apart from the tutor."

"So you won't be going back then. Why, what was wrong with this one?"

"She's a jumped-up little madam," Annie said, putting her handbag on her lap. "Then again, I wouldn't have expected any ch-" she stopped herself. "But in answer to your remark, yes I'll be going back. The teacher aside, I enjoyed the class very much. So, which didn't you do in the end, the window or the garden? Or did you just plump for both?"

Without bothering to answer, I drove us home.

A week became two, then three, and apart from a few barbs at 'the ageing hippy' in charge, Annie seemed to be enjoying herself, if that's the correct term. I wondered if part of it was the smell of clay that she always brought with her when she came home, an odour that for some reason I've always despised.

"Is that your excuse for not mending the window?" Annie asked when I brought up the smell of it in the car one evening.

"I think you'll find that's putty, not clay. And besides, they only use that on old-fashioned windows."

"Aren't *we* the expert," she said quickly.

But by and large the arguments had dropped off, which if I'm being truthful, I found rather unsettling. Then one week, the fourth I think it was, Annie came out of the class carrying a small box. As she marched towards the car, the smell became overpowering. Ignoring all my questions until she was safely belted up in the passenger seat, she opened the box and shoved its contents in my face.

"It's a gnome," she said, beaming.

Only just, I thought.

Inside the box was the ugliest-looking gnome I'd ever seen in my life, which when you consider what the average gnome looks like, is quite something. Imagine a badly-beaten Quasimodo looking into a fairground mirror and you're on the right track.

"It stinks," I managed to say eventually.

"Oh that's typical of you," Annie said, snatching the box back. "Trust you to say something hurtful."

"I meant the smell," I said, wrinkling my nose. "Aren't you supposed to fire them or something?"

She gave me a look which suggested the question wasn't worth answering. "Well I can't smell anything so it must be you. I can't understand why everybody else *likes* the smell of clay but you don't. And you'll just have to get used to it, because I'm well onto finishing the next one."

"You're making more of *that*?" I asked, stunned.

"Yes, I am. I thought I'd do two more and put them in different parts of the garden. If you won't let us move, the least I can do is make our garden a bit more attractive."

I snorted. "What, by plonking piles of gaseous clay all over it?"

She turned round and glared at me. "And what's *he* got to do with it?" she demanded.

"What?"

"I said, what has a dead boxer got to do with it?"

"What are you talking about?"

"Cassius Clay. He changed his name to Mohammad Ali. He was very successful as I recall –"

"I know who Cassius Clay is," I snapped. "I said *gaseous* clay, clay that smells."

"Well you should learn to speak properly. And it's pronounced 'gays-see-us'. I thought someone of your intellect would know that."

"'Gays see us'? Don't be ridiculous. And for your information, he's not dead either."

"Well I heard someone pronounce it that way on TV, so it must be right. And I thought he was dead. And anyway," she added as I drove away, "I've still to paint him yet."

We were nearly back home before I realised she was talking about the gnome.

The following week, after the first attempt had been painted (imagine a badly-beaten Quasimodo looking into a fairground mirror after he's been given a makeover by someone who's colour-blind) and displayed in a prominent place in the garden, Annie came out of the class with another one. It wasn't really any better. Neither was its odour.

"I'll need you to come inside next week to bring out the other one," she informed me. "He's much bigger than the first two."

"Bit of a monster, is it?" I asked, letting a smile play across my eyes.

She didn't reply. Instead she stared at me the whole way home. In the quarter of an hour it took to get there, I don't think she blinked once.

Annie's behaviour over the next week puzzled me. Instead of being all bright-eyed at the prospect of finishing another masterpiece and the added bonus of annoying me with the stench of her badly-rendered efforts, my wife seemed oddly subdued, nervous somehow. When she thought I wasn't looking, she kept giving me worried glances followed by contemptuous sneers. This was strange in itself as Annie was one of those people who seemed to have eyes in the back of her head, and had a habit of telling me what I was doing or thinking without appearing to look at me at all. But now, I was catching her do it. It wasn't until I went into the class that night that I realised what it was all about.

I got there as usual bang on nine. Parking up, I made my way over to what looked like a draughty community centre. A few feet away, the door opened and an elderly woman came out, cradling a pot in her arms. While the door was still open, I slipped inside.

The class was mainly full of women, most of them slightly older than Annie. The smell of clay was pretty strong, but not as bad as I'd expected it to be. In fact, in the short time I spent there, I found the smell quite manageable, although that's probably as much due to what happened next as anything. But I was left with the impression – which is even stronger now – that the clay Annie used was somehow more pungent than the stuff everybody else was using.

I spotted Annie at the far end of the room with her back to me, as was that of a thin woman in a long, brightly-patterned dress with thick, long brown hair. Reminded of Annie's description of an ageing flower child, I smiled.

And then, the ageing flower child turned round and smiled, right back at me. It was thirty years since I'd seen her, but apart from an odd line around the eyes and mouth she looked exactly as I'd remembered her.

"Kirsten," I said, my voice in a whisper.

They say it's your olfactory sense that takes you back to the past quicker than any other. But for me it was the optical; the sight of those small, almond-shaped green eyes, the olive-coloured skin, the red lips.

Her smile.

"Er, hello," she said, uneasily. Then, "Well, let's get it ready to take home, shall we?" It was then that I noticed Annie next to her, staring at me as though I'd just slapped her. Together they walked away, towards a door in the back wall.

"Lovely, isn't she?" a voice said at my elbow as I stared after them.

"Hmm?"

Standing beside me was a man of about seventy, nodding. "I don't much care for the classes," he told me confidentially. "It's her I come for! She fair puts a smile on my face! Aye ..." Nodding to himself, the man toddled off before I could reply. Not that I could've done; I wasn't exactly in the habit of falling head over heels in love, and the whole thing had rather knocked me for six. That smile took me back thirty years, to a vivacious, and (so I'd thought at the time) rather flighty girl. Too flighty for me by half; how wrong I was! Creative, idealistic, fun-loving – my God, how had I forgotten about her? And why on earth had I passed her over for –

"When you've quite finished daydreaming," Annie said, appearing out of nowhere, "you can give us a hand with this."

"Huh?" It seemed to take a few seconds for my eyes to focus. When they did, it wasn't on the most beautiful thing I'd ever seen in my life as I'd hoped, but on the most ugly.

It was slightly taller than the first two gnomes Annie had made, but was about twice the width, and had a disgusting batrachian quality to it – imagine a badly-beaten Quasimodo looking into a fairground mirror and seeing Toad of Toad Hall staring back at him. *That* ugly.

Needless to say, the smell was atrocious.

"This is him, is it," I said eventually.

"Yes," Annie replied, through gritted teeth, "this is him."

Not trusting myself to look at her, I looked at Kirsten instead. The smile on her face, a warm and genuine smile that showed she was pleased Annie was satisfied with her creation, was so bright it almost brought a tear to my eye.

"Annie's worked very hard on this," she said. "I think she's done really well."

"Yes," is what I should've said to her. Not "You've hardly changed in thirty years," as I did.

"Thank you," Kirsten said, her face flushing.

"Here," Annie growled. At first I thought she'd punched me in the chest; but looking down I saw that I was holding a large box containing the gnome.

"Yes," I said, trying to snap out of it. "Right. Well. Let's take him home, then."

"Bye Annie. Bye Phil," Kirsten called out as we walked away. *Phil ...* Annie never called me *Phil. Phil* sounded wonderful. Struggling under the weight of my burden, I managed to get the 'gnome' to the boot of the car, where it damn near cracked my suspension.

"I knew you'd go all gooey-eyed over her," Annie said once we'd set off. By the time I'd thought of a suitable reply, the moment had passed and we drove the rest of the way in silence.

That's why she's been in a funny mood all week, I thought. *She knew I'd meet Kirsten.* But how could she be so sure about what would happen?

I foolishly decided she couldn't and was just using it as an excuse to have a go at me. Pulling up in the drive I decided the best thing to do was pretend that nothing had happened, so I said "Well, that's three of them now. Are you going to give them names?"

"I'm thinking of calling this one Phil," Annie said, getting out of the car and slamming the door as hard as she could.

It was half term the next week, so there was no class. For me it was a double agony; the atmosphere at home was more poisonous than usual, and being deprived of even a glimpse of Kirsten made it even worse. I had hoped that it would turn out to be an aberration and the feeling would pass, or that Annie wouldn't want to go back after the break. But it wasn't to be.

"In case you're wondering, I still want a lift to the class tomorrow," Annie informed me the night before, as if reading my thoughts. "And a lift back of course. Just wait outside, in the usual place."

Of course I couldn't; it was hard enough driving away when I dropped her off, but a few hours later the idea of sitting in the car with Kirsten only a few feet away proved impossible. I had to go in. I even had my excuse lined up.

"Before you say anything, I just wanted to see what you were working on next," I told Annie when she saw me, all the while looking round for Kirsten.

"If you'd been listening to me over the past couple of weeks you'd know," Annie told me. "Obviously it's slipped your mind. You might try looking in front of you," she suggested.

Steeling myself for the worst, I looked at the table behind her. And god help me, I laughed.

"It's ... an owl?" I said, hedging my bets before putting my hand clumsily to my face.

"Oh, so you recognise it," Annie sneered. "As the gnomes obviously didn't meet with your approval, I thought I'd better do something else too. So I decided to get some use out of that bird book I bought you and do something from that instead. It's not finished yet, but – was it something I said?"

I had to stop myself from saying that it wasn't so much what she said as what she was turning into. When I think about it now, I'm sure that's the reason I didn't want to go bird-watching with her; I got enough of it at home – her squat, barrel-like frame, the barely-visible neck, her small, sharp nose, the beady hazel eyes magnified by prescription lenses; even the highlights in her cropped hair reminded me of feathers. It had never fully hit me until that moment.

"Well?" she snapped. "What do you think?"

"Er …" I started, looking at its bulky, malevolent form. "It's –"

What did I say next? I don't remember, because Kirsten appeared. The next thing I knew she was leading me out of the building and I hadn't given a thought to where my wife was. My emotions in turmoil, I stumbled towards the car.

Annie was already there, wiping her eyes with a hankie. She had an expression on her face I'd never seen before. I was still trying to work it out when I asked why she was sitting in the back seat.

"Oh, I don't know," she said, her voice all jumpy. "It just feels like the best place to be. Please, just take me home."

Her words conveyed her expression perfectly: defeat. I've never felt so wretched in my life.

Not for the first time, we drove home in silence.

Unsurprisingly, Annie didn't want to go the class the following week; besides her air of defeat, she seemed generally out of sorts – the few glances I dared cast in her direction showed that her skin was taking on a horrible translucent grey tinge. I offered to take her to the doctors but she told me it wouldn't do any good. The week after that, with no sign of improvement, I suggested that she go to the class anyway as it might make her feel better. As always, she saw through my logic straight away.

"What, so you can bump into your fancy woman again?" she hissed back. She was right – it had been nearly two weeks and it was driving me crazy. So crazy that on the night of the class I slipped out of the house while Annie was watching the telly. When I got back, apparently without her having taken her eyes off the screen, she said, "You went to explain to her why I wasn't there this evening, didn't you? But don't you worry – I'll be there next week."

Like I said earlier, eyes in the back of her head. Blushing all the way down to my shoes, I decided to have an early night.

When the next class came around I didn't think Annie was in any fit state to go, but I knew better than to say so. Dropping her off, I realised with a sickening sense of guilt that I had a real reason to go inside this time – to see if Annie was okay.

On my way back, I thought I spotted Kirsten standing between a row of cars outside the building. Getting closer, I saw that she was standing at the side of the road where I usually parked the car. My heart thumped. I started to smile at her; then I saw the expression on her face.

"I'm sorry, you can't park here. We're – oh –" Seeing who it was, the colour drained out of her.

"Why, what's wrong?" I asked.

"Well, I'm afraid you can't park here because –" she looked like she was going to burst into tears. "Because –"

The sound of the siren told me why. And instinctively I knew who it was for.

"She was working on her owl and, and – then she just seemed to double over, and –" suddenly the dam broke, and she was clinging to me, as if she loved Annie more than I did.

Moving out of the way, the ambulance parked up outside the class. The pavement was full of people now, whispering among themselves.

In the time it took to blink, or so it seemed to me, a stretcher passed by with Annie on it, her face even greyer than it had been earlier, her eyes closed. Moving away from Kirsten, I followed Annie into the back of the ambulance.

As I sat beside her, the smell of clay was even worse than usual; fanciful as it sounds, I'd even go so far as to say it was *frightening*. Then I saw the smears on her jumper.

"When she collapsed, she took what she was working on with her," one of the stretcher-bearers explained. "We had to prise it out of her arms."

At two o'clock that morning Annie died, the result of a massive heart attack.

I hung around the hospital for a while, not wanting to go home. Eventually, I decided to walk back, which took about an hour. I had so many things I needed to think about but I couldn't focus on any of them. Dawn was just starting to break as I got home, and suddenly I was very tired, too tired to take in whatever it was that looked different about the garden through the window. It could wait until morning.

In the living room, only the blood-red number '4' on the answerphone lighted the gloom. Pressing PLAY I listened to as much of Kirsten's first panicked message as I could stomach before going upstairs, leaving her talking to herself in the living room. The second before I fell asleep, I decided that when I called her in the morning it would be the last time I spoke to her.

The call was brief. Kirsten, still sounding more upset than I was, made me promise to get in touch if I needed anything, and to let her know when the funeral was. But I had no intention of telling her. It would be painful enough as it was.

Hanging up, I looked around at the living room. It looked bigger somehow, greyer and colder. With a sick feeling in my stomach, I headed for the kitchen to put the kettle on. The second I opened the door and looked towards the window, I saw what it was that was different outside. Dry swallowing, I stared back for a few seconds before unlocking the door and going out.

In the garden, the ugliest of the three gnomes was standing on top of the rain barrel under the kitchen window, staring in. Grabbing it around its middle, I lifted it and put it back at the far end of the garden where it belonged. Then, with considerable effort, I dragged the rain barrel back ten feet or so along the ground to its usual position beside the garage.

Going back into the house I started to make arrangements for the funeral.

I kept my promise not to talk to Kirsten again for five months.

During that time I'd settled into a routine of sorts, and despite the nagging feelings of guilt I kept experiencing, I found I was coping quite well. I'd managed to get used to the quiet of the house and its increased size, and for the first few months I didn't think about Kirsten at all other than with a faint sense of embarrassment.

Then one day I literally bumped into her in town.

It was still a month until Christmas but that seemed to be all people were talking about. I'd had an uneasy couple of nights wondering what the festive season would be like on my own, and had come up with the idea of maybe going away over the holidays. As I looked in the travel agents' window at the offers for short festive breaks, I'd made up my mind to go in and enquire further when I collided with someone coming out.

Would it sound silly if I said I knew it was her, even before our eyes met?

It happened quite quickly after that; a coffee here, a movie and a meal there. At first we talked about Annie, then about the old school we'd been to and what we'd thought of each other in those days, which led onto what we thought of each other now. We discovered we had a lot in common.

A couple of weeks later we both went back to the travel agents and booked a cottage in the country until the New Year; by the time the taxi dropped Kirsten off at her flat after the holidays we were talking about getting engaged.

As the taxi drove me home, I looked up and down the local streets in a way I hadn't done in years. In the cold winter sunshine they didn't look depressing to me, the way they had to Annie. The area wasn't a bad one, I decided. Good enough for Kirsten to move in, which we'd also discussed.

Paying the fare, I walked down the drive to the back door and, dropping the bags, let out a loud, contented sigh.

I was still letting it out when I saw the overturned dustbin in the back garden.

There wasn't much rubbish strewn about – since Annie died, there didn't seem to be as much any more – but what there was was scattered about among the frost, along with several uprooted plants and the soil they'd been growing in, as well as a handful of shattered plant pots.

Maybe Annie had been right after all. Letting out a different kind of sigh, I unlocked the door and dumped the bags inside. Looking out of the window as I washed my hands, I noticed that the gnomes at least were still in the same place, gurning at me like gargoyles from the back of the garden.

Turning my back on them, I picked up a towel and dried my hands.

A couple of months later Kirsten and I were married, and she moved in. A few days after that, I realised she wasn't the only new tenant in the area.

"I see what you mean about your garden," Kirsten said one day when I came home from work. "You have let it go, haven't you?"

"*Our* garden," I reminded her. "Perhaps you could weave some of your creative magic on it."

"Well, I could give it a go," she said doubtfully, her hands on her hips. "But where do I start?"

"How about over there," I said, pointing over to the gnomes.

She looked at me like I was kidding. "But Annie made those," she said, like I could possibly have forgotten. "Besides, I think they lend the garden a certain quirky charm."

Not wanting to have our first argument, I went inside to get a drink.

I'd just about finished it and was thinking about a second one when I heard Kirsten cry out. Wondering if one of the kids at the back of us was giving her trouble, I shot out of my chair and into the garden, only to find Kirsten laughing.

"What is it?" I asked.

"A mouse!" she said, her face flushed. "Scurried out of the hedge when I started clearing away the weeds. It scared the life out of me!"

"I'll have to get some traps, I suppose," I said.

"You'll do no such thing," Kirsten told me, her voice as close to anger as I'd ever heard it.

"But they're vermin," I reminded her.

"They're also living creatures," she informed me. "No, we'll just have to make allowances for it. No traps!" she said, wagging her finger at me and smiling. I smiled back, happier than I'd ever have believed possible a year earlier. Incredible how things can change, I mused as I poured that second drink and one for Kirsten.

Incredible how things change.

I think one of the most incredible aspects of that change was the way my life opened up after I met Kirsten; we started to go out, visit places, people; I made friends with Kirsten's friends and we also made new friends of our own. In fact we made so many good friends that we found ourselves being asked over to stay with some of them for weekends. And when Kirsten went so far as to suggest that *we* should invite them in turn to stay with us, I amazed myself by saying yes, that would be nice, *if* we had the room. But we *do* have the room, Kirsten informed me. We have the spare bedroom.

Ah, I thought. *The spare bedroom.*

Until that moment I don't think I'd given it a thought since Annie died. We'd never had children, and as neither of us had any friends as such, the spare bedroom had been used almost exclusively by Annie as part sanctuary, part storeroom. It was her space, and I hadn't minded at all. The thing was, in a closed-off compartment of my mind I still thought of it as hers. And Kirsten knew it.

"Come on," she said, dragging me by the arm towards the stairs. "Sooner we have a look at what needs to come out the better."

Opening the door, Kirsten went in ahead of me, coughing. "God, the dust in here," she said, pushing her way through the cluttered shelves, old clothes and discarded ornaments. "Let's have this window open."

Looking round, I couldn't see any reason for keeping anything in there; to me, the room seemed to be full of things Annie couldn't bear to throw away. I was just about to say something to that effect when I saw Kirsten looking out of the window into the darkness, frowning.

"Are all the telegraph poles around here that big?" she asked.

Frowning myself, I looked over to where she pointed. Above the bungalows in the next street, the telegraph pole there did look bigger than normal.

"Hang on a minute," I said, rooting around among the junk.

Beneath a pair of old curtains which I remembered Annie replacing just before she died, I found the fabled binoculars. Picking them up, I trained the lenses on the pole.

"There's a bird perched on top," I told Kirsten.

"It's a big one then," she said. "Let me see."

"You won't be able to see much, it's too dark."

Nevertheless she took the binoculars, staring at what was little more than a bulky shadow in the distance.

"It's very still, isn't it?" she remarked eventually.

She wasn't kidding. I was in there every evening after work, clearing the stuff out of that room, and every time I looked the bird didn't appear to have moved. I couldn't help wondering what it was waiting for. Then, the following week when the clocks went forward and we had an extra hour of daylight, I decided to have another look with the binoculars. What I saw made me feel distinctly uneasy.

"Where are you going?" Kirsten asked as I passed her on the stairs. I didn't stop to answer.

Walking quicker than I had done in years, I turned into the street next to ours and didn't stop until I was about two-thirds of the way along it. Looking up at the pole, I couldn't believe what I was seeing.

"Gave me a turn too when I saw it," a voice said behind me.

Looking round, a man of perhaps sixty was standing at his gate, smiling. "I reckon they must've gone up the ladder in their stocking feet in the middle of the night," he said.

"But," I mumbled, "it's –"

"A bird scarer. I suppose the idea is that if there's already a bird up there others won't land on the pole. They must peck through the wires or something. I've heard about 'em before but never seen one."

"But – but who put it there?" I asked stupidly. "How long's it been there?"

"I've no idea. Maybe it was the council or the phone company or someone. As to how long, I first noticed it at the beginning of this month."

Beginning of this month. About the time we came back from our honeymoon. I think he said something else then, about how sorry he was to hear about my wife, but I didn't catch it all. Instead, I rushed back home and found Kirsten in the spare room, sorting through some of Annie's stuff.

"The night Annie had her heart attack," I asked, badly out of breath, "what happened to that owl she made?"

She seemed amazed by the question. "What? I don't remember seeing it after that," she said when she'd thought about it. "When the ambulance left, we all went back inside, but nobody was in the mood to carry on so I sent everyone home. I didn't even think about the owl until a couple of weeks later, and by then it must've been long gone. I just assumed that someone had either taken it with them or it was put out with the rubbish in all the confusion. Why, you don't want it, do you?"

"No," I said, looking out of the window at the telegraph pole and its unmoving inhabitant, "I only hope it isn't the other way round."

A week later I felt much better, if a little silly. Our plans for the spare bedroom were really starting to take shape – we'd sorted through all of Annie's belongings, and earlier that day taken some of her clothes to the nearest charity shop. But best of all, I wasn't constantly looking at that blasted owl every time I went in the room. In fact it occurred to me that the last time I'd been in, I hadn't even looked out of the window.

The curse broken, I looked outside once more, this time without fear. It was still there of course, as I knew it would be; only now there was something sat on top of it.

Perched on the owl's head was a sparrow, sitting there seemingly without a care in the world, ruffling its feathers. As it went about its preening, a small white globule escaped it, and dribbled down the owl's face.

That's his theory shot down in flames, I thought, remembering what the neighbour had said. *Bird scarer indeed.*

But a few minutes later while I was looking for a pair of scissors to cut through the cellophane on a roll of wallpaper, I heard a brief screeching, followed by panicked squeaking. At first I wondered if our mouse had come to a sticky end, but then realised that the noise wasn't coming from the ground. Dropping the wallpaper, I looked out of the window just in time to see something small and brown falling out of the sky close to the telegraph pole, hitting one of the wires as it went. I was still looking out of the window when Kirsten appeared.

"Did you knock for something?"

"Hmm? Oh, no. I, er, dropped the wallpaper on the floor."

"Oh, while I'm here and I remember," she said, putting her arms round my waist as I continued to look outside, "I like where you put the gnomes."

I turned around sharply. "What?"

Turning back to the window, I looked down at the fence and saw the gnomes weren't there. It took me a second or two to locate them; one was in the middle of the lawn, while its 'twin' was over by the garden bench. The bigger, uglier one was now standing in front of one of the solar lights we'd just put in.

"I'd never have thought of it myself," Kirsten was saying, hugging me again. "When it gets dark, it'll look like its glowing. Luminous gnomes! When did you do it, after you came back from the charity shop?"

"I think something's just had a bird over in the next street," I said, not quite managing to change the subject. "I'm surprised you didn't hear the racket."

"Oh, that's a shame," Kirsten said sadly.

The next day, when we took the curtains down and greased up the windows, I'm ashamed to say it was with a great sense of relief.

It was around this time however, that things began to escalate. Only fool that I was, I didn't realise why at first. Annie always said I never remembered the important things.

It all started the night I tried to read *Papillon.*

It'd been quite a while since I'd had the house to myself. Not that I was complaining; I loved every minute that Kirsten was around – but the downside of being blissfully happy was that my reading addiction had suffered over the past few months – I'd bought the book nearly six months earlier and hadn't got past the blurb – but, with Kirsten away for a couple of hours, I could settle down to the book in peace. And, with a few fingers of good single malt by my side, that's what I intended to do.

Until the wind started blowing.

I'd never had to do anything about that gap in the seal or whatever it was, as we hadn't had any strong gusts for ages. But on that night, the wind howled round the house and inside it with a forlorn cry.

Half an hour later, I'd managed to read a grand total of four pages. I struggled on for the next hour or so, but by the time Kirsten was due to come home I'd given up completely.

Typical, I thought, slamming the book down. The first night I get to read in months, and what happens? Our stupid windows start playing up. Not a peep from them in almost a year, *a whole year,* nothing at all since –

– the previous April, when Annie started her pottery class.

It hit me like a punch in the gut. Ten minutes later, Kirsten came in, smiling as usual.

"Hi," I said, my voice hollow, "how did the class go?"

"Oh, the usual. The first one's always a bit awkward," she said, kissing me on the cheek. As she leaned forward, the smell of clay made me feel giddy.

"Good grief," she said, looking past me into the back garden. "Look at that."

"What?" I said, turning round.

She didn't have to tell me. In its position in front of the solar light, the ugliest of the ugly gnomes glowed with a spectral brilliance, its distorted face looking right in through the back window.

"I think I'll put it back in its original place," Kirsten said, heading out to the garden. Opening the door, the wind howled once more.

That night after finally managing to get to sleep, I was awoken by a terrible screeching sound outside. Fumbling my way over to the window in the darkness, I opened the curtains, squinting against the orange glow from the streetlight.

Beyond it, on top of the nearby telegraph pole, an owl was staring straight in at me, its eyes wide.

That uneasy feeling rearing up in me again, I went into the back room and looked out of the window. The owl on the telegraph pole had gone.

In the morning however, so too had the owl outside our window; but the one in the street behind had returned.

The following week when Kirsten went to her pottery class, the wind started to howl almost as soon as she left. We hadn't had any wind in the intervening seven days.

After half an hour's futile effort, I put *Papillon* down in frustration.

Then there was the night I came home from work to find Kirsten waiting for me at the gate. She looked like she'd been crying.

"What's wrong?" I asked, touching her arm.

"I found these when I was in the garden," she said, opening her hand to reveal several small brown objects in her palm.

"What are they?"

"Owl pellets," she said. "The past few nights I thought I heard squeaking and it reminded me I hadn't seen that mouse for a while."

"So?"

"When an owl eats something, it coughs up what it can't digest in the form of pellets; I looked it up in your bird book. And if you break them open you can see what they've eaten." As she broke open the pellet between her fingers, she let out a little sigh.

Among the remnants of the shattered pellet were several small bones. Her eyes welled up with tears once more.

It became a recurring problem – every other day we seemed to find more of the pellets, filled with fur, feathers and bones. There certainly seemed to be fewer sparrows in the garden. Kirsten was really quite distressed by it all.

For myself, I was more concerned with the faint odour of clay I noticed when we opened the pellets.

On top of that there was the wind, which by now I was really having my suspicions about. Every Monday night, without fail, the noise subtly changing as the weeks went by.

That and the gnomes, of course.

"Oh, this is getting silly now," I said, pointing up at the garage roof. Putting her hand over her mouth, Kirsten giggled.

"It's like those stories you hear," she said eventually, "where the gnome leaves home and starts sending postcards from New Zealand." She looked around the garden. "They're just not that well-coordinated yet."

"It's not funny," I told her. "When I opened the door I thought it was that owl at first." I tried to hide my shudder.

The gnome, which was perched on the edge of the garage roof, was staring at the space between the back door and the upstairs window. The other two weren't quite so adventurous, it seemed, although I didn't like the fact that one of them was standing at the base of the drainpipe, as if it were ready to climb up. The third one was stood in the middle of the back garden, along with several new pellets.

"I think this is a bit more important than a few kids moving garden gnomes around in the middle of the night," Kirsten said, picking up the pellets. "Those bird screams I keep hearing go right through me." Breaking one of them open, another small collection of bones was revealed.

"I think we should kill it," I said, the reek of clay in my nostrils.

Kirsten gave me a look I hadn't seen before. "Over my dead body," she said.

After work, I came home and had a look in the bird book to see if there was anything we could do.

There wasn't.

Then finally, there was the evening when I put down my copy of *Papillon* for the last time and admitted what I'd suspected for some weeks: that the wind, which was now hooting around the house instead of howling, *was talking to me.*

I couldn't deny it any longer. I'd heard it too many times to be deceived.

Guilt of course, that's all it was. I'd read enough books on psychiatry over the years to realise that. It was getting close to the anniversary of Annie's death, and I was guilty.

My face flushing, I picked up the book and headed for the hall. Opening the door, an almighty gust of wind blew through the house.

Phillip, it hooted. *Phiiiilllliiiippppp …*

When I came back down, I poured myself a large whisky and put the TV on as loud as I could stand it.

And then, on the week running up to the anniversary of Annie's death, the worst thing of all.

Silence.

Nothing all week – no pellets, no wind – even the gnomes stayed where they were supposed to. And I didn't like it. By the day itself I was a nervous wreck.

"Come on, hurry up and finish that," Kirsten said, smiling at me as I nursed my scotch after work that evening. "We're going out."

"What?"

"We're going out. For a meal. I've booked a table. So get yourself changed and we can go."

"Kirsten, I really don't feel like going out tonight. It's –" I couldn't finish the sentence.

"Don't think I don't know what's going on," she said. "I do. And it's no good sitting there brooding over it. It wasn't your fault Annie died."

"That's not how it feels to me," I said. *Or to Annie*, I almost blurted out.

"Just go upstairs, get washed and changed and we'll go. No arguments."

Surprisingly, we had a lovely meal, and the wine helped to relax me. We talked of the good times we'd had and the good times still to come. We laughed. Picking up my wine glass as Kirsten went to the bathroom, I breathed in its aroma contentedly, then stopped. Seeing the waiter was close by, I called him over.

"Is that a replacement you've just had put in?" I asked, pointing to the open window behind Kirsten's chair.

"I don't think so, sir. Why?"

"Nothing," I said, my mood suddenly changing. "It's just that I thought I could smell putty, that's all."

Looking up at the rapidly darkening sky, I wolfed back my dessert as quickly as I could.

"Have you got a cold coming on?" Kirsten asked as we walked home. I must've looked confused. "You haven't stopped sniffing for the past ten minutes," she informed me.

"No, but I think we should get home as quickly as possible. I'm sure it's going to rain."

"Well it isn't forecast," Kirsten said. "Besides, there's no hurry. Slow down. *Relax*." Linking her arm through mine, she slowed our pace to an agonising dawdle.

It was only a short walk from the restaurant to the house but to me it was torture. The night fell quickly; by the time we reached the neighbouring street all the curtains were closed and the streetlights were on. On top of the telegraph pole, I could just make out the owl. I wasn't sure if that was a good thing or not. Turning into our street, I looked up at the lampposts and telegraph poles but all were empty. Breathing heavily through my nose, I tried to hurry Kirsten along past the last couple of houses, but she was having none of it.

"Phil," she said, her voice slightly slurred by the wine, "take your time, we're almost home. I'm sure the gnomes won't have got *that* far." She giggled. "So, who do *you* think it is then? That pair behind us? We could always have a word with their mother if it c-"

Her words were drowned out by what sounded like large pieces of stone grinding above us. My first thought was that a couple of slates on the roof had come loose after all the wind we'd had recently. But as I was pulling Kirsten into the safety of our front porch I caught the overpowering odour of clay.

We were like sitting targets; with nowhere to run to, the owl dived down at us shrieking and spitting, its talons sinking into my scalp while its beak pecked at my forehead, aiming for my eyes. When I did manage to get it loose, it took a chunk of my hair with it.

"Open the door!" Kirsten screamed.

Fumbling for the key, I didn't see what happened next. But there was a sharp cutting sound followed by a scream. Turning round, I saw the owl fly off into the night. Kirsten had her hands clamped tightly to her face, but it wasn't enough to stop a thin trickle of blood from running down between her fingers.

As I had exactly a year earlier, I spent the evening and most of the night with my wife in hospital. The difference this time was that I got to come home with her.

Fortunately, the doctors seem to think the gash on Kirsten's face will heal in time. Kirsten being Kirsten, all she'd say was that the owl must've been distressed about something and we just happened to be in the way. It was one of those things, she said. As for its wholesale ransacking of the local rodent and bird population, we'd just have to keep sweeping up the pellets we found. It was after all, Kirsten argued, only doing what came naturally.

"Suppose it attacks us again?" I said. "And then there's the gnomes."

"What about the gnomes?" she asked.

"Well," I blustered, "can you remember the last morning we came down and they *hadn't* moved?"

"Hadn't *been* moved," Kirsten corrected me, smiling. "Kids, remember?"

"I don't know, Kirsten," I said, screwing up my face. "Perhaps we should move. Have a fresh start somewhere."

"Oh, *Phil*," she said with a little shake of her head, as if talking to a favourite child, "so a few little devils move the gnomes about – it's not the end of the world, is it? Neither is an owl defending its territory or whatever it's doing. And if there's one thing I've learned, it's that you can't outrun life's problems – they'll always be closer than you'd like them."

Later, I came to the conclusion that it must've been this last statement which triggered my nightmare, and the absolute worst part of this whole business.

Must've been.

One of the things I love most about Kirsten is the fact that in bed she sleeps facing me. Annie never did, but the way things turned out between us, that wasn't such a bad thing. But waking up and seeing Kirsten's peaceful face in front of me is something I've always cherished. Even after the attack, with her scar shining in the moonlight, it was still a comfort to me.

Understandably over the past few months, but particularly since the attack, I've had trouble sleeping. Kirsten on the other hand, has no such problem. Luckily, I've found that even I can drop off eventually, so long as I have her beautiful face opposite mine.

On the night in question, after a few hours' sleep, I awoke and found that I had to go to the bathroom. I remember I'd got to sleep relatively quickly that night, and hoped that seeing Kirsten's sleeping face would ease me back into sleep just as quickly. But when I got back into bed, she'd turned over. Still, it wasn't the end of the world; all was quiet outside, I had the love of my life beside me, and instead of her face I could drink in her beautiful, long brown hair glowing in the beams of moonlight coming through the curtains. With sleep once again descending on me, I reached out to touch it. But, sensing some kind of change, I stopped.

What it was that was different exactly, I wasn't sure – its lighter shade I put down to the moonlight; but the hair appeared to be somehow thinner as well, as if large chunks of it had been cut away. To reassure myself this wasn't the case, I once again reached out to touch it.

My fingers must've been about an inch away when I saw the two eyes, staring at me among the hair.

Great big round, unblinking hazel-coloured eyes in the back of Kirsten's head. And in my nostrils, the suffocating stench of clay.

It felt as if someone had stolen the breath from my body. I couldn't scream, I couldn't move. And the only thing in the world I wanted was for those eyes to blink, just once. But they never did.

Eventually I got my head under the bedclothes and waited for morning.

"You were making some strange noises during the night," Kirsten said when daylight finally arrived. "Bad dream?"

"Yes," I eventually managed to say.

"Well, if it's any consolation my night wasn't much better," she said, grimacing. "I think I've cricked my neck or something. It hurts like hell."

"Maybe it's because you were sleeping on your other side," I said nervously.

She stopped massaging her neck long enough to give me a strange look. "But I wasn't. I always sleep the same way – on my stomach, facing right. I don't think I could sleep any other way, even if I wanted to."

"But I saw you," I told her, "your head was definitely facing the opposite way r-" at that moment I felt colder than I've ever felt in my life.

"What?" Kirsten said, holding her neck again.

"Nothing," I said, leaping out of bed. "Must've been the dream. Y-you haven't seen that bird book anywhere, have you?"

"I imagine it's where it's always been," Kirsten replied. "Why, what do you want it for?"

I found it in the spare bedroom, beside the window. My hands trembling, I turned to the index, and finally to the section on owls.

I had hoped it was a myth, that story about owls being able to turn their heads all the way round. And when I read that it *wasn't* true, I could've shouted for joy. But when the next sentence in the book informed me that they can turn their heads *nearly* all the way round, I thought that I must still be dreaming. Because it meant that if Kirsten was right, and she *did* sleep the way she said she did –

"You found it then," Kirsten said, standing at the door, wincing as she rubbed her neck. Stepping forward, she looked down at the open page.

"You're still worried about that owl?" she said. "Oh that's *sweet.* But I'm fine, really. And I'm sure it'll go in the end. Not like that one." She pointed outside, to the owl on the telegraph pole. "That's one's there for the duration. Hey, do you think that's why the real one's hanging around? You'd have thought it'd have figured out it isn't real by now."

Downstairs, we found the three gnomes standing in a row on the back step. At that moment I could have burst into tears.

"Oh, come here," Kirsten said, hugging me fiercely. "If you're still that bothered about the area in a few months we can always move."

No, it wouldn't make any difference, I thought as she held me, the gnomes still on the step beside us, *the problem will always be closer than I'd like it to be.*

Catching the faint odour of clay on Kirsten's skin, I did my best to release myself from her embrace without drawing attention to the fact I was shaking. Then, instead of having my usual cup of tea, I went straight into the shower and tried to wash the smell from my skin.